DARLING
GIRLS

Also by Sally Hepworth

The Secrets of Midwives

The Things We Keep

The Mother's Promise

The Family Next Door

The Mother-in-Law

The Good Sister

The Younger Wife

The Soulmate

DARLING GIRLS

SALLY HEPWORTH

ST. MARTIN'S PRESS
NEW YORK

First published in the United States by St. Martin's Press, an imprint of St. Martin's Publishing Group

DARLING GIRLS. Copyright © 2024 by Sally Hepworth International Pty Ltd as trustee for the Sally Hepworth International Unit Trust. All rights reserved. Printed in the United States of America. For information, address St. Martin's Publishing Group, 120 Broadway, New York, NY 10271.

www.stmartins.com

Library of Congress Cataloging-in-Publication Data

ISBN 978-1-250-28452-5 (hardcover)
ISBN 978-1-250-34187-7 (international, sold outside the U.S., subject to rights availability)
ISBN 978-1-250-28453-2 (ebook)

Our books may be purchased in bulk for promotional, educational, or business use. Please contact your local bookseller or the Macmillan Corporate and Premium Sales Department at 1-800-221-7945, extension 5442, or by email at MacmillanSpecialMarkets@macmillan.com.

First U.S. Edition: 2024
First International Edition: 2024

10 9 8 7 6 5 4 3 2 1

For Jen Enderlin,
who made me an author.
There will never be enough thank-yous
in the world.

DARLING
GIRLS

THE OFFICE OF
DR. WARREN, PSYCHIATRIST

Dr. Warren sits in a gray folding chair, one ankle resting on the opposite knee. His suit is brown; his tie, red. His thin-rimmed glasses lie against his chest, on a chain. When I knock on the open door, he points to the vacant chair facing him, his gaze fixed on an old-school manila folder in his lap. His bald, liver-spotted head is as waxed and shiny as a freshly buffed sports car.

"Hello," I say.

No response. After a brief hesitation, I squeak across the floors in my sneakers and sit.

Dr. Warren remains bent over his file.

The room is bare apart from the chairs, a potted plant, and a battered wooden coffee table. While I wait for him to acknowledge me, I observe a couple of sparrows pecking at the peeling paint on the windowsill outside.

"Excuse me," I say, after several minutes, when Dr. Warren still hasn't greeted me. The clock on the wall says five past the hour.

He looks up, faintly irritated. "Yes?"

"Are we . . ." I feel silly. ". . . going to start?"

He looks at the clock, then back at his paperwork. "Whenever you like."

I haven't seen a therapist before, but this feels a little unorthodox. Perhaps he is one of those therapists who uses unconventional means to bring about a particular result—like failing to provide a chair because he believes people get to the heart of things faster when they are uncomfortable?

That, or Dr. Warren is an asshole.

"So I just . . . talk?"

"Yes."

"About what?"

He sighs. "It's up to you. But I'd suggest that you might want to talk about what happened at Wild Meadows."

It shouldn't be jarring, hearing the name of my childhood home spoken in such a familiar way. These days everyone is familiar with Wild Meadows. The media love the juxtaposition of the whimsical country estate and the atrocities that happened therein. They also love anything to do with foster children. The headlines practically wrote themselves.

Wild Meadows or House of Horrors?
The Secrets Buried Beneath the Wild Meadows
What's Lurking in the Wild Meadows

These headlines have put Wild Meadows on the map. Apparently people even drive up there to see it . . . or what's left of it. But while it's a headline or novelty to most, it's my life. The place where I learned about loss, and shame . . . and hate.

"I can't talk about Wild Meadows," I say. "Not yet."

Maybe not ever.

Dr. Warren leans back in his chair, clearly disappointed. I don't like to disappoint people. And yet, if I just come out with it, he won't understand. No one understands what it was like for me, growing up at Wild Meadows. The suffering that woman caused me. The only ones who understand are those who lived it.

"Well, we can just sit here if you'd prefer."

He looks back at his file, which I now realize is folded to conceal a newspaper. It confirms something I'd suspected for most of my life: that no one cares.

1

JESSICA

essica!"

Jessica had nearly escaped through the magnificent double front doors of Debbie Montgomery-Squires's home when she heard her name. Again.

She had just finished up a "room overhaul." Three hours of painstakingly ordering her client's bathroom cabinets into a Pinterest-worthy vision of color-coded, labeled, and stackable containers. The result looked spectacular—all of Debbie's friends said so. The fact that all of Debbie's friends were present to say so was the reason Jessica was dangerously close to being late for her next client . . . even with the extra fifteen-minute contingency time she built into her schedule.

Her first instinct was to keep walking. Nothing—nothing!— vexed Jessica more than tardiness. Except perhaps messiness. And people who cut corners, or people who missed RSVP deadlines. Jessica always RSVP'd to invitations the moment they landed in her hand or inbox. Then she diarized the event, made a note in her Organization app to buy a gift, if necessary, and created a block of time in her calendar to ensure she had an appropriate outfit to wear. At least forty-eight hours before the event, she decided on appropriate transport and mapped out the approximate time it would take to get there (with fifteen minutes added for contingencies).

Jessica had agreed to today's job only as a personal favor to Tina Valand, a beloved client, who'd purchased the voucher for Debbie as a birthday present and begged Jessica attend personally (rather than sending one of her excellent staff) because "Debbie is such a dear friend."

These days, Jessica could afford to be choosy. Since her home-organization business had taken off a few years back, Jessica left the grunt work to her team of staff while she concentrated on positioning herself as Australia's leading expert on home organization, appearing on *The Morning Show* and *Better Homes and Gardens* with handy tips for a more structured life.

When Debbie finally got around to booking her session with Jessica, she'd done it on the same day she hosted a post-Pilates coffee morning for her class. It wouldn't have bothered Jessica had Debbie not seen fit to bring each woman into the bathroom one by one, announcing, "Jessica is my home-organization whiz" before inviting the guest to tell Jessica all about their own organizational struggles.

"You don't mind, do you, Jessica?" she'd say.

"Of course not, Mrs. Montgomery-Squires," she replied.

Jessica did mind, of course. Now, Jessica was running late for her next job.

"Jessica?" Debbie said again, jogging to catch her at the door. Jessica sighed. Pasted on a smile. Turned around.

"This is awkward," Debbie said, "but I've noticed some items missing from the bathroom. I feel awful even bringing it up . . ."

Debbie did not feel awful. Debbie could barely breathe through her delight. Behind her, in the living room, seven women in active-wear sipped lattes and pretended not to listen. The eighth leaned forward in her chair and gawked unashamedly.

"I reorganized your bathroom cabinets," Jessica said, trying for patience, "which means everything will be in a slightly different place. I left a cheat sheet showing you how to find—"

"I understand that," she interrupted. "But I've looked carefully."

Jessica wondered how carefully she could have looked in the four minutes that had passed since she left the bathroom. She also wondered if there was a way to go back in time to the moment she agreed to the do the job so she could slap herself in the face.

"May I ask what is missing?"

Debbie glanced back toward her Pilates friends, suddenly less assured. She lowered her voice and leaned a little closer. "A bottle of Valium."

Jessica pulled herself up to her full five-foot-nothing height. She felt humiliated, as well as appalled for service people everywhere. "I can assure you, Mrs. Montgomery-Squires, I have not taken anything from your bathroom. But, if you are concerned, I'd be very happy for you to search my bag."

She held out the bag, glancing away, over her shoulder as if she couldn't bear to watch. For a shocking moment, Jessica thought Debbie might actually search it. But the other woman said, "That won't be necessary."

After a momentary stalemate, Jessica's phone began to ring, saving them both from navigating an awkward exit. "Well," she said, "if there's nothing else, I do need to get to my next appointment."

Jessica waited a moment. When Debbie didn't speak she turned and strode away.

"Love Your Home Organizational Services," she said as she slid into the leather seats of her new Audi. If the traffic lights were all miraculously green, there was a chance she could still make it on time. She started the car. "Jessica Lovat speaking."

"Ms. Lovat? My name is . . ."

There was a pause as the phone synced with the car's speakers. "Sorry," Jessica said, pulling into the traffic. "I missed that. Who is calling?"

"My name is Detective Ashleigh Patel."

No, Jessica wanted to scream. *No, no, no.*

There was only one reason detectives contacted her. Norah. But Jessica didn't have time for it today. She'd already used up her fifteen-minute buffer!

"What can I do for you, Detective?" Jessica said.

Last time the police called, her sister had assaulted a minor. Upon investigation, Jessica discovered the "minor" was a fifteen-year-old boy whom she'd jabbed with a broomstick after catching him peering through her window while she was getting dressed one morning. Still, it wasn't Norah's first assault, and her motives weren't always quite so reasonable. The court had imposed a community corrections order; if she reoffended in a twelve-month period, the sentence would be considerably harsher.

"It's time to stop this pattern of behavior," the judge said to Norah. "If I see you in this courtroom again, it will be to decide how long you'll go to prison for."

"Did you hear that, Norah," Jessica had cried on the way home. "Next time you're going to jail! In the real world, you can't use violence to deal with your feelings."

"How do you deal with your feelings in the real world?" Norah had asked.

"You bury them," Jessica replied. "Good and deep."

It was a philosophy Jessica had always lived by. But a couple of weeks ago, Jessica had stumbled across an article which claimed that burying toxic feelings could cause cancer. Immediately Jessica decided she must be riddled with cancer. After all, no one repressed more toxic emotions than she did. The idea of a physical manifestation of her suffering held a perverse sort of appeal. She found herself visualizing her insides, admiring the spoils.

"You," she'd say to the tumor wrapped around her spleen, "were caused by that time I had to bail Norah out of jail for the four thousand five hundred and sixty-seventh time. And you," she'd say to the masses in her ovaries, "you are the product of every time I had to worry about Alicia. And you," she'd say to the tumors dotted across her pancreas like confetti, "are the product of my childhood."

She'd almost been disappointed when her doctor gave her a clean bill of health All that repressed anger and nothing to show for it.

She'd been repressing anger about it ever since.

"I hope I'm not calling at a bad time," the detective said. She sounded young and unthreatening and polite—which was something, Jessica supposed.

"I have a few minutes," Jessica said. She put on her indicator to switch lanes. "What can I do for you?"

A learner driver pulled in front of Jessica, and she had to slam on the brakes to stop from hitting him. The mother waved in apology, and Jessica waved back, repressing her anger yet again.

"It's a little sensitive, to be honest," the detective said. "If you're driving it might be an idea to pull over."

"I'm not driving," Jessica lied. She had seventeen minutes to get where she was going—with no allowance for contingencies. She could listen and drive.

"Good. I'm calling to ask for assistance with an investigation I'm working on."

Jessica frowned. An investigation. Perhaps it would be like the time she was summoned for jury duty? A man was being tried for murder after strangling his wife in front of their three small children. Of course Jessica had been selected as a juror. A small, neat, thirty-something-year-old woman with honest brown eyes, scrupulous morals and tasteful nude flats—she'd been born for the role. Perhaps the judge had given this detective her name?

"What are you investigating?"

"I understand that you lived at Wild Meadows Farm back when it was a foster home in the 1990s?"

Jessica slammed on the brakes. A cacophony of horns sounded behind her.

Suddenly she understood why the detective had asked if she was driving.

"Are you all right?"

"Fine," Jessica squeaked. She pulled over to the side of the road, feeling strangely distant from her body.

"As you may or may not have heard, Wild Meadows has recently been demolished to build a McDonald's."

Jessica *had* heard. Even though she was now living in inner-city Melbourne, a two-hour drive—and another world—away from the country town where she grew up, her meticulous level of organization in all aspects of her life meant she kept tabs on everything she needed to know—and quite a lot that she didn't. She probably had a better idea of the goings-on in Port Agatha than most of the locals.

"Well," the detective continued, "the excavators had to dig quite deep to make room for the parking lot, and . . . they uncovered something."

Jessica thought she might vomit. She'd heard about these kinds of moments. One minute you're living your life, caught up in the trite little everyday stresses, the next you're blindsided by a full-blown crisis.

She started fossicking in her handbag.

"I'm afraid that what I have to tell you is quite upsetting," the detective was saying. "There's really no way to sugarcoat it . . ."

Jessica's fingers wrapped around the bottle of pills she'd tucked into the secret side pocket of her bag. With two Valiums in her hand, she reached for her bottle of water. *Thank goodness,* she thought, *for Mrs. Montgomery-Squires.*

"What did you find?" she asked the detective.

2

NORAH

At a secluded table in the back of a cheap Mexican restaurant opposite the train line, Norah was counting the number of ways her date had disappointed her. One: in his profile, Kevin professed to be "interesting," yet he'd already mentioned his passion for *Dungeons & Dragons* twice. Two: he'd called himself "intelligent" but wore the gormless dull-witted smile of a simpleton (it was common knowledge that, on average, smiley people had a significantly lower IQ than the somber). Three (the most glaring of the disappointments so far): his profile picture resembled Harry Styles, yet the man who sat before her bore a striking resemblance to a weasel.

"So," Kevin said, beaming like a fool, "I noticed that you were Norah with an *h*? What's that all about?"

Norah stared at him. "I noticed you were Kevin without a *h*?" she said. "What's that all about?"

"A *h*?" Kevin replied, perplexed. "In Kevin?"

She closed her eyes. Four: his self-professed "great sense of humor" appeared to be in the eye of the beholder.

Norah was starting to wonder if this was worth it. All she wanted was a few odd jobs done. Probably only a couple of hours' work.

A few years ago, when she'd discovered she could get the majority of her household maintenance taken care of easily—and, of more importance, cheaply—by having dinner with a man and planting the faintest suggestion of sex in his mind, she'd thought herself a genius. Particularly since she rarely had to deliver on the sex. Even on the occasions when she did, it was worth it; growing up with a scarcity mentality, Norah was nothing if not parsimonious. And as Kevin had listed "handyman" as a quality in his online dating profile (something that would inevitably be the fifth disappointment), she'd thought this would be a fairly straightforward transaction. They'd wake up Saturday morning, he'd complete a few odd jobs, and be gone by lunchtime.

No such luck.

Norah's therapist, Neil, was forever telling her she had a dysfunctional attitude toward sex.

"Actually," she said, "the opposite is true. I have sex with a man, and he fixes my hot-water service. Or cleans out the gutters. Or pays a bill. Sex, quite literally, allows me to function."

Neil was unmoved. "Sex isn't supposed to be quid pro quo, Norah."

"No?" She considered that. "Then what is it supposed to be?"

Neil hadn't responded straightaway, which made Norah think she'd won. But it turned out he was just taking his time to answer, acting thoughtful when he was probably just taking advantage of the fact that he was getting paid by the hour.

"It's an act of mutual pleasure," he said finally.

"Exactly," Norah said. "He gets pleasure from the sex, and I get pleasure from free help around the house."

Neil had got exasperated then. "Norah, I suspect your skewed idea of sex and its power stems from your childhood. Do you want to talk about that a bit?"

"No." Norah wanted to keep proving her point. She knew she could go several more rounds with Neil, each time reinforcing the fact that sex was, in fact, a transaction. Instead, Neil wanted to talk about her stupid childhood. It was a crying shame.

"Do you like kids?" Kevin asked her eagerly.

"No," she said. "I like dogs."

Specifically, she liked the big stupid ones, the ones that barked at the wind and got underfoot and bowled you over every time you walked in the door. Norah had three of this particular type of dog—a greyhound–Great Dane cross named Converse, a regular greyhound named Couch, and a mutt named Thong who almost certainly had some bullmastiff in him. They were all named for the first item they destroyed after coming to live with Norah.

Kevin beamed, revealing comically large front teeth. He resembled a marketplace caricature. "I have a Jack Russell called Harvey!"

For the love of God.

The worst part of dating, she'd told Neil at their last session—far worse than the sex if it happened—was the conversation. It was not only tedious but also pointless, given that if they *were* to become life partners eventually, then they would most likely spend the next thirty or forty years gazing at either the television or their phones in companionable silence. Why not practice some of that silence now, to get the feel of it? See if the silence felt *right*.

Norah signaled to the waiter, who was lurking nearby.

"Can I get you anything, ma'am?"

"A lobotomy," Norah said. "And make it a double."

The waiter smirked.

Outside the window a couple of dachshunds passed by with their owners. Norah waved at them. Kevin ordered a margarita.

"What is it you do for a living, Norah?" Kevin asked as the waiter shuffled off.

"I run my own business."

"Really?" Kevin leaned forward to get a better look at her boobs. "What kind of business?"

"I complete online IQ and psychometric testing on behalf of idiots who are applying for jobs."

Kevin's puzzled face demonstrated that he would almost certainly need her services if the circumstances arose. She wondered if she should give him her business card. "Psychometric testing?" he repeated.

"Businesses these days are stupid enough to think that they'll get better employees if they force them through a rigorous screening of ridiculous tests," she explained. "Instead, they get the most inventive cheaters. Which, admittedly, often translates to success in the workplace . . ."

"So you complete the test for them?"

"Guaranteed pass or your money back," she said in an American infomercial-type voice. She liked her infomercial voice, and often wondered if she should audition to use it professionally. "I usually get a few wrong so they don't mistake the person for a genius. That would be irresponsible."

"How does it work?" Kevin asked.

"It's pretty easy. I use a VPN that places my IP address at the client's location, then I log on at the same time as the candidate and complete the test while they sit there. They fill out all their own details and submit it from their own computer. For the privilege I charge them three hundred dollars a pop."

"Three hundred bucks? You must be pretty good at those tests."

"What's shocking is how *bad* most people are at them. Makes me worry for the world, it really does."

She'd been enjoying her monologue—Norah liked nothing more than talking about what idiots people were—but her mood dipped when she noticed Kevin staring at her. His eyes were all gooey.

"What?"

Kevin bared his teeth in a weaselly smile. "It's just . . . you're really pretty."

Norah was aware that she was attractive. She wasn't blind and, unlike Kevin, she wasn't a half-wit. She was six feet tall—and most of it was her legs—with unblemished olive skin and tumbling brown hair, courtesy of her Lebanese mother. She also had bright blue eyes—unusual for her complexion. People went *wild* for her eyes, regularly stopping her on the street to comment—or at least trying to, but usually Norah forestalled them, saying, "Yes, I know I have amazing eyes, thanks for noticing." Presumably she had her father to thank for her bright blue eyes but as she didn't know who he was she hadn't bothered.

It baffled Norah that her breasts weren't given more attention. They were, objectively speaking, an exercise in perfect symmetry, scale, and shape. A few years back, when Neil asked her to think of one thing she was grateful for, she hadn't hesitated. "The girls," she said, glancing down. Neil had appeared confused, so she'd lifted her top. She'd had to endure a lengthy lecture on "appropriate behavior in therapy" after that.

Kevin was still smiling at her. "I just . . . I can't believe I'm on a date with you."

Norah had just come to the conclusion that no amount of help around the house was worth spending time with Kevin when her phone began to ring. The gods, it seemed, were smiling on her.

"Must take this," she said, seizing the phone. "Hello?"

"Am I speaking to Norah Anderson?"

"Yes." Norah pressed a finger into the ear not holding the phone to block out the ambient noise. "Who is this?"

"My name is Detective Ashleigh Patel."

Norah frowned. The fact that Norah couldn't recall any dealings with a Detective Patel didn't mean anything necessarily. When you were in trouble with the cops as often as Norah was, the names and voices tended to blur.

"Sorry, Detective," Norah shouted, "I'm in a restaurant and it's a little hard to hear. I'm just going to step outside."

She waved at Kevin, who nodded, and walked out of the restaurant, onto the busy street. "Okay, I'm outside. What's this regarding?"

"It's to do with an investigation I'm working on."

"What investigation?" Norah kept walking away from the restaurant. She wasn't planning to return. She doubted Kevin would be able to fix the fan in her bathroom anyway.

"I'm part of a team investigating a crime we think may have occurred around the time you were living at Wild Meadows foster home."

Norah stopped walking so abruptly that a man crashed into her. She spun around and shoved him away, glaring as he called her a "psycho bitch."

"Are you all right?" the detective asked.

Norah didn't reply. She couldn't. Her heart was pounding in her ears, like when she swam laps underwater. "Yes."

"What I have to tell you is a little distressing," the detective cautioned. "It might be helpful if you were with someone right now."

"Norah!"

She glanced back over her shoulder. Kevin was striding toward her. Shit.

"I grew up in foster care," she told the detective as she began to jog. "I'm comfortable with distressing. Shoot."

Norah began to jog away.

"Hey!" Kevin called. "Wait up!"

"Are you *sure* you're all right?" the policewoman asked.

"I'm fine." Norah slowed, partly out of shock and partly because she was out of breath. She hadn't run since the last time she'd been chased by police, and she was out of shape.

"Well, some excavation work has been done at your former foster home. And while they were down there, they uncovered—"

"Norah!" Kevin called again, closing in her.

For fuck's sake.

She stopped short. It was all too much. Police. Wild Meadows. Kevin. Something had to give.

"Hold on a second," Norah said to the detective. She lowered the phone a waited until Kevin was right behind her before she spun around, taking him down with a right hook. It was a solid punch. Strong and from the chest.

Kevin stared up at her from the pavement, his nose spurting blood. "Jesus! What did you do *that* for?"

"Are you there, Norah?" the police officer was saying.

Norah lifted the phone back to her ear. "Yes," she said. "Sorry about that. Go ahead."

3

ALICIA

Seven hours. That's how much time had passed since Alicia collected two-and-a-half-year-old Theo from the police station and brought him to his new foster home. *Seven hours* since he scampered out of her grasp and disappeared under the dining room table. *Seven hours* since Alicia sat on the linoleum floor and promised him she would wait until he was ready to come out. Alicia always kept her promises to the kids. Which meant now she might have to die on this linoleum floor.

"Hey, buddy, I think *Bluey* might be on the TV," Alicia tried, without much hope. "Should we go and see?"

Theo didn't turn his little blond head from the wall. She had to admire his resolve. Since they'd arrived, he hadn't spoken, he'd refused all food and drink, and, if smell was anything to go by, he'd soiled himself. Still, he wouldn't budge.

Last night, he'd been taken to the police station by a neighbor who'd discovered him playing on the road at midnight, wearing nothing but a dirty nappy. Apparently his father had been too inebriated to realize he was gone. His mother had yet to be located and it wasn't looking hopeful. Alicia had hoped that returning Theo to Trish's, where he'd spent a few months earlier in the year, might provide Theo with some reassurance; but, if anything, his understanding of what was happening made things worse. His head remained down, his tiny, twiggy arms remained ramrod straight by his sides.

"Do you like chocolate?" she asked, as another foster kid, Aaron, sloped into the kitchen, and started rummaging in the cupboards, presumably for food. "I've got a Kit Kat here. Want some?"

Alicia broke off a chocolate finger and held it out to Theo under the table. To her delight, he scooted across the floor to inspect it.

"Ow!" she cried, as she felt the sharp milk teeth clamp down hard on her own fingers.

"You walked into that one," Aaron said, sitting at the table now, devouring a bag of crisps.

His comment delighted Alicia no end. In her experience, when kids felt comfortable enough to dis you, in her experience, it meant you were doing something right. As for the bite, Alicia had suffered worse. The fact was it took a certain kind of person to choose a woefully paid, underappreciated career in which most of the people you dealt with wanted to cause you physical harm. Alicia didn't blame the kids for disliking her—after all, in most instances she was the one who separated them from their parents. Of course they wanted to hit her, kick her, spit on her. It wore a lot of social workers down after a while, but for Alicia the opposite was true: knowing these kids had some fight left in them buoyed her. If there was one thing foster kids needed, it was fight.

Besides, Alicia had learned to accept being poorly treated a long time ago. It felt familiar, and in a way—even comforting. Like coming home.

"Oh yeah?" Alicia said to Aaron. "You think you can do better?"

"Five bucks says I can."

"Make it ten." Frankly Alicia would have paid a hundred, but Aaron held out his hand to shake on it, so Alicia did.

Alicia wasn't Aaron's caseworker, but she had a soft spot for him. At seventeen, Aaron had reached those precarious months before he aged out of foster care, and she always felt for those kids. The last time she'd seen Aaron she'd given him her card and told him to get in touch if he wanted some information about services and programs for kids aging out, or scholarships if he was interested in university. So far he hadn't reached out, and she suspected her card was in the rubbish bin, but there was always room for hope.

"Watch and learn," Aaron said, grabbing a fistful of his crisps and holding them under the table, palm up, like a kid feeding an animal at a petting zoo.

"Be careful," Alicia said. "He's got a sharp set of chompers."

As Theo glanced toward Aaron's outstretched hand, Alicia's phone rang. Normally she wouldn't answer the phone in this situation, but given that she likely wasn't getting out of here anytime soon, she decided to make an exception.

"Ten bucks," she said to Aaron. She stood up and accepted the call. "Hello?"

"Am I speaking to Alicia Connelly?"

"If you're a debt collector, no," Alicia said. "If I've won the lottery, yes."

She glanced at Aaron, who rolled his eyes. Theo was looking at Aaron's outstretched palm.

"Alicia, my name is Detective Ashleigh Patel," the woman said. "Have you got a minute?"

Alicia glanced at her watch. Six P.M. Not the latest call she'd had for crisis care, but late enough that it would be a struggle to find a family who'd be ready to take in a child tonight. Usually, it was a case manager who called to give her the particulars of a child's situation, but occasionally she did receive a call direct from the police. She got out her notebook and clicked her pen, waiting for the onslaught of grisly information—about the physical and emotional state of the child or children, their age or ages, and any previous history in the foster system.

"Sure. What have you got for me?"

A pause. "Actually, this is related to an investigation I'm working on. I'm hoping you might be able to help me."

Alicia unclicked her pen. "What investigation?"

Theo started eating the crisps directly from Aaron's hand, like a baby goat. Aaron made a grossed-out face, but he kept his hand there. He held his other hand out to Alicia, rubbing his index finger and thumb together. "Ten bucks," he mouthed. Alicia reached into her pocket for her wallet.

"It's in relation to a discovery made at Wild Meadows foster home in Port Agatha. I understand you grew up there?"

Alicia froze, her hand still in her pocket. "What?"

"I said it's in relation to—"

"Yes, sorry. I heard." She walked to the kitchen counter and leaned against it for support. "And yes . . . I . . . I spent a few years at Wild Meadows foster home when I was a kid."

Alicia's chest became tight. She had been waiting for this phone call for twenty-five years. Not *looking forward* to it . . . but waiting. It felt terrifying and exciting and important. Like the part of the movie when the truth starts to come out and the prisoner begins to believe they might have a shot at escaping death row.

"Well, as you may or may not be aware, Wild Meadows has recently been demolished. And while excavating, the construction workers uncovered . . ."

Aaron lowered another fistful of crisps under the table for Theo. Salt and crumbs were all over the boy's face and the floor.

". . . human remains. Bones, really. It looks like they've been there awhile. Possibly since the time that you were living there."

Alicia began to shake. She may have been waiting for this call for years but that didn't mean she was prepared for it. How could one prepare for something like this? Something that would, *should,* blow up her entire life?

"Are you there?" the detective asked.

"I'm here," she said. But she wasn't, not really. She was already back at Wild Meadows, reliving everything that had happened there twenty-five years ago with new, clear eyes.

4

JESSICA

After the call from Detective Patel, Jessica canceled her afternoon appointment (citing food poisoning, and offering the client a free Garage Storage Intervention session valued at $599—a little excessive, perhaps, but warranted under the circumstances) and drove directly home. By the time she got there, her sisters were already waiting in her living room.

Jessica hadn't told them to come; they just showed up. It wasn't a surprise, they always gathered at Jessica's house—perhaps because it was the most centrally located, but also because it was the nicest. Both Norah and Alicia lived happily in student-like accommodations, whereas Jessica lived in a beautifully renovated Edwardian home with three bedrooms, ceiling roses, two original fireplaces, and floor-to-ceiling windows that overlooked a sparkling aqua-tiled pool that she never swam in and, frankly, found it difficult even to look at. (Jessica hated pools. Every so often she considered filling it in.)

"Who do you think it is?" Alicia asked.

Norah frowned. "Who do I think *who* is?"

"The body, you goose."

"Oh. Right. Don't know."

Jessica looked at her sisters, who were *flopped* across various pieces of her furniture. Jessica had no idea how they could flop under the circumstances. Jessica never *flopped*. Jessica stood. Usually while tidying or cleaning or filing paperwork. *Doing*. Even when she was home alone, she sat upright, her feet on the floor or maybe tucked neatly underneath her. A few years back, Norah told Jessica that she always needed a nap after spending time with her because her energy was so exhausting. Evidently it was true, because a few weeks ago Norah had actually *taken* a nap midvisit, which frankly was a little rich as the purpose of the visit was for Jessica to do Norah's taxes (though, admittedly, Jessica preferred to work alone).

"Jess?" Alicia said, sitting up. Her hair was pulled up in a bun and her face was ringed with staticky ginger curls. "Who do you think it is?"

"How should I know?" Jessica snapped. "Wild Meadows is an old farmhouse. These bones might have been buried there for a hundred years for all we know. It could be anyone!"

"Okay," Alicia said, hands up like she was soothing a skittish horse. "Calm down."

Jessica laughed. *Calm down?* She couldn't remember the last time she'd felt calm. Panic was her constant state of being, as familiar to her as breathing. She imagined that even as a newborn she'd awoken each day with her heart in her throat, asking, *What will today be like? Will I forget something, or say the wrong thing? How can I make everyone happy? What if I can't?*

Despite her inner panic, a glance in the mirror above the mantel told her she looked utterly unflustered. Her muted makeup was flawless, her black hair was glossy and smooth, there wasn't a hint of color in her cheeks. Her white shift dress looked as fresh as when she'd put it on that morning. Of course it did. Alicia once joked that Jessica's linen shirts were too afraid to wrinkle. Quite right, Jessica had thought. They wouldn't dare.

As Jessica dragged in a breath she was reminded of an episode of the Mel Robbins podcast that she'd listened to recently. It was about how to deal with panic. Apparently panic felt quite a lot like excitement, and if you told yourself you were excited you could trick your feelings. She decided to try it now.

I'm excited that bones were found buried under Wild Meadows. Woo-hoo.

Great. Now she was a psychopath.

"The detective wants us to go to Port Agatha," Norah was saying. "Tomorrow."

Her tone was neutral, almost indifferent, but there were little giveaways that she was unsettled. The repetitive bounce of her right leg. The thumbnail she'd chewed down to the quick.

"Tomorrow?" Jessica exclaimed. "We can't just drop everything and go to Port Agatha."

"It's a police investigation, Jess," Alicia said. "I don't think we have a lot of choice. Besides, it's Saturday tomorrow."

"Of course we have a choice!" Jessica felt heat creeping up her neck. "We're not under arrest. We don't have to go there just because they asked us to."

Alicia, as usual, remained calm. "I'm just saying we might want to consider it. After all, we haven't done anything wrong. And if we refuse to go, how will it look?"

Jessica felt dangerously close to tears. This wasn't how she'd planned to spend the evening. She hated changing her plans; hated surprises and calls out of the blue, even when it was good news. And there was nothing good about this. This was her worst nightmare.

"I just . . . I just don't think I can go back there."

A long moment of silence passed, broken only by the jangle of Phil's keys in the door. From where she stood, Jessica heard him toss his keys, miss the bowl, and then chase after them as they skittered across the marble floor of the foyer.

"Hey, Phil," Alicia and Norah said in unison when he appeared in the living room a moment later in his Victoria Golf Club polo shirt. Phil had worked as a greenskeeper at the club for the past ten years, and he'd likely continue to do it for the next twenty. Jessica found herself irritated by this lack of ambition, even as she envied his contentment. And if there was one thing Phil radiated, it was contentment.

"Hey." He grinned. "I thought that was your car parked across the entire driveway, Norah."

He said it cheerfully, and Norah confirmed that it was indeed her car, equally cheerfully. She did not suggest moving it, nor did Phil ask her to. *He is so chill,* everyone always said. His mates called him "Chill Phil."

Now, for example, he looked so happy to see them all. And it was *actual* happiness, rather than the forced, polite kind. Jessica often tried to mimic his joyful demeanor, ever since a marriage counseling session a few years ago when he'd commented, "You just never seem happy to see me. I'd love it if you looked at me how you look at your sisters. If you cared about me the same way."

She felt awful when he said that. Particularly as she usually *was* happy to see him. She enjoyed his lanky, lingering presence in the house, his thoughtful commentary about whatever he'd listened to on the radio on the way home. She enjoyed caring for him—cooking his favorite meals, booking golf or surfing weekends, only buying one hundred percent cotton sheets, because any other kind made him itch. But the relationship could never compete with what she had with her sisters. Nothing could. They might not have been related by blood, but their time together in foster care had made them closer than biology ever could.

"It's a sister thing," Jessica had once said, glancing at their female therapist for solidarity. "No one loves their husband as much as their sisters, am I right?"

The therapist clearly didn't have any sisters, because she'd stabbed Jessica in the back. "I wouldn't say 'no one'—but it's interesting that you would think so."

They'd discontinued therapy shortly after that because Jessica was too busy helping Alicia move house and dealing with Norah's anger-management problems to attend appointments.

"There's lasagna in the oven," Jessica said to Phil. "You go ahead—I'm not eating."

"You didn't need to cook for me," he said.

They went through this dance every time: Phil pretending he knew how to cook, Jessica pretending she wouldn't have an anxiety attack if Phil started messing about in her kitchen. *Their* kitchen.

"I'm happy to do it," Jessica said. "But, Phil, would you mind giving us a minute? We're dealing with some family stuff."

"Cool," he said, and wandered toward the kitchen without another word. Chill Phil.

"Thank you!" she called after him, smiling extra hard.

"We need to go to Port Agatha," Alicia said when he was gone, her tone more decisive now. "If we leave in the morning, we'll be there by lunchtime and you can be home by tomorrow night. It's only a day. We can do this."

"We'll be together," Norah added.

Jessica stared at her sisters. They'd gone mad.

"If we go to Port Agatha they're going to pore over every detail of our childhood and analyze every moment we remember from Wild Meadows!" Jessica cried. "Have you forgotten what happened last time we did that?"

"They didn't believe us," Alicia admitted.

"They thought we were batshit crazy," Norah added.

"Exactly. So you'll forgive me if I don't want to go running back there after one vague phone call."

Jessica sat in an attempt to present an air of finality. As far as she was concerned, the matter was settled. There was no need to go to Port Agatha. The discovery of the bones was tragic, but nothing to do with them. They couldn't shed any light on them, even if they wanted to.

"But what if we *weren't* crazy?" Alicia said quietly.

Norah and Alicia were no longer flopped. They sat upright, spines straight, their eyes wide like the vulnerable little girls they'd once been.

"Alicia," Jessica warned, but it was too late. Pandora's box was open. Maybe it had been open from the moment the detective called.

"If we weren't crazy," Norah was saying, almost to herself, "it explains why human bones were found under Wild Meadows."

This was exactly what Jessica was afraid of.

5

JESSICA

Jessica only had a handful of memories of life before she came to Wild Meadows. According to her social worker, she'd lived in a tiny studio apartment that was perched above the shop where her mother—a Chinese immigrant—worked as a seamstress. When Jessica sent her mind back to that time, she could unearth only a few small details—the smell of instant noodles cooking in the microwave; the sound of her mother's slippers scuffing on the kitchen floor; the women standing on chairs while her mother hemmed their skirts and trousers. As for her father, she always associated him with the smell of cigarettes and the prickle of his stubble when he kissed her cheek, but she might easily have invented those things. There was no information about him in the social worker's file for him.

She did distinctly remember the day her mother died. She'd

been at day care. When the police officer came into the room, Jessica had thought it was going to be like the firefighter's visit they'd had the week prior. But the police officer spoke only to the teacher, who immediately looked at Jessica.

They told Jessica her mother had been very sad, and then she died. Jessica didn't know you could die from being sad. She remembered being very careful not to cry about her mother in case she died too. To distract herself from her pain, she focused on practical matters. Jessica didn't have any aunts or uncles, and no one knew anything about her mother's parents.

"Who will look after me?"

"Where will I live?"

"What will I do for money?"

Jessica hadn't known about the foster system back then, of course. She pictured herself living out of a cardboard box on the street. She was already wondering if she'd be allowed to go back to her home to get some cushions and blankets when the social worker, Scott, told her "the good news." He'd found a place for Jessica to go—wasn't that lucky?

Jessica's instinct was to agree. Yes. That was very lucky.

"She's a single woman, who doesn't have any children of her own. She lives on a country estate called Wild Meadows with horses and a swimming pool!"

Her social worker's eyes popped, like Jessica had won a prize. Jessica remembered conjuring up a smile. She didn't want to disappoint him. And she didn't want to be sad, in case she died.

When she arrived at Wild Meadows later that day, Jessica smiled again—and not just because she didn't want to disappoint Scott, the social worker. The house looked like something out of a storybook.

A classic white weatherboard farmhouse with shutters and a wide porch, overlooking the pastures and stables, complete with a huge swimming pool. Still, despite its grandeur, she felt a pang of longing for her mother and the cozy little apartment they had shared.

"I'm going to live *here*?" she said.

"Lucky, eh?" Scott said, using that word again. It prompted Jessica to reframe it in her mind. In the past, she'd thought being lucky was an unequivocally good thing. But there was another side to it, she realized. If you were lucky, it implied that your good fortune hadn't been earned. You couldn't question it, or take it for granted. You had to be *grateful*. Because what had been given to you could just as easily be taken away.

The woman standing on the porch looked like a fairy princess. She had wavy golden hair, blue eyes, and wore a white dress covered in tiny blue flowers. Her feet were bare and she *smelled* of flowers.

"Darling girl," she said, squatting down. "My name is Miss Fairchild."

To Jessica's surprise, the woman wrapped her arms around her. It was the first time someone had hugged Jessica since her mother died. It brought tears to her eyes. When she pulled back, the woman saw her tears. "What's the matter?"

"I miss my mummy."

"I know, poppet," Miss Fairchild said, kissing each of Jessica's eyelids. Her voice was sweet as honey. "But I promise I'm going to make everything better."

"You are?"

Jessica felt an agonizing burst of optimism. No one—not the day-care teacher, the police officer, or the social worker—had said that to her. Maybe this woman *could* make everything better? Maybe she could bring her mother back and make everything okay again?

Miss Fairchild beamed. "I'm going to make you forget all about your mummy," she said. "Wait and see. Before long, you'll forget she ever existed."

Miss Fairchild blasted into Jessica's world with everything a four-year-old girl needed. Love, security, devotion. Grand gestures, like allowing her to paint her room pink with purple stripes, and small gestures, like leaving tiny letters in envelopes from the tooth fairy. It was hard not to be swept up in it. Jessica didn't try. After all, she was *lucky*.

She didn't let Miss Fairchild out of her sight. If Miss Fairchild was raking the leaves, Jessica was too. If Miss Fairchild was running errands, or cleaning the house or going to the bathroom, Jessica was by her side. Miss Fairchild used to joke that the only time they were apart was when Jessica was sleeping, but even that wasn't true, because most nights Jessica crept across the hall into Miss Fairchild's room, climbed into her bed and snuggled up close to her.

Miss Fairchild didn't seem to mind Jessica's clinginess. If anything, she encouraged it. She even dressed them alike. "So we look like mother and daughter," she explained, even though the dresses were the only similarity between them. Miss Fairchild's hair was as golden and curly as Jessica's was dark and pin-straight; her eyes were as blue as Jessica's were brown.

"That child's feet haven't touched the ground since she arrived," people around town said. Or, worse, "You baby her," when Miss Fairchild pushed her along the main street in a stroller that she was too big for. Jessica always wanted to tell them to mind their own business. She loved that stroller, loved being held on Miss Fairchild's hip or sitting in the antique high chair in the kitchen while Miss Fairchild fed her. It made her feel safe. But if Jessica worried that Miss Fairchild might change her behavior in response to people's comments, she needn't have. If anything, it made Miss Fairchild more determined.

"Darling girl," she'd say, "I didn't get to push you or hold you or feed you when you were a baby, so this is our time with each other, and no one is going to take it away from us."

It was exactly what Jessica needed. She had only one thing to offer in exchange, and she gave it freely: her utter devotion.

"A party fit for a princess," Miss Fairchild said.

It was Jessica's fifth birthday and she was dressed in a pink tutu, with pink lipstick and a pink tiara. Miss Fairchild wore a pink sleeveless dress with a drop waist and a ruffled skirt that she'd made on her sewing machine. In the past few months, Jessica had become accustomed to feeling excited whenever she heard whirring in the kitchen.

The party was held in the garden. The porch was filled with pink balloons, the trestle tables were draped in pink tablecloths, and the napkins, the cake, the piñata and the goody bags were all pink. Pink was Miss Fairchild's favorite color—which made it Jessica's too.

Miss Fairchild had invited all the local kids, most of whom Jessica hadn't met before. Several of them tried to play with her, but Jessica felt shy, preferring to stay wrapped in the folds of Miss Fairchild's pink skirt instead. Jessica was grateful for the party, as she was grateful for everything Miss Fairchild did for her. But she preferred it when it was just the two of them, cleaning and organizing the house.

At the end of the afternoon, everyone lined up to thank Miss Fairchild for the lovely party.

"Anything for my darling girl," Miss Fairchild told them.

That night, as they lay in bed, Jessica whispered to her, "I wish I was really your girl."

She was unable to look at Miss Fairchild when she said it. As close as they were, and as much as Miss Fairchild doted on her, Jessica understood the tenuous nature of their relationship. Miss Fairchild wasn't her mother. There was no permanent agreement. It troubled Jessica, and she knew it troubled Miss Fairchild.

"We could pretend," Miss Fairchild said.

"Really?" Jessica whispered.

"Why not? You could call me Mummy. I like the sound of it, don't you?"

Jessica *really* liked the sound of it.

"Say it now," Miss Fairchild instructed.

"Mummy." Jessica giggled.

"Sat it again!"

"Mummy!"

"Shout it!"

"Mummy! Mummy! Mummy!" Jessica screamed at the top of her lungs.

"Yes," Miss Fairchild said with a nod. "I like it. It's settled, my darling girl."

Jessica's heart was so full she thought it might burst.

6

JESSICA

BEFORE

School came as a rude shock. To Jessica and Miss Fairchild both.
"I don't want to go," Jessica said on her first day. Her arms
were wrapped around Miss Fairchild's legs tightly, a pair of hand-
cuffs. "I'm *not* going."

The classroom felt loud and cluttered and chaotic and made
Jessica yearn for home, where she knew where everything was and
who was looking after her. Compared to Wild Meadows, school
felt barbaric.

"It's all right, honey," said Miss Ramirez, her prep teacher. She
squatted beside Jessica, whose head was buried in Miss Fairchild's
skirt. "We're going to have a lot of fun. And at the end of the day,
Mummy will be here to pick you up, okay?"

Jessica looked up at her. Miss Fairchild nodded; her eyes were
also full of tears.

"Maybe I should stay for a bit . . ." she started, but Miss Ramirez was firm.

"No. Let's start as we mean to go on."

Jessica howled as Miss Fairchild walked away. And, for the next few hours, she stared out the window, hoping to see her mother hurrying back to declare it was all a misunderstanding. It was only when Miss Ramirez asked her to organize the colored pencils into containers that Jessica turned away from the window. Since she was stuck here, she might as well help.

After the pencils, she did the crayons and the textas. When she was done, she asked Miss Ramirez if there was anything else that needed organizing.

"Jessica!" the teacher exclaimed. "Have you done all this? My goodness, aren't you a *miracle*. Class, what do we say to Jessica for organizing all our things so beautifully?"

"Thank you, Jessica," they droned at her.

Jessica had to admit that she didn't hate it.

By the end of the day the craft supplies cupboard was in perfect order. It broke Jessica's heart a little to hear that, tomorrow, they'd be getting things out of there again. Just when it was looking so good!

When they burst out of the classroom, Miss Fairchild was standing at the front of a pack of anxious-looking mothers watching the gate. Jessica ran headlong into her arms.

"I was so worried!" she said, bending to cover Jessica in kisses. "Are you okay?"

"Yes!" Jessica said. "I organized the craft cupboard and washed the paintbrushes and sorted the paper into color piles. And I made a friend! Bonnie and I colored in a picture of a fish!"

"Bonnie?" Miss Fairchild stood up straight. Blinked. "How wonderful."

Jessica slid her hand into Miss Fairchild's, ready to answer all her questions and describe every minute of her day. But Miss Fairchild didn't say another word. Didn't ask a single question about school. They walked the entire forty-five minutes home in silence.

That afternoon, Miss Fairchild suggested a swim.

"No," Jessica said. She had a fear of swimming. Jessica had a fear of most things she didn't know how to do. She'd been in the pool just a handful of times, and only under duress while wearing her float. Each time Miss Fairchild had said, "Next time, no float, okay?"

"Come on, you have to learn to swim sometime," she cajoled. "Everyone else at school will be able to swim. You don't want to be the only one who can't swim, do you?"

It was a smart strategy. Jessica wanted to fit in. She certainly didn't want to be the only one who couldn't do something. More important, she wanted to please Miss Fairchild.

"All right," she said. "But I want to wear my float."

Miss Fairchild agreed, but filled the float with so little air that Jessica doubted it would be very helpful.

"It needs more air!" Jessica whined.

But Miss Fairchild was firm. "I'll keep you afloat. You trust me, don't you?"

Jessica nodded, but on the edge of the pool she hesitated.

"Come on," Miss Fairchild said, her arms outstretched. "It'll be Christmas soon."

Jessica jumped. She broke through the water's surface and into the thick, aquamarine silence. It seemed to take forever for her to rise to the top. Panic set in quickly and intensely. Through the water she could see Miss Fairchild's pale skinny legs and navy one-piece swimsuit with the frill. She thrashed her arms wildly, trying to propel herself over to her mother. And it worked—she was getting closer. But just as Jessica reached out for her, the last of her breath disappearing from her chest, Miss Fairchild *stepped away*.

Jessica thrashed her arms harder. Each time she got close, Miss Fairchild retreated.

It went on and on. Jessica began to feel light-headed. Her panic started to slide into something blacker. Her arms stopped thrashing. Her lungs filled. And then . . . she broke through the water's surface.

"You did it!" Miss Fairchild was holding her, smiling brightly, beads of water sparkling on her forehead.

Jessica coughed, then vomited—once and then again. When she was finally able to drag in a breath, she rested her head against Mummy's chest.

"You swam, my darling girl," Miss Fairchild said.

"The float didn't work," Jessica told her when she could finally talk, still gasping for air between words.

"No," Miss Fairchild agreed. "Floats can let you down. So can people. But Mummy will never let anything happen to you."

Jessica coughed up some more water.

"You can't rely on anyone or anything except Mummy."

Jessica was too tired to reply, so she just clung to her mother's neck. Judging by Miss Fairchild's smile, it was a good enough response.

The months went by, and Jessica's world became smaller. There were no playdates, no parties, no visitors to Wild Meadows other than the postman. Apart from at school, Jessica didn't see anyone other than Miss Fairchild. Slowly, Miss Fairchild became Jessica's entire universe.

Jessica became intimately attuned to her moods. She learned how to please her, how to charm her, how to soothe her. She knew when it was a good time to ask for something, and when to accept that all was lost. Miss Fairchild was the center of her life, her everything. And if she kept it this way, she'd be rewarded with love, which was all Jessica wanted.

They had a strict routine at Wild Meadows. It involved a great deal of cleaning. Each morning after they woke they made the beds, wiped down the bathroom sinks and mirrors, and carried the laundry downstairs. Then they swept the porch and path, dusted and hoovered and polished, all before breakfast. Only when the laundry had been put on could they start to think about breakfast.

"You are the best helper, darling girl," Miss Fairchild always said.

Jessica was always quick to jump up after breakfast to wash, dry, and put away the dishes (Miss Fairchild didn't like dishes being left to dry in the rack). After that, they hung out the laundry, which was brought in, folded, and put away as soon as it had dried. Any rooms that weren't used in the course of the day were cleaned in the afternoon before dinner.

By the time Jessica was eight, she could clean Wild Meadows from top to bottom single-handedly. It wasn't a chore. Their cleaning routine gave her a sense of purpose that was hard to describe.

If Jessica's purpose was cleaning, Miss Fairchild's was balancing the books. She was obsessed with it.

"People see this place and think we're wealthy," Miss Fairchild often said. "But if we don't keep on top of our costs, we could lose everything in a heartbeat, do you understand?"

Jessica didn't really, but she nodded, as she always did when Miss Fairchild said anything. She knew that Miss Fairchild was careful with money. She made a small income by renting out paddocks to neighboring farms, and she was given a stipend with which to care for Jessica, but it wasn't a lot. To make it last, they needed to be frugal. Electricity and gas were a luxury. Food had to be bought on special or past its best-before date. Clothes were purchased at charity shops, or made on the sewing machine.

"Waste not, want not," Jessica would say, parroting one of Miss Fairchild's favorite phrases.

"Quite right, darling girl."

By the time Jessica was ten, Miss Fairchild's money concerns were becoming more of an issue. Interest rates were going up and, according to her, they needed to tighten their belt. But they lived so frugally that even Miss Fairchild was forced to admit there wasn't much left to tighten.

"Did I pay the electricity bill?" she'd ask from time to time, her eyes widening as she tried to recall. She always had paid it, and Jessica tried to reassure her of this, but Miss Fairchild could never relax until she'd checked for herself.

"I did," she'd say after she'd checked, as if someone was reprimanding her. "See? I did pay it."

When things got really bad, Miss Fairchild stopped sleeping. Jessica knew this because she often felt her slip from the bed in the night and tiptoe down the stairs to "balance the books." Often, on those nights, she never came back to bed.

One day after school, the doorbell rang.

It was . . . unexpected. They didn't have visitors at Wild Meadows. The only time the doorbell rang was when a package was delivered, and that was always first thing in the morning.

Jessica was so surprised she actually screamed. "Who is *that*?"

Miss Fairchild smiled and smoothed Jessica's hair back from her face. "No need to overreact, darling girl. Shall we answer it?"

It was Scott Michaels, Jessica's social worker.

It was odd. Usually when Scott was scheduled to visit, Miss Fairchild made sure they had the house in tip-top shape—even more so than usual—and Jessica was dressed in her nicest clothes. Not today. Now that Jessica thought of it, it had been a while since Scott had been to Wild Meadows. At first he'd come every few months. On those occasions, they'd sat alone in the living room while he read out questions from a sheet of paper, ticking off each item on his list with a lead pencil. Jessica always gave Miss Fairchild a glowing report. She supposed that was why he'd decided it wasn't necessary to show up anymore.

"Hello, Jessica," he said to her now, smiling to reveal small yellow teeth. He was just as she remembered: thin and weedy, with dirt under his fingernails. As usual, his shirt was unbuttoned a little too far, and a tuft of black chest hair was visible which Jessica thought was gross.

Jessica had always felt uncomfortable around Scott. She couldn't put her finger on why—he was always polite, and he'd certainly found a wonderful home for her. Yet, the feeling remained. In light of this, when Miss Fairchild told her to go and play while she talked to Scott in the living room, she felt relieved. She didn't go and play, of course. Jessica was a good, well-behaved child, but she could eavesdrop just as well as the next kid.

"There is a girl, around Jessica's age, available for placement now," Jessica heard him say. "As far as payment goes, the allowance would be the same as you're paid for Jessica. It will start the day she is placed with you."

So this was why Scott was here, Jessica realized. *This* was how Miss Fairchild was going to sort out their money worries.

"I've got to be honest, though," the social worker continued. "She's pretty troubled. She's been in and out of care since she was six and has had several violent episodes. She's claimed some predatory behavior from her current foster father, but I must admit, I have my doubts; she could be—"

"I'll take her," Miss Fairchild interrupted.

Scott laughed. "I know you're desperate, but you might want to take a look at her report before agreeing to anything."

"I said I'll take her."

"All right," he said, as if he thought she was crazy. "I'll get the wheels turning then."

Jessica could tell from the noises in the room that he was standing up. She crept out of the hallway and slipped into the kitchen. As the two adults walked toward the front door, she heard Scott say, "I can also organize for the clothing and miscellaneous allowance to be released immediately, if that helps."

"That would be great," Miss Fairchild said.

When she'd closed the door behind him, Miss Fairchild called, "Jessica, you can come out now!"

Jessica slunk into the hallway.

"I assume you heard that?"

"Another girl is coming to live with us?"

Miss Fairchild nodded. "I'm sure it feels strange—and it *will* be strange for a while. Change is hard for everyone. It will be especially hard for this new girl."

"Do we really have to do this?" Jessica said, looking up at her. "Scott said that the girl is troubled. Violent!"

"Not everyone has been as lucky as you have, Jessica," she said sharply. "It's time we showed some charity to people less fortunate than we are."

"You're right," she said hastily, in response to her tone. There was nothing she hated more than Miss Fairchild being unhappy with her. "I'm being silly. *Of course* we should help this girl. I've been so lucky."

That must have been the right response, because Miss Fairchild stepped forward and kissed the top of Jessica's head. But there was something robotic about the gesture. It was as if she'd already moved on from Jessica and was thinking about her new child—the troubled, violent one they were going to save from her unfortunate life.

THE OFFICE OF DR. WARREN, PSYCHIATRIST

"Right," Dr. Warren says. He is wearing a different tie—green today—but everything else is the same: the brown suit, the crossed legs, the manila folder in his lap. I've been sitting in silence for six minutes so I'm surprised when he suddenly addresses me.

I blink. "Right . . . what?"

"Right . . . are you ready to talk about Wild Meadows?"

When I shake my head, he sighs heavily. Clearly, he wants to hear about what happened there. Who wouldn't? Despite his show of acting disinterested, he probably thinks it's a real coup, getting to speak to me. It makes me wonder about the kind of man who does a job like his. The kind of stories he must hear, day in and day out . . . I imagine it does something to a person.

"In that case," he says, "you may as well talk about something else."

He scribbles something in his file. He is probably playing su-doku or doing the crossword. Perhaps if I were in his position, I'd do the same.

"Like what?" I ask.

"Childhood?" he says with a shrug, as if he is making it up as he goes along. "Tell me about a time when you were happy."

"Okay." One thing to be said for having a horrific childhood is that pinpointing the happy parts is easy. "In the early days of my childhood, believe it or not, I was spoiled. No one forced me to eat my vegetables, to make my bed, to contribute much to the house-hold chores."

I try to assess Dr. Warren for a reaction, but his expression is bland. Carefully neutral, or perhaps bored. A sixth sense tells me he'd prefer to hear about the gory stuff.

"I was an only child," I continue. "My dad was my hero. When I was little, I wanted to go wherever he went. Even at dawn, when he got up to milk the cows, I was right by his side. My mum liked to sleep in, so that was a time just for us. When I got older and started school I couldn't go with him to milk the cows anymore, but I still stood on the back porch every morning and waved to him when he left. I did it for years. Then, one morning, he didn't come back. Massive heart attack, apparently. And that's kind of it for the happy memories."

Dr. Warren jots something down. A note about me, or perhaps he just figured out the answer to seven across.

"After that it was just me and Mum," I continue. "The commu-nity rallied, as country folk do. People brought food and arrived to help with the farmwork. It was a relief because Mum didn't have the faintest idea how to run a farm—she was a city girl. I overheard some of the neighbors saying that they assumed we would move into town eventually. I hoped they were right. Dad's absence hurt anew every day. I thought a fresh start would be good for us. But six months passed, and Mum didn't suggest we move. When I brought it up, she said, 'Maybe.'"

Dr. Warren is looking at me now. Whether it is intentional or I just happen to be in his line of sight is unclear.

"She slept a lot," I go on. "She stopped showering, started drinking and taking pills. She sent people away when they came to help with chores, even though they needed doing and she wasn't attempting to do them herself. She stopped opening the bills and notices that appeared in our letterbox, each more urgent than the last. When I drew her attention to them, she threw them in the fire." Even all these years later, I can feel rage building at the memory. "Her ineptitude and her inability to keep us afloat terrified me. It also made me furious."

Dr. Warren cocks his head with something resembling interest. His buffed scalp catches the sunlight, reflecting it brilliantly across the room.

"I don't know how much later it was, but at some point a group of women from the local church came to the house. I recognized a couple of them. They told us the church had funds for people who'd fallen upon difficult times. I'd never been much of a believer but when they said that, I was willing to suspend my disbelief. The women said Mum would be eligible and that they were going to help her get her life back on track. They also suggested that we think about coming to church services. 'The only one who can help with your spiritual recovery is the Lord,' they said. We weren't churchgoers, but if they were going to help us I didn't care if they represented the Devil himself. They handed me a pocket-sized prayer card on the way out the door. It was the Our Father, printed and laminated.

I kept it for a long time. At that point, I thought God might really be the only one who could help. Unfortunately, it turned out that even He couldn't."

Having finally aroused Dr. Warren's interest, I talk and talk. Turns out you start to crave attention after a while, when no one pays you any. Dr. Warren only looks at his crossword once or twice. Before I know it, there is a knock at the door to indicate that our time is up.

"You did well today," Dr. Warren tells me. "See you next time."

I'm still not sure about Dr. Warren, but I have to admit, I blush a little at his compliment. I never wanted to be in therapy, but since I appear to be stuck with it, I plan to graduate at the top of my class.

7

NORAH

Around 9:00 P.M., Norah stood up from Jessica's couch. They'd managed to convince Jessica to go to Port Agatha and speak to the police first thing in the morning. Like Jessica, Norah didn't relish the idea, but as it seemed to be an inevitability it felt wasteful to keep the debate going. Besides, a part of her was intrigued by the discovery of the bones. She wanted to know who they belonged to. She wanted answers.

Norah was a big fan of answers. It was, undoubtedly, why she was so fond of maths. The knowledge that the square root of this equaled that had always been a balm for her soul. Even when she took into account irrational numbers—numbers that could not be expressed as the quotient of two integers—there was certainty in knowing that combining an irrational number with a rational would form something real. Norah had thought she'd done that with her memories of her childhood at Wild Meadows. She'd taken her irrational memories—the ones that the police and psychologists had deemed to be false—and combined them with rational facts to form truth. But the discovery of the bones meant she was back to square one: stuck with an irrational number, with nothing rational to help her make sense of it.

It was why she needed to go back to Port Agatha.

As Norah slipped out, Alicia waved but Jessica didn't even notice. The irony of Jessica always worrying about *her* was not lost on Norah.

In the driveway, Norah unlocked her car and got inside, taking a minute to bask in the silence and the comforting scent of old dog vomit that had dried into the seats. Today had involved far too much talking. Norah appreciated the great wonder of communication as much as the next person, but she despised it in excess. She particularly despised it when the topic had anything to do with her childhood.

She started the car and was preparing to drive when her phone flashed with a new message.

> My nose is broken. I've spent the entire night in the
> emergency room. You can't just go around assaulting
> people, Nora.

The message was from someone called Kevin. Norah was about to reply that he had the wrong number when she remembered the man she'd put into a cab to the hospital a few hours earlier, blood dripping down the front of his shirt.

Shit.

She hadn't told her sisters about him. She'd been distracted by the news of the discovery at Wild Meadows, but even if she hadn't, she probably would have kept it to herself. After what the judge had said about Norah running out of chances, Jessica would just worry, and what was the point of that? Norah could take care of this herself.

She picked up the phone and thumbed in a reply.

> Send me a list of your medical expenses and I'll pay them.
> P.S. It's Norah. With an 'h'.

Three dots appeared immediately. A second later, another message.

> It was a public hospital. It's not about the money.

Jesus H. Christ. Now the man had principles?

She turned on the car light, lifted her top, and snapped a photo of her breasts. Let's see what his principles thought of that.

> For your pain and suffering.

She sent it. For a moment, there was no response. Then Norah saw dots.

> That's . . . not what I expected. Wow.

She could practically see his revolting smile. That should take care of it. Hallelujah. Norah thumbed another quick message.

> Just don't go to the cops, okay. I have a community
> corrections order. It's like a suspended sentence.

> Lol. Seriously?

Seriously. You should count yourself lucky. The last guy didn't
come off as well as you.

Kevin sent back a laughing face, which was weird, but Norah
figured she'd got her point across. She chalked up Kevin's easy
acceptance of the situation to the fact that she was extremely attractive, and men tended to make poor choices when it came to
extremely attractive women. It was one of the few certainties in
Norah's life that she could rely on.

She dusted off her hands theatrically, and tossed the phone onto
the passenger seat. There, she thought. She'd taken care of it. If there
was one thing Norah had learned from growing up in foster care,
she thought as she drove away, it was how to take care of things. Her
methods were a little unorthodox, perhaps, but they had to be. Back
when she was a little girl, it was undoubtedly her unorthodox methods that kept her and her sisters alive.

8

NORAH

Y ou're lucky to be coming to this home," Norah's social worker, Scott, told her as they pulled up at Wild Meadows.

Norah looked up at the house doubtfully. "Why am I lucky?"

It was an important question, Norah had determined. She was ten years old, and it was her seventh foster placement. She'd been told she was lucky to go to the last place, where she'd shared a room with a teenage boy who liked to crawl into bed with her at night. (When she'd told her foster mother, the woman was unconcerned. "If he does it again, kick him in the balls," she'd said. Good advice, as it turned out.) She'd been told she was lucky to go to the place with the cat who bit her so deeply she'd needed eight stitches and an IV drip. She'd been told she was lucky when she was sent to the place that made the kids eat hot sauce if they asked for more food. This time, she wanted to understand why she was lucky.

Scott pulled up the handbrake. "Because you have somewhere to live."

He smiled, too stupid to be ashamed of his disgusting little teeth. But his eyes remained dead, empty holes in his face.

Scott, Norah had learned, was an asshole. The type who muttered around kids and laughed too loudly around grown-ups. When he'd collected Norah that morning he'd said, "My, haven't you grown?" and his eyes had lingered on her a little too long.

Norah *had* grown in the previous few months. She was the tallest in her class at her last school, taller even than the boys. Taller even than Scott, which wasn't hard. She had also started to become soft and curvy in the breast area ("early for your age," her last foster mother told her), which, from the way Scott's gaze skimmed her chest, had not gone unnoticed.

She crossed her arms and stared him down. *I see you, asshole.*

"Miss Fairchild is a very nice woman," he continued. "She has another foster daughter around your age."

"Is there a Mr. Fairchild?"

Also an important question. At another placement, there had been a Mr. who always sat very close to Norah on the couch. Norah had seen the writing on the wall long before the day he'd opened his trousers, so she had her pocketknife ready. If she was going to need her pocketknife here, it would be useful to have a heads-up.

"No Mr. Fairchild," Scott said.

As they walked toward the house, the front door opened, and a woman emerged. She had blond hair and blue eyes, and she reminded Norah of the Barbie she'd played with at her therapist's office, except that the Barbie's hair had been hacked off and this woman's hair was shoulder-length and mousse-scrunched-wavy. She wore a pink sleeveless dress with a drop waist.

"Hello!" said Barbie. "I'm Miss Fairchild."

"I'm Norah," Norah said. "With an h."

The woman blinked.

"You look like Barbie," Norah said.

The woman let out a short, high-pitched laugh. "My goodness," she said. "Aren't you funny?"

"Call me if she gives you any trouble," Scott said to Miss Fairchild. "I'll be back in two weeks to check in."

Scott always said that when he left Norah at a new placement and then she didn't see him again for months. She wondered why he bothered. He didn't make eye contact with Norah as he climbed back into his car.

"Won't you come in?" Miss Fairchild said when he was gone.

Norah, clutching her garbage bag full of possessions, followed her into the house.

"Isn't she pretty, Jessica? Miss Fairchild was saying to the other child. "She could be a model!"

Norah snuck a look at Jessica. Despite Scott saying she was around Norah's age, she was about half Norah's height and—judging by her behavior—a quarter of her intelligence. She sidled alongside Miss Fairchild, oddly close, perhaps territorial. Norah wanted to tell her to relax; she could have the freakish blonde all to herself, thank you very much.

"First things first," Miss Fairchild said when they reached the stairs. "I want you to know that whatever happened at your last place will not happen here."

"What happened?" Jessica asked.

Miss Fairchild nudged her sharply. "Jessica!"

But Norah didn't care. She looked directly at Jessica. "I kicked my foster brother in the balls when he crawled into bed with me. He was a perv."

Miss Fairchild exchanged a glance with Jessica, the two of them raising their eyebrows in sync. They reminded Norah of Tweedledum and Tweedledee.

"Well," Miss Fairchild said finally, "I want you to know that you're safe here."

"Good," Norah said. She was genuinely relieved to hear it, but she had her pocketknife for backup all the same. After the experiences she'd had, she wasn't inclined to take anyone's word for it. "So what are the house rules?"

It was yet another question she'd learned to ask up front, before she could be found guilty of an infraction she didn't know about, or that had been newly created.

"We all pitch in with the cleaning," Miss Fairchild said. "It's a big place so there's a lot to do."

This was fine by Norah. At her previous placement the house had been verging on squalor. The kids all had to share a bed, and in three months the sheets hadn't seen the inside of the washing machine. When she offered to wash them herself, she'd been told she was a snobby little brat and made to sleep on the floor.

"Is there a particular chore you'd enjoy doing?"

"Laundry?" she suggested.

Miss Fairchild smiled. "That would be perfect."

"But that's my job," Jessica protested, tugging at her foster mother's skirt.

Miss Fairchild ignored her.

"Do we have a bedtime?" Norah asked.

This tended to vary wildly from place to place. At one foster

home, she'd been put to bed at 6:00 P.M., along with the toddlers
and babies, so her foster parents could drink beer. At another, she'd
been left to her own devices and put herself to bed whenever she
was tired.

"How about eight o'clock? You can sleep in the bedroom opposite mine. Jessica will make up the beds for you both."

Jessica looked surprised. Actually she looked *appalled*.

"Come now, Jessica," Miss Fairchild said, "you can't sleep in my
bed forever. Of course, if *you* are scared during the night, Norah,
you're welcome to come into my bed. You're in a new environment."

"Mummy—" Jessica started.

"*Enough!*" Miss Fairchild's reaction was so swift that even Norah
was startled. She gripped Jessica's arm just above the elbow, tightly
enough to lift Jessica's heels. Her face became white as chalk. "It's
not just the two of us anymore, Jessica. The sooner you understand
that, the better." Miss Fairchild's fingernails were digging into Jessica's skin. Their faces were almost touching. "And enough of this
'Mummy' nonsense. From now on you're to call me Miss Fairchild."

When Miss Fairchild let go, there were marks on Jessica's arms
and she was blinking back tears.

"Right," Miss Fairchild said, her smile returning. Her eyes,
Norah noticed now, weren't like Barbie's. Rather than being
startled-looking, this woman's eyes were sharp. "I'll get you some
fresh sheets and towels."

With that she disappeared, leaving Norah and Jessica blinking
in her wake. It wasn't the outburst that unsettled Norah; she'd seen
plenty worse. The speed of her recovery, though, complete with a
fresh maniacal smile—that was new. Norah didn't like new.

"You'd better not go into her room," Jessica said softly, not looking at Norah.

"I won't," Norah said.

She wasn't trying to make peace. It was simply that the idea of visiting that woman's bed in the middle of the night was infinitely scarier than any nightmare Norah might be trying to escape.

At her first foster home, Norah had received a fist in the stomach before she'd even made it in the door. She'd just climbed out of the social worker's car and was standing on the nature strip when the boy approached from behind. She was six, the boy was thirteen.

She didn't see it coming. One minute she was standing there, the next she was doubled over, struggling for breath. Her caseworker, who'd been fetching her garbage bag from the trunk, scolded the boy, demanding to know why he'd done it.

"Because she's new," he said. His tone said *duh*.

Norah hadn't understood at the time, but she soon did. She even came to appreciate it. A swift punch was akin to an orientation. It taught you who was in charge, who to look out for, and where you stood.

Before long, Norah had learned to brace for the first punch. Not long after that, she learned to throw it.

It vexed Norah that the rest of the world didn't operate this way. It would have been useful, for example, if Miss Fairchild had given her a swift punch that first day. At least then she would've known what was coming.

At bedtime, Jessica used the bathroom first, then Norah. Jessica explained this to Norah as if it were very important. When Norah was finished, she returned to find the room in darkness.

She stopped in the doorway. The bedroom had a sloping ceiling and a dormer window and the blind was drawn. Once the door was closed, it would be hard to see anything at all. Norah had never liked darkness. She had a dim memory of having been blindfolded once. The details were hazy, but she remembered laughter (someone else's) and terror (her own). Years later, even though she understood she wasn't in danger, her body didn't seem to care. It still heard the laughter and felt the terror.

"I put your clothes away," Jessica said. She was already in one of the wrought-iron twin beds; Norah could see the S-shaped mound under the covers. "I think you'll find the system makes sense. Undies in the top drawer, then tops and jumpers, then pants. Dresses are in the wardrobe."

"Thanks," Norah said. If the exacting way Jessica lined up her things on her dresser was any measure of the way she did thingsc—everything at right angles and organized by like (hair care, dental care, etc.)—Norah assumed she would have done a reasonable job of it.

"Are you going to come in?" Jessica asked.

Norah didn't move. Her heels dug into the floorboards, as if someone was preparing to push her inside.

She was still standing that way when Miss Fairchild appeared a moment later. She was still wearing the floral dress from earlier, but the lipstick and eye shadow had been washed off and her face looked like a blank, creamy moon. "Is everything all right, Norah?"

"I don't like the dark."

"Well, why didn't you say so?" She seemed delighted to be able to help, marching downstairs and returning a minute or two later with a lamp. "Will this do?"

Norah took the lamp. There was a white wooden bedside table next to her bed, and an outlet was visible beside it. "Yes, thanks."

"Is there anything else you need?"

"Nope," Norah said. She crossed the room, plugged in the lamp and climbed into her bed, pulling the blankets around her. To her surprise, Miss Fairchild followed her, sitting on the edge of her bed. When she bent to plant a kiss on Norah's forehead, Norah held her breath.

After she'd left the room, Norah wiped furiously at the spot Miss Fairchild's lips had touched.

"That was a mistake," Jessica said.

Norah rolled over in bed. "What was?"

"Telling her what you were afraid of," Jessica said. "One day, that will come back to bite you."

9

NORAH

For the first few weeks at Wild Meadows, Norah *watched*. Having been a foster child for most of her life, she'd learned it was a good idea to get the lay of the land early. The more information you gleaned in the early days of a placement—a foster father's pet peeves, the fact that meals come only once a day or that the first one up got their pick of the shared clothing—the better. So she learned that Miss Fairchild was a woman of routine who spent most of her time cleaning. She drank wine, but not a worrying amount, and thus far it had not preceded violence or rage. She liked conversation to revolve around herself. And she was exceptionally frugal.

"It's not cheap to run the farm and to feed and clothe you," Miss Fairchild said, as she served up a meal that seemed to Norah to be lacking in both quantity and nutrition. After a few weeks of it, Norah felt the hunger gnawing day and night.

Also notable to Norah was the fact that Miss Fairchild knew things. Things she shouldn't rightfully know—like the fact that Norah ate her entire lunch at recess rather than splitting it into recess and lunchtime, or that she'd stopped at the skate park for a few minutes on the way home from school to play on the abandoned board that she'd found.

Miss Fairchild also appeared to like Norah, which was both good and bad. She'd had foster parents who had taken an instant dislike to her, and that never worked out well. At the same time, she'd learned to be leery of adults who liked her too much.

"You did the laundry?" she'd exclaim, when Norah would perform her allocated chore. "What on earth did we do without you?"

It was bizarre. Norah might have written her off as one of those oddly nice people—like Dulcie, the receptionist at her previous school, who called everyone "sweet babycakes"—except that, unlike Dulcie, Miss Fairchild wasn't nice all the time. She was unpredictable—lashing out at unexpected times—usually at Jessica, who followed her around like a puppy dog, working overtime to get her attention. Sometimes it worked, sometimes it didn't. For the life of her, Norah couldn't work out why she bothered.

Still, Norah fell into a routine. (It was annoying, because getting into a routine usually guaranteed she'd be yanked out of it without notice or explanation and planted somewhere new. For this reason, she hadn't bothered asking Scott if this would be a permanent placement. She knew the answer would be "If you're lucky," and if Norah had figured out one thing by now, it was that she wasn't.) School was part of this routine. Unlike most kids her age, Norah enjoyed school immensely. It was one of the few places where she could know with reasonable certainty what was going to happen. At her new school—one of those small-town places housing prep through to Year 12 and grouping two or even three year-levels into one classroom—each day started with circle time, then literacy, then maths, then sport. As usual, maths was her favorite subject, but she enjoyed nearly all the lessons, apart from art, which was unnecessarily messy and had no discernible point.

Norah was aware that she was extremely intelligent. The teachers were always saying so. Norah and Jessica were grouped together, so Norah knew that Jessica was also (surprisingly) smart too, and (unsurprisingly) eager to please, always with her hand up, always volunteering to help the teacher. Like Norah, she seemed happiest in the classroom. Jessica spent most of her lunchtimes in the library or alone in the playground, while Norah spent them scavenging for leftover food or picking fights. One such lunchtime, she had just discovered an uneaten apple on the grass when she heard a commotion.

Turning toward the sound, Norah saw a large girl pointing a menacing finger at Jessica, who was sitting on a swing. The large girl was Sandra. Sandra was the youngest child of a dairy farmer and had six older brothers. She was as tall as Norah, with wide shoulders and hips, and as strong as one of her father's cows.

"I—I'm sorry," Jessica was stammering.

Norah moved closer.

"Not sorry enough." Thrusting her hand forward, the girl knocked Jessica backward off the swing onto the tanbark. A couple of onlookers shrieked, high on the scandal of it.

When Sandra advanced on Jessica, now sprawled on the ground, Norah sprung into action. It wasn't that she was a fan of Jessica. Truth be told, she found her annoying and whiny. But a strange code existed in foster care. While you could torment your foster siblings all you wanted at home, out in the real world, you were a pack.

Norah easily knocked Sandra off balance with barely a push. Once the girl was on the ground, Norah kneeled heavily on her side.

"Get off me!" Sandra cried.

"What's going on?" Norah asked Jessica, who was crab-crawling away from Sandra. When she stood, tanbark hung from her like ornaments on a tree.

"I said get off me!" Sandra shouted, trying to wriggle free. "What's *your* problem?"

"That's what I was about to ask you," Norah said.

Sandra pointed at Jessica. "*She* was supposed to do my homework, but she didn't. Now I have a detention."

"I was going to do it last night," Jessica said weakly. "But I . . . I . . ."

She drifted off. Norah understood. Miss Fairchild had been in a volatile mood and had tasked Jessica with extra cleaning duties right up until bedtime.

"I tried to do it in class this morning," Jessica continued, "but Mr. Walker caught me."

"How much are you paying her?" Norah asked Sandra, who was still pinned beneath Norah's knees.

When Sandra looked baffled, Norah looked at Jessica, who was scuffing her feet. Her cheeks were pink. "Jessica?"

"She's not paying me," Jessica muttered.

Norah frowned. "Well . . . what's she doing for you?"

"Nothing."

Norah stared at her. "Then why are you doing *her homework*?"

Jessica shrugged. "Because she asked me to."

"Will you *get off me*?" Sandra spat.

Norah responded by adding more pressure. "From now on it's

two dollars per worksheet," Norah said to Sandra. "Ninety percent or above, or you get your money back."

It took a minute for Sandra to catch her breath. "I'm not paying—"

"We'll also take payment in food. Homework in exchange for lunch. Your mark will vary in direct correlation to the quality of the lunch."

When Sandra didn't respond, Norah leaned forward to put more weight on her knees.

"Fine!" Sandra gasped.

"Good."

The bell went then, so Norah stood up, releasing Sandra. The girl's face contorted as she struggled to her feet. "Who the fuck are you anyway?" she said to Norah.

"The name's Norah. With an *h*." Norah said. "I'm Jessica's sister."

By the end of the day, Norah and Jessica already had two additional customers for their homework racket.

"Why did you tell Sandra I was your sister?" Jessica asked that afternoon as they trudged home from school.

Norah considered that for a moment, then shrugged. "Announcing you're a foster child rarely leads to anything good."

"What do you mean?"

"You know. Strange sad looks from parents. Kids asking what happened to your parents. Teachers who want you to stay late after school to help them organize the sports shed." Norah drew air quotes around the words "organize the sports shed."

Jessica's eyes widened as understanding dawned. *"Oh."*

"I know you're not my actual sister, obviously," Norah said. "Maybe I shouldn't have said that."

When Jessica replied, her voice was small. "Actually," she said, "I liked it."

Norah didn't know what to say to that, and clearly neither did Jessica, because they walked the rest of the way home in silence.

"Why hasn't the laundry been put away?" Miss Fairchild demanded.

Jessica and Norah had been having a nice afternoon until that point. As they did their chores, they'd actually *chatted* a little. Norah wasn't a huge one for chatting, but she had managed to turn the conversation to dogs and before she knew it she was enjoying herself. Until Miss Fairchild had arrived home from running errands and found them taking the laundry off the clothesline together.

"How sweet," she'd said, in a voice that made it clear she meant the opposite. "You two are friends now."

Ever since then she'd been in a *mood*. Norah could have sworn that it was brought on by the sight of Jessica and Norah getting along. Norah had finished folding the laundry and had ducked into the bathroom before putting it away when she heard Miss Fairchild holler.

By the time she got back to the kitchen, Miss Fairchild looked incensed. "Well? Why hasn't it been put away?"

Their foster mother was wearing a lolly-pink dress with puffed sleeves. Her lipstick was a similar shade; she resembled a children's party entertainer or host, which made her thunderous expression even more terrifying.

"Laundry is Norah's job," Jessica protested. She shot Norah an apologetic look, but Norah didn't mind. It was accurate, after all. Besides, she could handle Miss Fairchild far better than Jessica could.

"I was just using the bathroom," Norah said. "I'll finish now."

She headed toward the piles of laundry, but Miss Fairchild's arm shot out, stopping her. Her gaze remained on Jessica. "*What* did you say?"

An alarm bell went off inside Norah. Danger—but not for her. Miss Fairchild was *glaring* at Jessica.

The other girl was already rigid with fear. "I said . . . laundry is . . ." But she couldn't finish the sentence. Tears welled in her eyes.

"You selfish, selfish girl. Only ever doing things if they are your job."

This was spectacularly inaccurate, given that Jessica spent the majority of her waking hours seeking out jobs she could do to win Miss Fairchild's favor, but Norah had already learned there was no point in arguing with her. Her wrath, when it came, was like a runaway train—once it got going there was no way stop it.

Jessica's chin trembled. It wasn't the first time Norah had watched as other kids were shouted at and punished. But in those instances, the kid typically hated their foster parent. Jessica loved Miss Fairchild. She was stupidly, hopelessly, loyal. It was like watching a dog being kicked.

"I'm sorry," she whimpered.

"You *will* be."

Miss Fairchild marched to the sink. A moment later she returned, clutching a fresh bar of soap. Norah watched in horror as she plunged it into Jessica's mouth.

"*This* is what we do to people who talk back!"

The soap was so large Jessica's eyes bulged as her lips strained around it. There seemed no possible way it would fit, but Miss Fairchild kept pushing until the entire bar was in Jessica's mouth. Then she covered Jessica's mouth with her hand.

Jessica's eyes became wide and panicked. Bubbles formed around the edge of her lips, leaking between Miss Fairchild's fingers.

"I think . . . I think she's choking," Norah said. But her uncertainty about the situation kept her rooted to the spot. Did Jessica want her to intervene? Or would that make things worse?

Miss Fairchild ignored her.

Jessica gagged. Tears leaked from her eyes. Bubbles came out her nose. Miss Fairchild kept her hand over the girl's mouth, staring into Jessica's rolling, terrified eyes.

Finally, Norah couldn't bear it any longer. "Stop it!" she cried, stepping forward and slapping Miss Fairchild's hand away from Jessica's mouth. Instantly, the soap shot from Jessica's mouth and skidded across the floor. Jessica ran to the sink and vomited. Her body heaved violently as she gripped the edge of the counter.

Norah looked at Miss Fairchild, who just stood there breathing heavily, as if recovering from a terrible shock.

"Put the laundry away," she said finally, and turned and walked out of the room.

There was no retribution for Norah for intervening—at least, not that day. When it came to vengeance, Miss Fairchild preferred to play the long game.

Scott returned for his first visit when Norah had been at Wild Meadows for four months. He smelled like the communal microwave at the police station, and the sweat patches under his arms dipped nearly to his waist. Norah found herself unable to look at him, focusing instead on the blue plastic clipboard on his lap. He'd scribbled Norah's name at the top, spelling it without an *h*. When she pointed this out, he didn't bother to correct it.

"How are things, Norah?" he asked.

Miss Fairchild wasn't in the room when they had their catch-up—that was one of the rules. Scott, like the social workers before him, always told Norah she should speak freely, and tell him if anything about her new home made her uncomfortable. Her previous two social workers had said the same thing, word for word, leading Norah to deduce they were all reciting from the same brochure.

"Which things?" she asked.

"Any things?" He looked up from his clipboard, already frustrated. "All of the things?"

"I don't understand what you mean."

Scott sighed. "Do we have to do this every time?"

Norah sighed back. "If you keep asking me about things without specifying what things you mean, then yes, we do."

"Are you settling in?" he said slowly, as if Norah were the dimwit.

"I guess," she replied equally slowly.

"School's okay?"

"Fine."

"Do you have any concerns that I can help you to resolve?"

That one was easy. Norah was completely confident that Scott was incapable of resolving any concern she might have. "No."

"Right then." Scott ticked a couple of boxes on his form. "I'll make a note that the placement is working out well."

"I didn't say that," Norah said.

But Scott was already on his way to the door, like he was in a big hurry. Fine by Norah. Except a few seconds later she heard him talking to Miss Fairchild in the hallway.

"I've got another one, if you're interested," she heard Scott say. "Same age as these two. A respite case. Her grandmother, who's been raising the girl, has been taken to hospital."

"A respite case?"

"Short-term. A few weeks or months. It's her first time in foster care and she's had a fairly stable upbringing, no trauma that we know of so she shouldn't give you any trouble."

Miss Fairchild didn't respond for a couple of seconds.

"You'd prefer a traumatized child?" Scott asked in disbelief.

"Of course not." She sounded irritated at the suggestion. "I just want to help the kids who need it the most, that's all."

"Well," Scott said, "respite money is quite good. But I can give it to someone else if you're not interested—"

"I'll take her," Miss Fairchild said. Money, of course, trumped everything.

But when Alicia arrived a few days later, Norah started to wonder if Miss Fairchild *did* want a traumatized child. Because this time, there was no honeymoon period of adjustment, no demented smile or declarations that she was safe at Wild Meadows. Rather, it seemed like Miss Fairchild hated Alicia on sight.

10

ALICIA

By midnight, Alicia was wishing she'd got up and left Jessica's house when Norah did. She was dog-tired, weary with emotion, aware that they were making the two-hour drive from Melbourne to Port Agatha early the next morning. And still her sister droned on. Jessica had prepared a list of possible questions, each one written in a different color, and she had been pacing the floor for hours, running through "parameters" around what they should say to "protect" themselves.

"But if we don't tell the cops everything," Alicia said, "how will they figure out who the bones belong to?"

Jessica threw up her hands. "I don't know. But with Norah's criminal record, I'm not prepared to take that chance. What if we become suspects? What if *she* does?"

Jessica was right to be cautious. Alicia was grateful for her caution, because it allowed her to think beyond it, safe in the knowledge that Jessica wouldn't let them do anything stupid. But the fact remained, there was more to what happened to them when they were children than even they knew. Alicia didn't want to do anything to put them in danger, but . . . what if this was their one chance to get to the bottom of it?

"Are you really ready to go back there, Al?" Jessica asked.

"What do you think?" Alicia said. In the twenty-five years since she'd left Port Agatha, Alicia hadn't gone anywhere near the place. She could barely bring herself to say its name aloud.

"I'm off to bed," Phil said, poking his head in.

"Good night," Jessica said, without looking at him.

"Why don't you go to bed with your husband, Jess?" Alicia said. "I'm calling it a night anyway."

"I think we should bring a lawyer with us," Jessica said.

Alicia sighed. Phil, who'd been waiting in the doorway hopefully, slunk away.

"Jess, no," Alicia said. "How will it look if we show up with a lawyer?"

"Smart," Jessica said. "It will look smart."

"Or guilty! Listen, we haven't been accused of anything. We're assisting. Showing up with a lawyer is going to give off the wrong vibe."

Jessica paused. "Maybe you're right."

It made Alicia nervous when Jessica accepted her counsel. After all, Alicia wasn't known for her wise, well-thought-out decisions. She was the one who threw caution to the wind, who took risks, who acted first and thought of the consequences later. An easy thing to do when you had so little regard for your own mortality. But Alicia had a very high regard for her sisters' mortality, not to mention their good health and happiness.

"Let's just play it by ear," she said. "We don't have to answer anything we don't want to. At the first hint of trouble, we'll get a lawyer."

"Okay," Jessica said. "Okay."

"Good." Alicia slung her handbag over her shoulder and walked toward the door. "So, you'll pick me up in the morning?"

"Eight o'clock," Jessica said.

Alicia had just started the car when her phone began to ring. The number came up as unknown, which, combined with the hour, meant it was work.

"Alicia Connelly," she said.

"You owe me ten bucks."

The voice sounded like it belonged to a child. Not a young child; more of an adolescent. It took her a moment to place him.

"It's Aaron," he said, registering her pause. "Trish's foster son."

Alicia kicked herself. She knew that to the kids she worked with, being remembered was significant. At the same time, she noted the hint of disdain, as if she were an idiot not to have realized, and it helped to ease her guilt.

"I know who you are, mate," she said, matching his tone.

"Sorry for calling so late," he said.

She started to drive. It wasn't the first time she'd received a nonurgent call from a foster kid late at night, but it *was* the first time anyone had apologized for it. It seemed there was something about those late hours that made kids think of her. Alicia considered it a compliment. "Late? I was about to go out clubbing."

"Seriously?"

"Of course not." She laughed.

Aaron didn't join in and Alicia could just about see him rolling his eyes.

"Is everything okay? How is Theo?"

"He's doing much better. We spent the night snuggling on the couch and watching movies."

"You did?" Alicia cried. That was so much better than she'd dared hope; she'd have been happy to hear that he'd come out from under the table.

Aaron snorted. "No! But he's eating as long as I handfeed him. And he let me put him to bed, though he wouldn't have a bath or change his clothes and I'm pretty sure he'd shat himself."

Alicia felt her mood lifting considerably, which under the circumstances was unexpected.

"Did you actually put him to bed?" she said, not wanting to be caught out twice.

"Someone had to. Clearly you and Trish weren't getting very far." This time he didn't pause for a response. "Anyway, the reason I'm calling is that I've been searching for information about university scholarships and you mentioned that you might know of some funding?"

"I certainly do. I can email you some links if you like." Alicia indicated right and made the turn. "If anything looks interesting to you, I'd be happy to help you fill out an application."

"Yeah, maybe."

"Cool," Alicia said. She gave him a minute to see if there was anything else. When he didn't speak, she asked: "Anything else I can do for you?"

"Nope," he said. "That's it."

"Okay." Then, on a whim, she said, "Hey Aaron . . . You don't have to tell me if you don't want to, but I wondered . . . what happened to your parents?"

It wasn't a question she typically asked—partly because, if the kid was one of her cases, she already knew, and in those instances where she spent time with a kid who wasn't one of her cases, she tended to avoid it as the answer was usually loaded. She wasn't sure what made her ask now. When Aaron paused, she worried that she shouldn't have.

"My mum has never been capable of looking after me," he said finally. "She has an intellectual disability, and some physical disabilities too. No one knows who my dad is. My gran raised me until three years ago when she went into a nursing home."

Alicia felt her breath catch. "Your gran raised you?"

He was quiet for a moment. "Her name was Doris. Good name for a gran, right?"

"Great name for a gran," Alicia agreed. She felt both sad and happy all at once.

"She died six months ago."

"I'm sorry to hear that."

"Yeah," he said. "*Vale*, Doris."

"*Vale*, Doris," Alicia replied.

Aaron ended the call and Alicia pulled to the side of the road. She felt emotional, which was hardly surprising after the day she'd had. What was surprising was that the particular type of emotion she felt in this very moment wasn't the terrible type. The brief interaction with Aaron had left her feeling . . . whole. Connected.

Looking out the window, she wasn't exactly shocked to find herself outside Meera's house. This happened from time to time. She'd be setting off for home and, without planning it or making the decision to go there, she would end up idling her car out front, as if by muscle memory, as if her body just knew where she wanted to be.

Meera was a colleague of Alicia's, a child protection lawyer. "One of the heroes," Alicia always said. Alicia fancied her, of course. Everyone fancied Meera. Whenever Meera was in court, everyone was mesmerized by her intelligence, passion, and commitment to her job—not to mention her long legs, dark hair, and deep brown eyes.

She and Alicia were friends. If Alicia had got out of the car and tapped on the front door, Meera would have been happy to see her. She'd smile and roll her eyes and say, "What's up, Anne Shirley?" (an old joke about Alicia's hair), then invite her inside. For a brief moment, Alicia considered doing this.

There was a light on in the living room. Meera was probably on the couch in her leggings, hair in a messy bun, laptop on her knees. They'd spent plenty of nights side by side on that couch, working or hanging out.

One particular night stood out in Alicia's mind. It had happened just over a year ago. They'd been discussing a six-year-old girl named Kasey whose foster family had been petitioning to adopt her when, at the eleventh hour, Kasey's biological father had come out of the woodwork, wanting custody. It wasn't an unusual case, and yet, while listening to Meera explain the merits of each petitioning party, Alicia had found herself overcome with emotion. Alicia had always known Meera was a caring lawyer. She knew she wasn't the type to just do what was easiest. But the lengths that she'd gone to in this case moved Alicia. It made her wonder how different things might have been if someone like Meera had been looking out for her and her sisters all those years ago.

At some point during Meera's speech, Alicia grabbed her friend's face and kissed her. It was a peck at first, but soon they were rearranging their limbs, and the file of carefully ordered paperwork was sliding off Meera's lap and onto the carpet. Alicia had been taken aback by Meera's enthusiasm. Having spent her adult life seeking out dysfunctional, commitment-phobic, and even abusive partners, Alicia hadn't known what to do with reciprocated attraction. And so she ended the kiss, apologized for crossing the line, and shut Meera down any time she tried to bring up that night ever since.

There was no point in entertaining the idea of a relationship. It would never work out long-term. How could it?

Alicia started driving again, taking the scenic route home from Meera's place along the river. No one was about. It was the still of night—dark, cool, and perfectly silent. As she drove, Alicia felt the heaviness of life closing over her. This happened from time to time. She'd be going along just fine when *wham*—a darkness descended, bringing with it a certainty that life wasn't worth living. That *she* wasn't worthy.

Alicia's gaze veered to the river. She imagined taking a sudden, sharp turn. Her car would barrel over the grass toward the water. There would be a rush of adrenaline followed by the slow calm of her chassis submerging. Alicia wouldn't try to claw her way out. She'd just close her eyes, reveling in the intoxicating feeling that soon it would all be over.

Alicia drew her eyes back to the road, her hands clasping the wheel tightly at ten and two. She wouldn't do it. She *couldn't* do it to her sisters. Anyone else, *everyone* else, yes. But not to them. They'd both gone through enough.

11

ALICIA

BEFORE

Smile.

It was Grammy's voice Alicia heard as she bounced along in the passenger seat of her social worker's Volvo. *Smile, be polite, and do what you're told.* That's what Grammy would tell her to do, so of course that's what she'd do. She was going to think of it like an adventure. Who knew? It might end up being a lot of fun.

"It's only temporary," Sandi said, tapping her pink nails against the steering wheel. She had permed blond hair and electric-blue frosted eyeshadow and reminded Alicia of Sarah Jessica Parker in *Girls Just Want to Have Fun.* "Before you know it, your grandmother will be better and you'll be back home."

Alicia nodded bravely, but she was nervous. Grammy had had a fall. At the hospital, the nurses had said it would take weeks, or even months, before Grammy would have recovered enough to return home. *Months!* It was hard to fathom waiting months to see Grammy again.

When Alicia had seen her at the hospital, she'd been shocked at the sight of her. Grammy looked so . . . old. So frail. It must have been the hospital gown and bed. Alicia wasn't used to thinking of Grammy as old or frail. She was so full of life! She sold raffle tickets for Rotary, volunteered at the local library, and chased birds off her plants by shaking her walking stick at them. She had wild hair, a heavy gait (both of which Alicia had inherited), and razor-sharp judgment. But hands down the greatest thing about Grammy was her laugh—raucous and boisterous, it reverberated around any room and even the most po-faced person couldn't help but laugh along. Once, when pulled over, Grammy made the police officer laugh so hard she wet herself. (Needless to say, Grammy got out of the ticket.)

Alicia's father had died when she was very little, and when her mother had a breakdown a few years later, Grammy hadn't missed a beat, scooping up her granddaughter and raising her. Alicia knew that her circumstances—being raised by her grandparents—were different from most of her peers, but in her opinion her circumstances were vastly superior. Unlike most parents, Grammy had no interest in forcing Alicia to eat vegetables or heed strict bedtimes, and if Alicia didn't feel like going to school Grammy urged her to take the day off and come along to mah-jongg instead.

"We're lucky to have found this place at short notice," Sandi said as they turned in to the driveway of a picturesque farmhouse. "There are two other girls around your age living here."

As they drew nearer, Alicia noticed the huge swimming pool and decided to look on the bright side. She'd always wanted a swimming pool. Life was all about your attitude, Grammy always said. Alicia was going to face this situation with the best attitude she could muster.

Sandi parked in front of the house. On the porch a pretty blond woman stood, waving. Alicia waved back. Beside her were two girls: one bow-lipped with glossy black hair and intense brown eyes; the other brown-skinned, blue-eyed, and gangly-tall.

"You must be Alicia," the woman said, when Alicia got out of the car. "I'm Miss Fairchild. Welcome to Wild Meadows."

Miss Fairchild ran her gaze ran over Alicia, as if appraising her. Alicia stood up straighter.

"Thank you," she said politely. "It's good to be here."

They lapsed into an awkward silence as Sandi retrieved Alicia's suitcases from the back of the car. She expected that Miss Fairchild would break the silence, perhaps by asking how far she'd traveled, or telling her what they had planned for the afternoon. But the woman didn't say a word.

Sandi put Alicia's suitcases beside her on the grass. She'd brought three with her—one containing clothes, another with books, and a final one with photographs and keepsakes from home. Overkill, perhaps, but she didn't know how long she'd be staying.

"Don't you have a lot of things?" Miss Fairchild said, a hint of disapproval in her voice.

"Oh, I probably overpacked," she'd said, embarrassed. "Grammy always told me to be prepared for anything."

"How sweet of Grammy." Miss Fairchild smiled tightly. "Why don't you head on inside, while I have a quick chat with Sandi. Jessica, Norah, help Alicia with her things."

The girls each grabbed a bag. Alicia picked up the remaining one and followed them inside.

"Thanks," Alicia said when they set down her cases in the living room.

"It's okay," the tall one said. The other one shrugged. After that, neither girl spoke. It wasn't exactly the instant chemistry Alicia had been hoping for, but they were probably as nervous as she was, she reasoned. Grammy always said that the best way to break tension was to make a joke, so when Alicia spotted the Russian dolls on the mantel, she knew what to do.

"I hate Russian dolls," she said. "They seem nice at first but when you get to know them, they're really full of themselves."

She raised her eyebrows at the girls, who blinked at her slowly. It was as if they'd never heard a joke before. Finally, several seconds later than she should have, Norah laughed. It was so sudden, so abrupt, that Jessica and Alicia couldn't help laughing too.

"Full of themselves," she said. "Funny."

"What's funny?"

Alicia hadn't noticed Miss Fairchild leaning against the doorframe, watching them. She was smiling, but her gaze was hard. Upon seeing her, Jessica and Norah immediately stopped laughing, putting Alicia on edge.

"Oh," Alicia said. "Nothing. I was just making a joke."

"How wonderful," the woman said coolly. "I didn't realize we had a comedian among us."

"Right then," Sandi said, from behind Miss Fairchild. "I'll call with news of your grandmother as soon as I hear something. You be a good girl!"

Before Alicia could respond, Sandi was heading for her car. Every instinct Alicia possessed was urging her to run after the social worker. But what would she say? "I have a bad feeling about this woman"? "Something about her doesn't seem right"? Sandi would tell Alicia she was just nervous. And maybe she was. Maybe, once she'd settled in, she'd laugh about how nervous she'd been. And in a few weeks, she'd tell Grammy all about it, and all about the lovely time she'd had at Wild Meadows.

Alicia *prayed* that would be the case. Then she prayed that Grammy would get better quickly, so she could come and get her out of here.

They spent the afternoon cleaning. It was odd, since as far as Alicia could see, the place was already cleaner than Grammy's had ever been, and Grammy was extremely house-proud. The other girls didn't even complain.

"You show her the ropes, Norah," Miss Fairchild said.

Alicia, as it turned out, wasn't very good at cleaning. She did everything so badly that Norah had to go over it again after Alicia had finished.

"Sorry," Alicia said as Norah peered down at the sink, which Alicia had been cleaning with a rag for several minutes. "I'm not very good at this. My skills lie more in the area of making a mess."

Norah frowned. "Have you ever cleaned anything before?"

"Not really. Grammy does the cleaning at home. I guess I am pretty spoiled."

Norah considered this for a moment. "What happened to Grammy? Did she die?"

"No, no," Alicia said. "She had a fall, but she'll be fine. She's recuperating in the hospital. When I go home, I'm going to start cleaning to help her out," Alicia decided on the spot that that's what she'd do. "So, I need you teach me how you get the mirrors sparkling like this one."

"All right." Norah seemed, if not flattered to be asked, at least prepared to help. She pointed to the edge of the tub. "Sit there. The trick is to dry it with newspaper . . . and don't use too much spray. Watch."

Alicia watched Norah's long spindly arms fly across the glass in quick, sharp movements. When she was done, she showed Alicia how to clean the toilet, including those hard-to-reach spots at the back.

"You're a cleaning ninja," Alicia said admiringly. "A wizard!"

"You should see Jessica," Norah said, before adding: "By the way, she'll probably reorganize your stuff and remake your bed if she's not happy with it. Let her do it; it's easier."

"Roger that," Alicia said, appreciating the intel.

"And she's weirdly territorial about Miss Fairchild. She's been with her since she was little and—"

As if on cue, Miss Fairchild poked her head into the bathroom. "Goodness," she said when she saw Alicia sitting on the edge of the tub. "You're finished already, have you, Alicia? You must be an excellent cleaner."

But her expression said that she didn't believe that at all.

Alicia rose awkwardly to her feet.

"She *is*," Norah said. "And fast! I still have the sink to go."

Miss Fairchild's gaze slid to Norah. Clearly she wasn't stupid and she didn't like being treated as such.

"Is that right?"

"Yep," Norah said, scrubbing the sink. "She's a cleaning ninja. A wizard!"

"A comedian and a wizard?" Miss Fairchild said, her eyes narrowing. "Lucky us. Since she's so good at it, maybe tomorrow the wizard can clean all the bathrooms by herself!"

She stared at Alicia, who wanted to disappear under the woman's gaze. After what felt like an eternity, she left the room and Alicia sank back onto the side of the bath.

"Thank you," she said to Norah.

"Don't thank me," Norah said. "Just learn quickly."

Alicia somehow knew she wasn't just talking about the cleaning.

Dinner was a tiny serving of rice and beans that made Alicia ache for Grammy's cooking.

Grammy was an old-fashioned cook. At home, Alicia's days started with waffles or French toast, or maybe scrambled eggs with bacon and baked beans. Lunches were thick-cut sandwiches of ham and salad, plus fruit, and dinner was meat and three vegetables, followed by a bowl of ice cream or jelly or trifle.

Alicia had always been a good eater. That's how Grammy described it. *My Alicia is a very good eater.* Like it was a talent of hers. And indeed it was. Alicia always finished everything on her plate, including the vegetables.

At Wild Meadows, apparently, they didn't even *get* vegetables.

"May I have some more rice, please?" Alicia asked that night after she'd scraped her plate clean.

Jessica and Norah glanced at Miss Fairchild. Their apprehensive expressions put Alicia on guard. What had she said? She could see leftover rice on the stovetop from where she sat.

She laughed nervously. "Grammy says I have a big appetite."

Miss Fairchild sat back in her chair, taking her time to finish chewing. After she swallowed, she laid her cutlery in the center of her plate. "Sounds like Grammy was overfeeding you." She ran her gaze over Alicia, then gave her a tiny smile. "It's not your fault. People overfeed kids, making little gluttons of them. It's why we have a childhood-obesity epidemic."

Jessica and Norah looked at their plates.

Miss Fairchild stood to clear up and Alicia blinked back tears of surprise and humiliation. The first thing she did, Alicia noticed, was empty the remaining rice from the saucepan into the bin.

The moment Alicia closed the bathroom door, the tears came in a flood. It was a blessed relief, after fighting them back since dinner. *Let them out!* Grammy always exclaimed when Alicia cried, pulling her to her bosom. *You'll feel better after.*

But after ten minutes of crying, Alicia didn't feel better. It was a scary feeling, being shunned by an adult who was responsible for your care. Alicia was used to people being *delighted* by her. Grammy, obviously. All of Grammy's friends. Her teachers at school, her friends' parents. In her world, people were warm and friendly and kind. This place felt like a horrible parallel universe.

When she had finally cried herself out she returned to the bedroom, expecting to find the girls sitting up in bed, reading or chatting. Instead, the room was quiet. Each bed butted up against a wall. Jessica and Norah were on their sides, facing the center of the room. By the light of the dim lamp at Norah's bedside, Alicia saw that their eyes were closed.

It was so odd, so abrupt.

"Are you guys going to go straight to sleep?" Alicia asked as she sat on her bed.

"What else would we do?" Jessica whispered. "And keep your voice down!"

"I don't know," Alicia said, lowering her voice. "Faff around. Chat. Plan what clothes to wear tomorrow. Read a book."

No response. Norah, Alicia noticed, was frowning.

"At home," Alicia explained, "Grammy tells me a bedtime joke every night. Every night a different joke! I never understood how she had so many of them until I found a book of jokes under her bed." Alicia felt a fresh stab of sadness.

"What's a bedtime joke?" Norah said.

"Shhhh!" Jessica hissed.

"What should you do if you can't go to sleep?" Alicia said.

Norah opened her mouth to respond.

"No, you don't answer. It's a joke," Alicia explained.

"Oh," Norah said, but she still looked confused.

"You lie on the edge of the bed and soon you'll drop off."

Alicia waited for laughter, but both girls remained silent.

Then Norah said quietly, "I get it. You meant drop off to sleep, right? That's funny."

Jessica said nothing. Perhaps she was too busy shushing them and stealing glances at the doorway to take it in.

It wasn't exactly the response Alicia was hoping for, but she suspected it was the best she was going to get. She closed her eyes, ready to put an end to this horrible day. In her mind's eye she saw Grammy sitting on the edge of her bed, resting her blue-veined hand on Alicia's hip.

"Good night, Grammy," she whispered, not caring if Jessica or Norah heard her. "I'll be home soon."

Alicia had never told Grammy a lie. She hoped this wouldn't be her first.

12

ALICIA

BEFORE

You girls had better hurry," Miss Fairchild said, "or you'll be late for school."

They were sitting at the breakfast table, which had been laid with bowls and spoons. Miss Fairchild sat at the head of the table, dressed and ready for the day in a floral skirt, white blouse and pearly pink lipstick. Her fingernails and toenails were both painted peach, and her hair was wavy with the exception of her bangs, which were blown-out straight.

"What time does school start?" Alicia asked, eating faster in case they had to leave before she was finished.

Alicia had spent the night before trying to ignore her rumbling tummy so she could get to sleep. When she did drift off, she dreamed of eating an ice-cream sundae the size of a basketball.

"Eight thirty," Miss Fairchild said. "But it's a forty-five-minute walk."

Alicia nearly regurgitated her breakfast. *Forty-five minutes!* It was already scorching hot outside and it wasn't even eight in the morning. At home, if the weather was even slightly too warm or too cold, Grammy insisting on driving her to school, which was a five-minute walk at most.

"The exercise will be good for you, Alicia," Miss Fairchild said pointedly.

Alicia's cheeks burned. Jessica and Norah didn't laugh, which was kind, but their obvious discomfort was nearly as bad.

Norah and Jessica walked as slowly as they could to accommodate her, but Alicia was still faint and had three blisters by the time they arrived at school. A little voice in Alicia's head wondered if maybe, just maybe, Miss Fairchild was right. Maybe Grammy *had* been overindulging her. She didn't clean, she was driven to school, she could eat whatever she pleased. Maybe she really was . . . what had Miss Fairchild said? . . . a little glutton.

At school, Jessica took Alicia to the office, where she filled out some paperwork. Then she was placed in a composite class with Jessica and Norah. On the walk to school she'd discovered there were eighteen months between them—Jessica was the oldest at thirteen, Alicia in the middle at twelve and a half, and Norah, eleven, was the youngest. The reverse order of their heights, Norah noted.

It was interesting, observing Norah and Jessica in this environment. They were, Alicia surmised, neither cool nor uncool. Norah was incredibly smart, and extremely hot-blooded—being sent out of the classroom twice in the morning alone: once for calling Matt Trotman a dickhead ("he is one") and another time for pushing Anthony White Reynolds off his chair (which she claimed was an accident but definitely wasn't).

Jessica, while not as smart as Norah, had her hand up much of the time, and was the very opposite of Norah's turbulence; she was the first to get her books out, or volunteer to be library monitor, or answer a question. Alicia, who had always been a solidly average student and comfortable with that—likely because of Grammy's incessant cheerleading—suddenly found herself feeling suddenly insecure about it. *Is there anything you are good at?* a little voice said. *Not cleaning. Not sport. Not studies. You're not the most attractive, the most talented, or the most helpful. What, exactly, is the point of you?*

By the time lunchtime came around, Alicia was starving and thoroughly miserable. In the canteen area, most people gathered in groups. Alicia looked around for Norah and Jessica, assuming they'd sit together, but when she saw them sitting separately and alone, neither of them so much as glancing in her direction, Alicia wandered outside and sat on the first step she found. Miserable as she was, she needed to eat. She didn't have high hopes for her lunch, which had been made by Miss Fairchild, but when she opened her lunch bag and found two rice crackers and a small, sad-looking apple, she thought she might cry.

The only thing that kept her going was the knowledge that there would be a message waiting for her from Grammy when she got home. There had to be. Grammy would be worried sick about her, desperate to know how she was getting on. When Alicia told her what it was like with Miss Fairchild, Grammy would move heaven and earth to get her out of there. And then Alicia could leave this whole experience at Wild Meadows behind her, like the bad dream that it was.

• • •

There was no message from Grammy. On top of the disappointment of it, she felt humiliated, even a little annoyed. *Why* hadn't Grammy called?

There would be a reasonable explanation; there had to be. But try as she might, Alicia couldn't figure it out. Grammy would have a phone in her room—and even if she didn't, surely she could ask a nurse to ring? She'd be anxious about Alicia being placed into foster care. She'd want to know that Alicia was all right. Her silence didn't make sense.

"Would it be all right if I called the hospital?" Alicia asked Miss Fairchild finally. She'd done her homework and finished her chores and couldn't hold back, even if the prospect of approaching Miss Fairchild made her want to throw up.

Miss Fairchild, who was dusting the mantelpiece, looked irritated at the interruption. "You heard what your social worker said," she said briskly. "She'll call when there is news." She resumed dusting.

"I know. It's just . . . I thought she would have rung by now."

Miss Fairchild stopped dusting and sighed before turning back. "Your grandmother is in hospital, Alicia," she said, enunciating every word clearly. "How is she going to get better if you don't leave her alone? It's not easy looking after a child. It's even harder, I imagine, if you're an old woman. All that cooking, cleaning, running around. Can you blame her for wanting to switch off for a little while? Who knows," she muttered, turning back to the mantel, "maybe *Grammy* is enjoying her little vacation away from you?"

Alicia felt like she'd been slapped.

"No," Alicia said, even as a little voice in her head said: *She's right.* "She's not enjoying it. She'll be worried about me. Wondering how I'm doing."

But Alicia was starting to doubt so many things. Maybe she was wrong about Grammy?

"If that's the case," Miss Fairchild said, "I can think of only one reason she hasn't got in touch."

Like a fool, Alicia was about to ask what it was. Then it dawned on her.

Miss Fairchild turned back to the mantel, dusting more vigorously now. The hem of her floral skirt bounced rhythmically.

Once again, Alicia's eyes filled with tears.

Where are you, Grammy? Come and get me. Please.

When Alicia climbed into bed that night, she felt something crunch underneath her.

"What on earth?" She fished between the sheets and found a small packet of barbecue shapes.

In the semidarkness, Alicia saw two pairs of eyes gleaming.

"Did you guys leave these here?" she whispered.

Jessica shrugged. "You looked like you needed them."

Alicia did need them. Dinner had been soup with no bread and no croutons. At home, it would have been a starter. She tore open the packet of biscuits and stuffed them in her mouth a few at a time.

"But where did they come from?"

"We have our ways," Norah said, propping herself on one elbow.

"Thank you," Alicia said through a mouthful of crumbs. "It means a lot."

"So, Alicia," Norah said, "do you know any more jokes?"

Alicia swallowed. "Only about a million," she said, before pouring the remains of the packet into her mouth.

"Tell us," Norah said eagerly.

Alicia lay back against the pillow. "Why does the man eat shoe polish before he goes to sleep?" she asked.

"Why?" the girls asked in unison. Even Jessica looked eager, eyes fixed on Alicia.

"So he can rise and shine!"

Jessica rolled her eyes and let out a soft *ha*. Thirty seconds later, Norah laughed. "Another."

"What do you call a sleepwalking nun?" Alicia asked.

"What?"

"A roamin' Catholic."

"More!"

Alicia continued. With each joke, the length of time between the punch line and Norah's laughter reduced. Slightly. And while Jessica didn't laugh out loud, she was grinning broadly, hardly glancing toward the door anymore. It wasn't much, but after the day she'd had, Alicia was prepared to call it a win.

Another week passed and still Alicia heard nothing from Grammy. The only thing distracting her from worry was her hunger. She spent her days obsessing about her next meal and planning what she would eat once she was home at Grammy's. She spent her nights trying to sleep through the rumble in her belly.

Norah and Jessica slipped her something every now and again— apparently they were running a homework racket that earned them some money and extra food—but it wasn't enough. They seemed to cope with the hunger much better than she did. Alicia's interior voice reminded her of this often. She was the only one who had the problem. She *was* a glutton. It undid her after a while—the hunger, the self-loathing. She became cranky, teary. Desperate.

One night, as she lay in bed unable to sleep, her hunger overcame her. She couldn't relax, couldn't think straight. It was as close as Alicia had ever come to feeling possessed—one minute she was lying in bed, the next she was out of bed and creeping downstairs in the darkness.

In the kitchen, she threw open every cupboard, every drawer. It wasn't rational. She knew Miss Fairchild didn't stock snacks—no Pop-Tarts, or crisps, or Savoy biscuits—but hope was a cruel thing. She fantasized about stumbling across a stash of hidden treats that had been forgotten. When she didn't find one, she settled for a box of cornflakes, stuffing great handfuls into her mouth. Finally she tipped her head back and poured the cereal straight into her mouth, trying to fill the ravenous hole inside.

It was only when the box was empty that she considered the consequences of her actions.

Miss Fairchild was right. She was a *glutton*.

She did her best to clean up the spillage, then crept back upstairs and slid back into bed. When the girls roused, she ignored their questions, too ashamed to tell them what she'd done. Besides, they'd know soon enough.

Miss Fairchild was waiting at the table when they came down the next morning, showered, and dressed and made-up, with not a hair out of place. The expression on her face was enough to make Alicia want to puke. Norah and Jessica sat in their usual spots, looking confused. The empty box of cereal was on the table.

"Someone had a midnight feast, I see," Miss Fairchild said, her voice soft.

Alicia had never longed for Grammy more in her life. She slid into her seat and hung her head. "I'm sorry."

"You made quite the mess of the pantry," Miss Fairchild continued. "What did you eat with, a shovel?"

Alicia assumed it was a rhetorical question, but when she didn't respond Miss Fairchild repeated herself. "Alicia? I said *what did you eat with?*"

"I didn't use anything," she said, her hands trembling. "I just . . . tipped the cornflakes into my mouth."

"Disgusting," Miss Fairchild said. "You are disgusting."

The wait to find out what was going to happen next was agonizing. The room was deathly quiet, apart from Jessica's panicked breathing. Norah looked less panicked, more resigned.

At last, Miss Fairchild pushed back her chair abruptly and stalked over to the pantry, retrieving a tin of baked beans. "Well," she said, "since you're not a fan of using utensils to eat, I will stop providing them. Crockery too. And don't think I'm going to let you get my tablecloth dirty."

She wrenched the lid off the beans, animated now, the blue veins pulsing in her neck.

Alicia didn't understand. Was Miss Fairchild going to make her eat beans straight from the tin? Alicia was still coming to terms with the idea of that when Miss Fairchild upended the tin and spilled beans all over the polished kitchen floor.

Alicia let out a gasp. So did Jessica. Norah closed her eyes.

"Go on," Miss Fairchild said, her mouth twisting into a perverse sort of smile. "I'm sure you're hungry. Don't let it go to waste!"

"You want me to eat off the floor?" Alicia stammered, beginning to cry. It was the shock of it as much as the humiliation.

"Why not? You seem to prefer eating like an animal." Miss Fairchild pulled Alicia from her seat and pushed her onto her knees. "So do it."

By the time Alicia lowered her head to the floor, she was sobbing so hard she thought she might be sick.

You deserve this, the little voice whispered to her. *You* are *disgusting.*

She slurped a mouthful of beans from the floor.

"And don't be leaving any behind," Miss Fairchild said, looming over her. "We've wasted enough food today already!"

13

JESSICA

Phil was asleep. He'd exited the bathroom approximately seventeen seconds earlier, and just like that he was curled up on his side, snoring.

Jessica didn't know how he did it. She had a very specific routine that she had to follow if she was to have the slightest hope of drifting off. Make sure the house was clean and tidy, take out the garbage, check every door and window to ensure it was locked. Once that was done, she showered and put on pajamas, brushed her teeth, took her Lexapro and melatonin tablets, applied her serums and moisturizer. Then she placed her phone on charge, told Alexa to turn on white noise, and got into bed to read a chapter of her book before turning off her lamp and staring into the darkness for hours until her body finally relented.

Tonight, as she slid between the sheets, she suspected it would take a while. Disturbing vignettes from her childhood circled in her brain—swimming pools and basements, birthday parties and horses. And fear, of course. Lots and lots of fear. It was a mistake to go to Port Agatha—Jessica knew it in her bones, in her blood. It wasn't just the memories the visit would unearth, either; it was more than that. After all, the police weren't just looking for information. They'd found *human bones*. If they determined that the cause of death was suspicious, they'd be looking for a murderer ... and they were foster children. Adults, technically, but always foster children. If people started pointing fingers, Jessica knew in which direction they'd be facing.

She rolled over in bed, wishing Phil would wake up. She understood the irony. She spent most waking hours ignoring Phil—too busy with work and her sisters to properly engage—but the moment he fell (instantly) asleep, she became desperate for his attention. She knew she could wake him. He wouldn't mind. He'd listen to her explain everything, and then say, "It'll be cool, Jess. The cops will believe you. Want me to come to Port Agatha?"

But she wouldn't wake him. Even after all these years, yearning for the love and attention of someone who couldn't give it to her was much more comfortable than actually receiving it.

She looked at him sleeping. So cute. People often referred to Phil as "cute." He was small and athletic, with earnest brown eyes and a warm smile. The two of them had been babies when they met—both of them working at an upmarket Italian restaurant in Melbourne. Jessica was the maître d'; Phil was a busboy. Jessica had been exceptional at the job. If her upbringing as a foster child had taught her anything, it was how to people-please. She knew how to adapt to people's moods, how to charm and please, how to make things look easy when they were extremely difficult.

Phil was also good at his job. On top of his day-to-day duties, he would do things to make her day easier, like bringing her a glass of ice-cold water as she stood at the front desk on a busy night, or quietly standing behind her in those few instances that customers became aggressive. It was nice knowing someone had her back.

"It's my job," he'd say, whenever she thanked him.

But one night, when they'd both stayed back for a couple of drinks at the end of their shifts, he'd made an admission.

"It *is* my job," he said, looking into his half-drunk glass of beer. "But I'll admit, I'm more diligent about it when you're on shift."

"Why?" Jessica asked. She wasn't fishing for compliments. Back then, the idea of someone doing something kind specifically for her was not something she was accustomed to.

"Because I like you."

He'd said it as if it were obvious—like she was an idiot not to have known. And so they started dating. Jessica never thought to ask herself if she liked him too. It didn't seem relevant. Being loved had been the goal of her life. Loving someone in return . . . that was just showing off.

She rolled toward her bedside table and picked up her phone, saw two new voice messages waiting for her. This was against the rules of her sleep routine, of course. It was too stimulating. According to an article she'd read, every minute spent looking at your phone in bed delayed sleep by six minutes. But tonight she couldn't help herself. It wasn't like she was going to be sleeping anyway.

She played the first message. Phil didn't so much as stir.

"Jessica, this is Debbie Montgomery-Squires."

Just like that, the uncomfortable face-off with Debbie over the pills came back to Jessica like a punch to the gut. It had only happened this afternoon, she realized in wonder. It felt like another lifetime.

She glanced at Phil; he hadn't so much as stirred.

"... I have searched high and low and cannot find my pills. I even moved the shelves to check they hadn't fallen down the back of them. I am *one hundred percent certain* they were in the cabinet when you started. I was starting to think I was going mad when one of the ladies mentioned that her cousin used your services and had also noticed pills missing afterward."

Jessica's stomach dropped like a stone.

"We were planning to go straight to the police, but I thought I'd do you the courtesy of speaking with you first. If you could give me a call at your earliest convenience, I'd appreciate it."

Fuck, Jessica thought. *Fuck fuck fuck.*

Panic feels a lot like excitement, she reminded herself, thinking of Mel Robbins's podcast. *I'm excited that Debbie Montgomery-Squires wants me to call her to explain what happened to her Valium. I'm glad her cousin also noticed pills missing from her bathroom cabinet.*

Nope. Mel Robbins's tip was bullshit.

What was she going to do now?

She thought about waking up Phil. "So what?" he'd say. "You took some Valium! They shouldn't have left it lying around."

It didn't matter that Jessica was in the wrong—not to Phil. His loyalty was blinding. Once, when they were first married, Jessica had reversed into a parked car. They hadn't had much money back then, and she'd been furious with herself for being so stupid.

"What kind of idiot leaves their car parked somewhere?" Phil had said when she told him.

She'd laughed and laughed. That was the point. But she'd stopped laughing somewhere along the line. Not just at Phil. She'd stopped laughing at all.

What she needed, ironically, was a Valium, to help her think. She'd been prescribed benzodiazepines three years ago, after having what she later discovered was her first panic attack. She'd been helping a client sort through her deceased mother's attic when it came on quite suddenly.

It started with acute, overwhelming nausea. Within minutes she was breathless, her palms were damp, her mouth dry. There was a pain in her chest: a sharp, stabbing pain that she thought might be a heart attack. She told her client—Mrs. Souz—not to call an ambulance; Jessica had never liked a lot of fuss. Sure enough, by the time Mrs. Souz fetched her a glass of water and asked if she might be pregnant, she was already feeling better.

She'd assumed it was one a one-off thing, a "funny turn." But then, three weeks later, it happened again.

"Panic attacks are very common," Dr. Sullivan told her, when she finally made an appointment. "But they can be quite frightening when you don't know what they are. If you do nothing, they will go away on their own. But if it's impacting your livelihood, you might want to consider medication."

"I don't want pills," Jessica had said. "I have a business to run. I can't be in a daze."

"It affects people differently, but many people find that all it does is the edge off. In any case, I think you should fill the script, Jessica. Some patients find just having the bottle with them makes them feel more secure. Knowing it's there if they need it is enough."

Being the rule-follower that she was, Jessica had the prescription filled. And the next time she had a panic attack—in the car on the way to a client—she pulled over and took the pill. The result wasn't instantaneous. By the time it kicked in, twenty minutes later, she'd all but recovered from the panic attack. Still, she felt it. Like a blanket of calm. Her thoughts slowed, her chest became loose. It was a fucking miracle. And it was available to her whenever she needed it.

It carried on this way for a while. She'd have a panic attack every so often, take a pill, and then have a wonderful day. After a while she started taking a preemptive pill before a busy day, just in case. They were excellent for sleep, too, she found. When she took a pill, she slept like the dead. She started to yearn for that feeling she got when the pill slid down her throat. The knowledge that calm was coming. No amount of meditation, yoga, or journaling could bring her that same sense of peace.

The pills ran out surprisingly fast, and at the speed Jessica was consuming them, the doctor was reluctant to prescribe more. But one of the great things about being a home organizer was that you had access to a lot of people's medicine cabinets. Jessica only took a few here and there. She had a reputation to protect, after all. Lately, though, she'd become a little more cavalier—hence the hullabaloo today at Debbie's house today.

Jessica sat up. For heaven's sake—if there was ever a time to take a pill, this was it. Tomorrow was going to be a big day, a difficult day, and she needed a good night's sleep if she was going to be on her game. In the morning, she'd call Debbie and smooth things over. It would be fine. Everything always looked brighter after a good night's sleep.

She opened her bedside drawer and fished out an emergency

bottle of pills that she'd placed there for moments like this. These were heavy-duty. Extra-strength. The label read EMILY MAKIV. Nice woman. Jessica had organized her pantry last year.

Jessica tipped two pills into her hand and reached for her water bottle. *Sleep is coming,* she told herself as she lay back down. *Sleep is coming soon.*

THE OFFICE OF DR. WARREN, PSYCHIATRIST

My next session with Dr. Warren starts much like the previous two—with him pointing at the vacant chair and then making me wait several minutes for no discernible reason before he appears to remember I'm there. This time, I don't sit in silence till he tells me to speak. I am a little short of people who are prepared to listen to me lately. And when no one will listen to you, the idea of an open forum stars to look quite appealing.

"Where was I up to?" I say.

His gaze is already back on his file. "The church ladies came to your house to help you out with your financial situation."

I might have been flattered that he remembered had I not spied the words "Church ladies / money problems" written on the notepad in front of him, under the date of our last session.

"That's right. . . . Well, the week after the church ladies showed up, they came back with the parish accountant, a man named John Wagner. He was there to help Mum go through the bills and get an idea of our financial situation. John was a big, tall man and he wore a shirt and slacks, which was unusual for the country. He reminded me of a strict schoolteacher." I grimaced at the memory of him. "He spoke very formally to my mother. He didn't even look at me. He and Mum spent the entire day in the formal dining room, going through boxes of bills, and looking at statements and payments from past years.

"Every few hours, John would yell out, 'Can we get some coffee in here?'; 'Can we get some tea in here?'; 'Can we get a sandwich in here?'

"I remember being surprised. I'd never made my parents tea or coffee or lunch before. Still, if John was helping Mum, I was happy to oblige—even when he failed to thank me for my efforts.

"After he left, Mum was more animated than usual. She heated up some soup for our dinner and, as we ate, she told me she was hopeful that, with John's guidance, she might be able to get on top of things. I threw my arms around her when she said that, which is saying something. Mum was so surprised she almost forgot to hug me back.

"'John was a bit weird,' I said to Mum when I'd resumed my seat. 'He didn't even make eye contact with me once.'

"'Really,' Mum said, frowning. 'I didn't notice. I thought he was nice.'

"'Oh, he *is* nice,' I said quickly. 'Helping us with our finances out of the goodness of his heart? He doesn't need to look at me. I'll always be grateful.'

"Mum looked relieved. 'Well . . . good. You can bring some of that gratitude with you to church tomorrow.'

"I blinked. 'Church?'

"'It's the least we can do after what they've done for us.'

"I groaned. 'Fine. As long as it doesn't become a regular thing.'

"But it *did* become a regular thing. Week after week we went to church every Sunday and listened to the pastor drone on about being a good Christian. We sat in a pew with the women who'd come to the house, and afterward we stood out front while the members of the congregation chatted. John, who played the organ during the service, joined us, and he and Mum would stay talking long after everyone else had left. At first, I was glad to see this, hopeful that his influence would keep Mum on the path toward financial competence. But by the fourth week, when I once again found myself waiting for my mother to finish up a conversation with John, I started to feel irritated.

"'Mum!' I whined, pulling on her arm. 'You've been talking for ages. Let's go!'

"'Do *not* speak to your mother like that,' John said, so sharply that both Mum and I startled. It was, I realized, the first time he'd acknowledged my existence at all, and the rage in his eyes felt incongruent with my infraction. I was just a child.

"'Don't just stand there gaping,' he said. 'Apologize to your mother.'

"I looked at Mum, who appeared as surprised as me. But after a moment, she nodded.

"I'd never felt so betrayed.

"'I'm sorry,' I said, looking at my shoes.

"After that I stood quietly while John told Mum that she'd allowed me to take advantage of my father's death. At my age, he said, I should be doing at least as much as she did around the household, and I should be speaking to her respectfully at all times. Mum listened without contradicting him.

"'Can you believe that guy?' I said, when the two of us were walking home. 'Asking me to apologize? Who does he think he is—my father?'

"Mum winced. 'He *is* very strict,' she conceded.

"'And then saying I've taken advantage of Dad's death! That I needed to do more around the household!'

"'He doesn't have any children of his own, so I think he's a bit of out step with his expectations,' my mother allowed. 'But I could hardly tell him that after everything he's done for us. Better to be polite. Besides, he's right—you could be doing a little more around the house.'

"'I don't like him,' I said sulkily. 'Why do we have to go to church anyway?'

"'Because the church gave us money—'

"'So now they own us?'

"'No. But we need to be respectful.'

"'To John?'

"'Yes. To John.'"

Dr. Warren listens avidly as I relate this, straightening in his seat every time I mention my relationship with my mother. I wonder what it is about her that interests him so much.

"And that made you angry?" he says. "Having her take his side like that?"

"I guess."

"Must have been lonely," Dr. Warren says. "Losing your father and then, in a way, losing your mother."

"Yes." The tears that spring to my eyes are born of surprise as much as anything else. "It did."

A long silence ensues. I'm not sure what is happening, but I sense that Dr. Warren is pleased with me. And even as a fully grown woman, I have to admit, there is something about pleasing people that still makes me feel good.

"I'm afraid our time is up," he says, a second before the knock on the door. He closes the file in his lap and opens the brown leather briefcase by his feet. It contains an alphabetical file organizer. A filing system in a bag. He flicks through the dividers until he gets to *F* for Fairchild.

"I'll see you next time," he says as he slides my file inside.

14

NORAH

From the back seat of Jessica's Audi, Norah reached between her sisters and grabbed the vanilla-scented cardboard air-freshener tab that hung from the rearview mirror.

"Hey!" Jessica cried.

"These are full of chemicals," Norah said, tossing it out the window of the moving car. "I read somewhere they can give you cancer."

Norah had read no such thing, but the smell of those things was like sandpaper against her brain, and she would never last the distance to Port Agatha with it in the car.

"I wouldn't need it if you didn't always insist on bringing your dogs in my car!" Jessica muttered. "Where am I dropping them anyway?"

Norah had been slightly duplicitous when she's loaded them into the car, telling Jessica she just needed to "drop them somewhere" and immediately changing the subject. She'd hoped Jessica would forget they were there, but they weren't being their best selves. Thong had already drooled all over the leather seats, and Couch had shed hair everywhere except for the blankets Norah had brought for him to sit on. Converse, who was resting his head on the center console, had been relatively quiet, but that was only because he'd discovered the bag of bougie dog treats in Jessica's bag and devoured the lot, meaning he would soon have terrible gas.

"Doggy day care?" Alicia suggested, when Norah didn't respond.

"As if," Norah said. "Those things cost an arm and a leg!"

"Jessica will pay," Alicia said, and Jessica nodded enthusiastically. Jessica *loved* paying for things. "It's only money," she'd say with a wistful, floating expression, as if she were a meditation teacher. "You can't take it with you when you die."

As for Norah, she was more than happy to take Jessica's money. In fact, lately, whenever Norah wanted new clothes, she simply emailed links to Jessica and a few days later the desired garments showed up in boxes on her doorstep. It was like Uber Clothes, except they didn't charge her card.

Alicia, however, refused to take Jessica's money. Recently, when Norah was giving her a hard time about it, Alicia told her it was because she was too proud.

"Proud of what?" Norah had cried. "Being poor?"

Sometimes Norah didn't understand her at all.

"Norah," Jessica said tightly. "Tell me where I'm taking these dogs, or I swear I'm leaving them on the side of the road."

"Jess," Alicia said in a conciliatory tone, "surely we can let them—"

"No. They can't come all the way to Port Agatha. Not in my new car."

"They're on blankets," Norah said. "And they've already drooled on the seats."

Jessica looked like her head might explode. Luckily her phone chose that moment to ring. "Fine!" she said. "But never again. I mean it, Norah."

Alicia gave her the thumbs-up, and Norah settled back into her seat happily, ready to enjoy the drive as they left the city behind.

"Jessica Lovat, Love Your Home," Jessica said.

"Hey, Jess, it's me." Norah recognized the voice that boomed over the speaker. It was Sonja, the manager of Jessica's business. "Sorry to bother you on a weekend."

Norah snorted. As if Jessica didn't work all day every day. As did Sonja, apparently, since it was Saturday morning. Trust Jessica to find such a high achieving employee.

"Hi, Son. What's up?"

"Just a quick one; I had a phone call from a client . . . Debbie Montgomery-Squires? You did her bathroom overhaul yesterday?"

Jessica's face darkened. "Is this about some missing pills? I reorganized her cabinets. Things were moved around."

Norah caught sight of Jessica's face in the rearview mirror. There was something off about her, Norah thought.

"I know," Sonja said, "I explained that. I just wanted to touch base because I'm a bit worried about her. She's the litigious type. The type to go to *A Current Affair.*"

Jessica's jaw flickered. "I'm headed out of town, bit of a family emergency, but I'll give her a call now, okay? I'll offer her a free wardrobe cleanse?"

"Can I suggest consulting with legal first?" Sonja countered. "In case that could be seen as an admission of guilt?"

"Good idea," Jessica said. "Thank goodness for you." She ended the call. "Never work with rich people or animals," she told her sisters.

"That's a bit rude," Norah said, "to animals."

"What was that about?" Alicia asked.

Jessica shrugged. "Nothing I haven't dealt with before." Her cheeks were pink.

"Pills, eh?" Norah said. "I remember when people used to steal jewelry."

"I didn't steal anything!"

"I know, I know," Norah said. "I'm just saying, if you did want to steal, go for cash. The safes are always behind paintings in those big houses. At least, that's where they are in the movies."

Norah trailed off when her phone beeped. Looking at the screen, she saw it was Kevin.

Loved that photo

Norah rolled her eyes. *Of course* he loved it. Who wouldn't? Meanwhile, she had a list of odd jobs still to be done. He sent another message.

How bout another one?

The audacity, Norah thought. For a broken nose? He should count himself lucky he didn't end up with two broken legs.

"Who's texting you?" Jessica asked.

"The man I went on a date with yesterday."

"Ooh," Jessica said. "Must have gone well if he's texting?"

Alicia spun around. "Let's see a picture."

Norah pulled up his profile pic and handed Alicia her phone.

"Is this him?" She sounded appalled. "He looks like a chipmunk."

"A weasel," Norah corrected. "And that photo is flattering."

Alicia shuddered. "Gross."

"I didn't expect you to fancy him," Norah said defensively, taking her phone back, "what with being a lesbian and all."

"She's bisexual," Jessica corrected, perking up. Jessica loved talking about the fact that Alicia was bisexual. She found it exciting. Norah also found it exciting, truth be told. She'd looked forward to the arrival of a sister-in-law, perhaps one with a dog, but so far Alicia had been a very disappointing lesbian-or-bisexual. She'd never even had a girlfriend.

"She's a nonsexual," Norah said.

"For God's sake," Alicia muttered.

"You *are*," Norah said. "When was the last time you had sex?"

"Alicia has an avoidant attachment style," Jessica said. "She pushes people away before they get too close."

"Okay, Brené Brown," Alicia said. "We were talking about *Norah's* date."

"Classic avoidant," Jessica said, throwing a small smile over her shoulder.

"Are you sexting him?" Alicia said, looking over her shoulder.

"I had to," Norah explained. "I broke his nose, so I needed to do something to stop him from pressing charges."

The sharp intake of breath that followed made Norah wonder if Jessica was having a medical episode.

"Relax," Norah said. "I sent him a photo of my boobs. He'll never do anything now. My boobs are magnificent."

"That's true," Alicia said.

Jessica was still gulping air. "Norah, you cannot assault anyone else, do you understand? You could go to *jail*!"

Norah rolled her eyes.

"I'm serious." Jessica glanced at her in the mirror. "I'm worried about you. I think you should try meditation again. That class you took in Sandringham really helped for a while."

Norah had never taken that class in Sandringham. She'd told Jessica she had to stop her from talking about it—a tactic that backfired, as Jessica now referred to the class regularly, asking for meditation tips or suggesting they go back together. Frankly, Norah thought her sister needed the class more than she did. "Maybe."

"Good. Because the next person you assault might not be happy to drop the matter for a photo of your boobs."

Jessica grossly underestimated the power of her boobs, Norah thought. But she let it slide.

For a few seconds they sank into glorious silence. Then Jessica stiffened. She turned slightly toward Alicia, her nostril twitching. Alicia's movements mimicked Jessica's.

"What?" Norah asked, as they both began to gag, jabbing wildly at buttons, trying to open the windows. "What is it?"

And then the smell hit her.

Wow, Norah thought. Those bougie dog treats were potent.

15

JESSICA

It was Friday night, and they were on the couch in their pajamas. Miss Fairchild had gone to a community meeting in town, leaving them home alone (obviously she was too cheap to pay a babysitter). Before she left, she'd told them, "If anyone comes to the door, say I'm upstairs in bed with a headache." Alicia had been nervous about the prospect of having to lie, but Jessica reassured her that in her entire life, no one had ever come to the door unexpectedly when Miss Fairchild was out.

But now someone was knocking at the door. They all looked at each other in horror.

"You said it never happened!" Alicia cried.

"I said it had never happened before," Jessica said.

"What do we do?"

"How should I know?"

"Do we answer it?"

The questions kept coming. Jessica didn't have any answers. Neither did Alicia or Norah. Jessica was about to suggest that they turn off the lights and hide when Norah started striding toward the door.

"No!" Jessica and Alicia hissed, jogging after her. "Norah! Wait!"

But she was too quick. By the time they'd caught up with her she was already at the door. As she opened it, her two sisters pressed themselves against the wall, out of sight of the visitor.

"Yes?" Her tone was haughty, expectant.

Alicia stifled a giggle.

"Package for Holly Fairchild."

Norah reached for the package. "Thanks."

"I need a signature."

"Sure thing." Norah leaned against the doorframe. "Where?"

Her confidence was impressive, Jessica had to admit. As Alicia's shoulders shook with repressed mirth, Jessica found herself stifling her own giggles.

"Sorry, sweetie, you need to be over eighteen." A pause. "Is Holly home?"

"I'm Holly," Norah said, cool as a cucumber.

Alicia slid down the wall, biting her fist to stop from laughing.

"No you're not."

"How would you know?"

"Because I've met Holly several times down at the post office."

Jessica and Alicia exchanged glances, eyes wide and worried.

Norah rallied quickly. "Of course! I almost didn't recognize you. Good to see you again, Logan."

The guy's patience had run out. "Listen, kid, I know you're not Holly. You're wearing Polly Pocket pajamas." Logan sounded tired. "And Holly looks . . . different."

"I didn't want to bring this up, but *you're* wearing a bottle-green uniform. And, frankly, *you* look different too. How do I know you're actually Logan?"

Now Jessica was shaking with laugher as Alicia wiped away tears.

"Just give me my package, Logan, if that's really your name."

Logan had clearly had enough, because the next thing they knew, Norah was closing the door, package in hand.

"Logan was an imbecile," she said, and the three of them broke into fresh gales of stomach-aching laughter that lasted the rest of the night.

16

ALICIA

I have good mind to leave you two and the dogs here and drive back to Melbourne," Jessica said crossly. "I don't understand how it can smell so bad. My eyes are watering."

They'd had to pull over and stand in the ditch at the side of the highway while they waited for the smell to clear from Jessica's car. Jessica's complete inability to see the funny side had Alicia and Norah in stitches.

"*You* bought the treats!" Norah said, wiping tears of laughter from her own eyes.

"I didn't know they would eat the whole bag!"

"I used to know a lot of fart jokes," Alicia said, "but I stopped telling them because everyone said they stunk."

She and Norah doubled over, laughing so hard Norah nearly toppled over. Jessica rolled her eyes, desperately trying to repress her smile. Alicia loved it when they made Jessica laugh. It was a rare treat. There was something about the whole interaction that fortified Alicia. When they finally got back on the road, it was with all four windows down and a sense that things weren't quite as bad as they had been a few minutes earlier.

When they were about twenty minutes from Port Agatha, Alicia decided to make a few work calls. Despite it being the weekend, she couldn't help but check in on Theo.

"Trish!" Alicia said, when the woman answered her phone. She closed the window of the car so she could hear better. "I'm glad I've caught you. How's Theo?"

"Better, thanks to Aaron," Trish replied. "Theo is quite infatuated with him. Won't leave the kid alone. Aaron would never admit it, but I think the feeling's mutual."

"Yes, I got that sense," Alicia said. "Listen, I've managed to get Theo an emergency appointment with an amazing pediatric psych. I'll text you the details. By the way, it looks like Theo's parents are going to relinquish parental rights, which means he'll be put up for adoption." Alicia paused. "I don't suppose you'd . . ."

Trish's response was swift. "Alicia, you know I'd love to, but I'm too old to be adopting babies now. Besides, people will be chomping at the bit for him, surely?"

Alicia knew what she meant. There would be no shortage of people wanting to adopt a two-year-old, who was white, cute, and had no known additional needs. Still, it wouldn't have felt right to move a traumatized child who was just starting to settle without asking the question at least.

She heard the sound of children squealing in the background. "Is that him?"

"Yep. Terrorizing Aaron."

Alicia smiled. "Remind me, who's Aaron's caseworker?"

"Louise? Louise something, I think. I have it written down somewhere. Why?"

"Just wondering." Alicia didn't know a Louise, but she made a mental note to track her down. She often did this, when she interacted with a kid who she wasn't officially responsible for. In Alicia's experience, the more people who cared about a kid, the better.

"I know you'll find Theo a good home, Alicia," Trish said out of the blue. "They always do well, the kids in your care."

"Thanks, Trish," Alicia managed through the lump in her throat.

But after she hung up, she wondered if Trish was right to have so much faith in her. Of course she would try to find Theo a wonderful home. But how would she really know? How sure could they ever really be that a foster home was good? It was a question that plagued her, day in and day out. After all, from the outside, Wild Meadows had seemed very good.

She dropped her phone into her bag. "I don't suppose you would consider adopting a two-year-old?" she said to Jessica.

"I've told you, I don't have the capacity. I run a business."

"Lots of working parents raise foster kids," Alicia replied.

"Great," Jessica said. "Then you do it."

"I live in a rented one-bedroom apartment!"

"So buy a house," Norah said from the back seat. "Jessica will pay."

"I will," Jessica said eagerly.

"Jessica *is not* buying me a house," Alicia said irritably.

She only wished her reasons for not adopting were as simple as accommodation. How could Alicia welcome a child into her life when she couldn't even have a proper relationship with an adult? She couldn't risk it. The stakes were too high.

"This is the turn-off!" Norah cried, pointing at the sign to Port Agatha. "Jess—here! Turn left. Here."

It was as if Jessica hadn't heard. Her hands were clutching the steering wheel, her gaze fixed straight ahead.

Alicia put a hand on her forearm. "Jess."

"I know. Just . . . give me a sec."

"You can do this," Alicia told her. "Norah and I are here."

"Okay." Jessica exhaled. "All right."

The turn was so late and so sharp that the dogs slid across the back seat, hitting the opposite door before landing in a pile in the footwell.

"Sorry," Jessica said to Norah, with an anxious glance in the mirror, as if bracing for her wrath. Alicia braced for it too. But to her surprise, Norah leaned forward, putting her hand on Jessica's arm where Alicia's had been a moment earlier.

"You did it," she said with uncharacteristic earnestness. "I'm proud of you."

Port Agatha was a small farming community two hours from Melbourne, comprising rural properties and a small township. According to the last census, it had a population of three thousand two hundred and eighty-five people. On the drive into town, they passed the Country Fire Authority building, a pair of tennis courts, a barbecue area, and a decrepit playground. Finally, they reached the local police station.

"I remember this place," Norah said.

The police station hadn't changed since the last time they were in Port Agatha, but the buildings around it had. Back then, the squat, 1970s flat-roofed single-story building had a concrete parking lot on one side and a paddock on the other. Now it was nestled between a coffee shop and one of those general stores that existed in every country town—the kind that sold everything from lawn chairs to hardware supplies to romance novels. Farther along the street were a hairdresser, a fish-and-chips shop, a newsagent, and a secondhand bookstore. Directly across from the police station was a beautiful, but weathered, old pub.

When they pulled up in the gravel car park, there was a pause as they each gazed out to the street. Even the dogs seemed suddenly pensive. No one was willing to make the first move out of the car, until Alicia broke the silence with an audible sigh.

"Right," she said. "Let's go."

As they made their way toward the station, Norah wrangling the dogs, Alicia's phone beeped with a voice message from Meera. Receiving a message from Meera here in Port Agatha felt jarring, like a bizarre clashing of worlds—a wedding and a funeral, a birth and a death. Her thumb hovered over the message for a second before she returned the phone to her pocket. Even though it was undoubtedly about work, Meera's messages needed to be savored. Cherished. Not listened to on the fly while approaching her worst nightmare.

Three detectives—two men and a woman—greeted them in the foyer of the police station, which smelled of curry and cigarettes.

"We really appreciate you coming in today," the female detective said. "I'm Ashleigh Patel, I spoke to you on the phone. This is Detective Hando and this is Detective Tucker."

They greeted each other with nods of the head. Hando was forty-odd, with sandy hair and stubble. Tucker looked to be in his fifties, with a gray mustache. Detective Patel was the youngest and the most impressive, in heels and a severe-looking ponytail, which told Alicia this team wasn't local to Port Agatha.

"I like your mustache," Norah said to Tucker.

Norah had always had a mustache fetish, ever since they were kids. She told them she'd read somewhere that men with mustaches were more trustworthy—but once, after a couple of drinks, she'd admitted that she merely found them sexy. Alicia hoped she wouldn't ask if she could touch it.

"Thank you," Tucker said, after a brief, puzzled pause. "My wife hates it." His gaze went faraway for a moment, as if he were thinking about his wife.

"Anyway," Patel continued, "we're from the homicide squad in Melbourne, but we've set up an office here for this investigation."

"Homicide?" Jessica said. "So you think the person was . . . murdered?"

"We think it's possible," Patel said. "That's what we're here to find out."

There was a short silence as they all digested this. Jessica got it together first.

"Well," she said, "we're hoping this won't take long. We all have responsibilities in Melbourne that we need to get back to."

"We understand," Patel said. "And I can assure you, we'll get through our questions as quickly as possible." Thong jumped up on Patel's black suit. "Ooof. Hello."

"Are these your dogs?" Hando asked, kneeling beside Converse and scratching his chin. "They're gorgeous. Unfortunately we can't have dogs in the interview rooms."

"They're service dogs," Norah said, without missing a beat. "So they have to stay with us."

Patel looked at the mutts dubiously. "*These* are service dogs?"

"Yes," Norah said serenely.

One of the things that Alicia had always admired about Norah was the fact that she was a committed liar. Not to be confused with a *good* liar; Norah's gift was the ability to come up with a lie on the spur of the moment and remain committed to it against all logic and reason.

"For . . . ?"

The pause was negligible. "Irritable bowel syndrome."

The detectives exchanged a look. Hando, still stroking the dog's chin, snorted. "You have service dogs for IBS?"

"Of course."

"And you require three?"

"One each," Norah said. "And I suggest you open a window in the interview rooms."

Jessica broke into a sudden coughing fit. Alicia patted her back.

Patel glanced at her colleagues, who appeared just as bewildered as she was. "And you all have a diagnosis, I take it?"

Norah nodded. "You can call our doctors, if you like." She reached for her phone, which, Alicia had to admit, was a nice touch.

"That won't be necessary," Patel said. "Would you and your, er, service dogs like to follow us?"

Patel led them to a small room with a wooden desk, a fiddle-leaf fig, and a window that overlooked the parking lot. Couch immediately ran inside and peed on the plant.

"Jessica," Patel said, "you'll be in here with me. Detective Hando will take Norah and—"

"You're splitting us up?" Jessica interrupted. She looked utterly panicked.

Norah, looking equally stressed, bent over to rub Thong's belly.

"We need to interview you separately, yes," Patel said.

Alicia had expected this, but the prospect of being separated from her sisters—in Port Agatha—triggered anxiety in her too. It was almost as if the clock had wound back twenty-five years. They were all young girls, begging to be believed. Except this time they weren't children. This time, they were going to demand to be heard.

"Okay." Jessica clapped her hands and smiled brightly at her sisters. "Let's do this."

Detective Tucker crossed his legs, exposing the white sports socks that he'd already apologized for. Apparently, he'd forgotten to pack black ones. He didn't seem like a detective. He reminded Alicia of a kindly uncle, with his unkempt graying hair and weathered skin.

"Let's start at the beginning, Alicia. How did you end up at Wild Meadows?"

Alicia had agreed that the interview could be recorded, and they'd been through all the official stuff—confirming the date, the location and the names of those present.

"I was a respite case," Alicia said. "My grandmother had a fall and was taken to hospital, so there was no one to take care of me."

"A respite case?" Tucker said. "So you weren't in the home for long?"

"I wasn't supposed to be. But as it turned out, I stayed."

Tucker glanced nervously at Thong, whose huge head was resting on one of his feet. "And why was that?"

"My grammy," Alicia said, with a wobble in her voice, "she . . . she didn't come out of hospital."

"My condolences."

It felt so ridiculous to be receiving condolences. It happened when she was a little girl, and now she was in her mid-thirties. She should be over it by now. She should be over everything that happened at Wild Meadows.

"Can you tell me about your relationship with Miss Fairchild?" Tucker asked, after a respectful silence.

"We didn't have a relationship."

"*Oh?*" Tucker's bushy eyebrows leapt up toward his hairline. "How so?"

"You can't have a relationship with a monster."

Tucker's expression became concerned. Alicia crossed her arms in front of herself—a makeshift shield.

"I'm sorry, Alicia, but I'm going to have to ask you to tell me about it."

She nodded. She'd known this was coming. But it wasn't until Thong moved over to lie at her feet that she was able to open her mouth and start.

17

ALICIA

BEFORE

I think it's my birthday," Norah said.

The three of them were in bed, looking up at the ceiling. Alicia had told all the jokes she knew, including the crappy ones. Norah laughed at them all indiscriminately. They were lying there, waiting for sleep to come, when Norah made the announcement.

Alicia propped herself on an elbow. "You *think?*"

"It's either the sixteenth or the eighteenth, I can't remember which."

"You *don't know* when your birthday is?"

Norah wasn't listening. "It's the eighteenth today. So either way, I must be twelve."

Norah seemed happy enough with that, but Alicia was appalled. "Can't you ask Miss Fairchild? Or your social worker?"

"Probably. But it doesn't really matter, does it?"

Alicia was about to say that yes, it did matter, because birthdays were special. Then it dawned on her that birthdays might not have been all that special for Norah.

"Have you ever celebrated your birthday?" she asked gently. "Had a party or anything?"

Norah thought for a minute. "There was a photo of me at Mum's house with balloons in the background. I think that was a party. But I don't know if it was mine or someone else's."

"Do *you* know when your birthday is?" Alicia asked Jessica.

She nodded. "May twelfth. I had a party the first year I came to Wild Meadows, when I turned five."

Alicia felt a tug of emotion. "That's the only birthday party you've ever had?"

Jessica nodded again, clearly not wanting to expand on this.

Alicia had had a party every year of her life, she was pretty sure. Certainly every year that she remembered. Not big parties. One year, she was allowed to pick a friend and go to the movies and have McDonald's afterward. Another year she had two friends over to Grammy's friend Judy's house to swim in her backyard pool. But there was always cake, a few balloons, and the birthday song.

"What's so good about parties anyway?" Jessica asked.

"Well," Alicia said, "the food, for one thing. Chips and lollies and sausage rolls. Soft drinks. Cake!" Her stomach rumbled at the thought. "And presents. Everyone who comes brings you one."

Norah and rolled over to face her. "What do you do at the party?"

"Sometimes you play games like pass the parcel, or there's an entertainer—a clown, maybe," Alicia said, enjoying their entranced expressions. "But when you're older, like us, you . . . I don't know— hang out. Talk. Listen to music. Dance."

"That sounds fun," Norah said. "I like to dance."

Jessica snorted. "When have you ever danced?"

"I dance," Norah said defensively. "If I hear music on the radio or in the supermarket or something. I'd dance at a party for sure."

"Fine." Jessica held her hands up in surrender. "You dance."

They were all quiet. The silence felt slightly wistful.

"Why don't we dance now?" Alicia said suddenly. "We can have a dance party for Norah's birthday."

Jessica scoffed. "Yeah right. Like Miss Fairchild wouldn't lose her mind."

"She wouldn't," Alicia said, "if it was a *silent* dance party."

Jessica and Norah looked unconvinced.

"Come on, spoilsports." Alicia rose, crossed the room and pretended to put a tape into a cassette player, feeling excited and a little foolish. "Norah, what's your favorite song?"

"'Kung Fu Fighting,'" she replied, without a moment's hesitation.

"Good choice," Alicia said. "I'm putting it on. There you go, it's playing. Now . . . dance."

Alicia closed her eyes and began shimmying her hips, her shoulders, her hands. Before long she was bopping wildly around the room. There was something about it—the sense of release—after the tension of the past few weeks. It felt fantastic. Alicia got lost in it.

When she opened her eyes a few minutes later to check on the others, Jessica and Norah were also dancing. Norah was standing on her dressing table, playing air guitar and kicking her legs high. Both girls were smiling.

And to her surprise, Alicia realized she was smiling too.

"Alicia? Can you come in here a minute, please?"

The next day, Miss Fairchild called out to her as soon as she walked in the door from school. It was her polite voice, which perhaps should have tipped Alicia off that they had visitors. Usually when they arrived home Miss Fairchild either ignored them or ordered them to do chores.

When Alicia saw the social worker in the living room, she squealed. "Sandi! You're here! Am I going home? I was worried when I didn't hear from you. I thought you would call in a few days. What happened?"

Even as she talked, her delight turned to irritation, and then tears. She hadn't known emotions could transition so fast.

"I'll give you some privacy," Miss Fairchild said, standing. She was dressed particularly nicely today, in a linen dress and *pearls*, and she'd curled her hair. Obviously she'd known Sandi was coming.

"What's wrong?" Alicia asked when she and Sandi were alone.

Sandi stood. She was wearing the same electric-blue—frosted eyeshadow as last time, with spidery mascara. Her nails were orange and she smelled of sickly floral perfume.

She took Alicia's hand in one of hers. "Your grandmother couldn't call, honey, she was too ill from the pneumonia."

Alicia blinked. "Grammy has *pneumonia*?"

"She did." Sandi clasped both of Alicia's hands now and looked at her desperately. Tears filled her eyes. "She became ill in the hospital. I'm so sorry, honey. Your grandmother passed away this morning."

Alicia pulled her hand away.

Sandi put her arms around her. "Shh . . . Oh, it's okay, honey. I know. I know. Shh . . ."

Sandi didn't need to shush her; Alicia wasn't crying. She stared, unblinking, over the social worker's shoulder. "Grammy's . . . dead?"

"I'm so sorry, sweetie."

Sandi hugged her tighter. Alicia just stood there. It was as though someone had turned a dimmer switch. Everything became dark. Her limbs became heavy and cold and she buzzed, like static was running through her.

Finally Alicia pushed Sandi's away. "Why didn't someone tell me she had pneumonia?"

"I thought you *were* told." Sandi glanced at the door Miss Fairchild had exited through.

"I didn't get to say goodbye to her," Alicia said dumbly. And then, almost immediately: "What will happen to me?"

Your grandmother has just died and you're already thinking about yourself! the little voice said. *You are a selfish girl. You didn't deserve her.*

"I've explained the situation to Miss Fairchild. Obviously, you were only meant to be a respite placement but under the circumstances she's willing to keep you on here indefinitely."

The lights seemed to dim further.

"I know this is distressing. And it's a lot to take in."

Alicia shook her head. "I can't stay here."

Sandi blinked her spidery eyelashes. "Oh. Well, we can look into another placement for you . . ."

"I don't want another placement. I want Grammy."

Sandi's face crumpled in sympathy. "Oh, I know, baby. Shh. It's all right. I know. Come here."

Sandi opened her arms, and this time Alicia sank into them. Despite what Sandi said, it wasn't all right. With Grammy dead, nothing would ever be right again.

Alicia lay in bed all afternoon, crying so hard her head ached and her throat became sore. Jessica sat on the edge of the bed, her hand resting on Alicia's arm. Norah was at the foot of the bed, her long legs stretched out, almost reaching Alicia's nose. Neither of them seemed to know what to say or do.

"Are you going to stay at Wild Meadows?" Jessica asked.

Alicia hadn't thought she had any tears left, but at this, her vision blurred again. "I told Sandi I didn't want to. She said she'd look into another placement. But I don't *want* another placement." She let out a sob. "I want *Grammy*. She was all I had. Now I've got nothing."

They let her weep for a minute or two. Alicia assumed it was because they knew she was right. She had nothing. But when she looked up, Norah was shaking her head.

"You have us," she said. "That's not nothing."

Alicia felt a stab of guilt. Before she could say anything, Norah continued, "You don't have to leave, you know. There are worse places than Wild Meadows."

Alicia nodded, but she didn't believe it.

"It's true," Norah said. "For example, the family that locked us outside from seven in the morning till five in the evening every day—boys in one paddock, girls in another, while the parents sat inside watching daytime television. Or the family that made us pick up dog poop with our bare hands if we forgot to wash up before dinner, to teach us a lesson. The place with the foster brothers who locked me in the cupboard and wouldn't let me out until I touched their ding-dongs . . ."

Alicia stole a look at Jessica. Her eyes were full of tears.

Norah crossed her legs, resting her ankles on Alicia's side. "And the family who made us watch movies with naked people in them . . . that was gross."

As the stories went on, each one definitely, unequivocally worse than Wild Meadows, Alicia began to cry too. No child should have to choose between this place and one of those others Norah described, just because their parents had died or were unable to care for them. It wasn't right.

"At least here, we have each other," Norah said at last. "Maybe if we stick together, we can become like . . . like sisters."

Even through the grief that pierced Alicia, it was hard not to be affected by what Norah was saying. Especially when, after a couple of seconds, she extended her pinkie. Norah wasn't one to be sentimental; it made the gesture all the more moving. "What do you say?"

Jessica offered her own pinkie without hesitation, which Alicia found equally moving.

She could see that, after the stories Norah had just shared, it did make sense to stick together, forge their own family. But that meant staying at Wild Meadows with Miss Fairchild. It felt like an impossibly cruel choice.

And yet, there were Jessica and Norah looking at her, their pinkies extended, their expressions painfully hopeful. Alicia sighed. How could she say no to *pinkies*?

She closed her eyes, sent up a prayer to Grammy. Extended her pinkie. Within seconds it had been snatched up into a three-way.

"Sisters," she said.

18

NORAH

Detective Hando, to Norah's delight, was a dog person. He had four dogs at home—one more than was legally allowed in his inner-city dwelling: a German shepherd called Roger, a Staffy named Ian, a beagle cross called Martha, and a terrier with one eye called Boris Johnson. Norah had already offered to take one of them, which of course would be one more than *she* was legally allowed to have, but like Hando, she cared not for silly dog rules.

After ten minutes of them sharing photos of their dogs on their phones, Hando glanced at his watch and suggested ruefully that it might be time for Norah to make her statement.

"Fine," Norah said, sitting back and crossing her arms. "If we must."

He pressed record on the device, then proceeded to state their names, the date and some file numbers corresponding to a manila envelope that was sitting on the coffee table.

"Right," he began. "I want you to tell me about your life at Wild Meadows, starting with how you came to be there."

"I was booted from my previous placement for kicking someone in the balls."

Hando blinked. "May I ask why you were in foster care? Where were your parents?"

"My mother was a drug addict," she said.

Hando made a sympathetic face, but life with her mum wasn't so bad. Norah had liked the predictability of it. The two of them had a routine. Her mother took drugs before she went out for the evening. She arrived home as the sun came up, then slept all day, waking up around the time that Norah got home from school. After dinner, she took drugs again. Rinse and repeat.

It was all fine until the day when Norah got home from school and found her mother still asleep. She was so still, and so pale, that Norah began shaking her.

"What are you doing?" her mum asked groggily.

"Just making sure you're not dead."

"Hold my hand, then," she said, closing her eyes and holding out her hand.

Though she scorned herself for it later, at the time Norah had interpreted her mother's comment to mean that if Norah was holding her hand, she *couldn't* die. Norah took her side of the bargain very seriously. She sat beside her mother's bed and gripped her hand tightly.

Three hours later, when her mother's boyfriend arrived with a couple of friends, Norah's mum was still asleep. He tried to wake her, even slapping her face, but her mother didn't stir.

"Norah, get out of there. I need to call an ambulance."

But Norah sat holding her mother's hand, even as the paramedics ran into the room, tailed by police. When one of the cops tried to prise Norah away, she went ballistic.

"No," she screeched. The strength of her voice surprised her. "I have to hold her hand."

"Honey, we need to help your mother," the police officer said. His eyes were bright with urgency. "I'm going to take you back to the cop car, okay? Have you been in a police car before?"

He started tugging Norah away from her mother, but she wouldn't release her mother's hand.

"You need to let go, honey," said the police officer.

"I can't," Norah cried.

"I'm sorry," he said. "You have to."

The cop gave a final tug, and her mum's hand slid from her grasp.

"I'm sorry about your mother," Hando said again.

Norah shrugged.

"What about your dad?"

"Already dead by then."

"Oh."

Through the window, Norah saw a man in a baseball cap walking toward the door of the police station. There was something familiar about him, the way he walked as if his feet were glued to the ground. Underneath the baseball cap, his hair was red.

"I know this is difficult," Hando said, "but I promise it's incredibly helpful to our investigation."

"If you say so. But I don't see how telling you about my childhood has anything to do with it. You'd be better off asking who the bones belonged to."

Hando sat up straight. "Do you *know* who the bones belong to?"

"No."

He looked so disappointed, Norah felt bad. She considered

making a guess, but before she could, he said, "In that case, talking about your childhood is all we've got."

Bugger.

"Perhaps you can tell me how you felt about Miss Fairchild?" the detective suggested. "Did you like her?"

"No. She was awful."

"Awful how?" Hando asked. "Violent?"

"Depends on your definition of violence."

"What do you mean by that?"

Norah sat forward in her chair and rubbed the belly that Converse had exposed tellingly. "Let's just say she found more interesting ways to hurt people."

19

JESSICA

BEFORE

It was Saturday afternoon, and Jessica was on the sofa, watching taped episodes of *Beverly Hills 90210*, while Norah, beside her, read a book. Unusually, Miss Fairchild had left them alone for the afternoon.

"What should we do?" Alicia asked.

"What do you mean?" Jessica said.

"I *mean* . . . what shall we do?" Alicia said. "With the afternoon?"

Jessica paused the TV on Brenda and Dylan making out on the couch at the Walsh house and frowned at Alicia. It was just such an odd comment. As if she expected them to suggest a trip to the seaside or an outing to the zoo. Alicia had been at Wild Meadows for six months—long enough to know that when they weren't doing homework or chores or running errands, they read books or watched TV or hung around the house. Which was exactly what they were doing now.

Norah looked equally confused.

"We're not allowed to go anywhere," Jessica said. Miss Fairchild had been very clear on this. She'd said it was for their own safety, but they knew she just didn't want people to know she left her foster kids home alone for hours on end.

"We don't have to go *out*," Alicia said. "We can stay here and do something."

"Like what?"

Alicia gestured toward the window. It was a beautiful sunny day. Beyond the pool, at the bottom of the field where the paddocks gave way to a wooded area, the horses were having a canter. "How about horse riding?"

Jessica laughed.

"What?" Alicia said.

Jessica stopped. She'd assumed Alicia was joking. "Do you even *know* how to ride a horse?"

"No," Alicia said. "But Grammy always said it was a crime to waste a beautiful day."

Jessica began to pulse with panic. She was torn. On the one hand, she was terrified to do anything that might make Miss Fairchild angry. On the other, four months had passed since Alicia's grandmother died and Alicia was yet to regain her spark. It was as if the spirit had drained out of her. Jessica could see that she tried her best, moving through the rituals of the day—playing, chatting, even laughing—but it was like an actor performing Alicia rather than the real thing.

And Grammy said it was a crime to waste a beautiful day!

"They're not even Miss Fairchild's horses," Jessica said desperately.

"But there's a man out there," Alicia said. Norah and Jessica followed her gaze to the man by the stables. "See?"

"That's the stable guy," Jessica said. "He looks after the horses."

"Maybe he can teach us to ride?" Alicia said. "I'll go ask."

She took off quickly, going through the kitchen, out the back door and down the porch steps. Jessica and Norah scrambled to follow, but by the time they caught her she was halfway across the lower paddock, striding confidently toward the stables.

"Hello?" Alicia called to the horse man as they approached.

He was bent over examining a horse's hoof when she called. He didn't rush to look over, but when he did it was only for a second—a quick glance before he looked back down again. "What do you want?" he said gruffly.

"I'm Alicia. I live over there at Wild Meadows." She pointed over her shoulder. "It's a beautiful day and . . ."

Horse guy looked up. He was younger than Jessica had thought. Maybe twenty years old, with orange hair, and freckles all over his face and arms. He wore a red flannel shirt and riding boots.

At the sight of his impatient frown, Alicia's confidence seemed to fade. "I was wondering if we could ride a horse," she finished quickly.

He shook his head, picking up a brush from the grass and putting it in his pocket. "They ain't my horses—I just take care of them."

Jessica exhaled in relief. She'd been agreeable and it hadn't worked out. None of it was her fault.

"Please?" Alicia said, stepping forward. "Come on. We're foster kids. Surely it couldn't hurt to give a few foster kids a bit of joy." She smiled winningly.

He stopped. "You're foster kids?" He appeared to consider this for a moment, then glanced up the hill toward the house. "And your foster mother . . . ?"

"Won't be back for hours." Alicia grinned.

Jessica wondered why them being foster kids had changed his mind. Whatever the reason, after a final glance toward the house, he relented. "Fine. You all want a go?"

Alicia didn't even turn around to check with Norah and Jessica. "Yes, please," she said. "All of us."

The horse guy's name was Dirk. After his coolness, he became a bit more friendly. He was a pretty good teacher, too, helping them mount the horses and paying close attention as they trotted around the paddock.

Jessica had to admit it was a lot of fun. She felt majestic sitting astride her horse, Almond, making gentle noises and saying things like, "Whoa . . . Good girl."

"You're a natural," Dirk told her as she trotted past. She beamed with pride.

Norah, on the other hand, was not a natural. Despite Dirk's encouragement she managed only about fifteen minutes astride Bangles before declaring that she preferred dogs to horses. Alicia did only slightly better, sitting on Bertha, who was barely taller than a pony, for only half an hour before calling it a day. But Jessica rode Almond for nearly an hour. She couldn't believe the way time had flown. She was so reluctant to stop that, in the end, Dirk had to take the reins and help her off.

"Thanks," she said, as she dismounted. "That was awesome."

"I don't see you guys around much."

"We're inside people," Jessica said. "Speaking of which, it's probably better that we don't mention this to our foster mother. She might be mad at us for bothering you."

"Your secret's safe with me." He grinned. "My boss wouldn't like it either."

"The perfect crime," Alicia said.

As they made their way up the hill, Jessica felt practically jubilant. It was a good idea, listening to Alicia, she realized. Alicia knew how to have fun, and that was one thing they all needed. Jessica was about to tell Alicia this as they crested the top of the hill and Wild Meadows came into view. Miss Fairchild was standing on the porch watching them.

"Where have you been?" she demanded, as they climbed the steps. She was unusually flustered—her hair a little windswept, her blouse untucked at the back. Her eyes glistened with rage.

None of them replied.

"Well?" Her tone was icy.

"We went horse riding," Alicia said, her voice barely audible.

"You went *horse riding!*" Her eyes were wide, nostrils flaring. "On other people's horses. After I *told* you to stay home. Can you imagine my embarrassment when I bumped into Sara Mitchell, who'd just driven past Wild Meadows and seen you girls riding her horses?"

This explained why she looked so disheveled. She must have run all the way from town when she'd heard.

"You *didn't have permission to ride them.* Not from me, not from the owners of the horses. Sara could move her horses elsewhere and I'd lose that income. Then who would feed you? Who would keep the farm running?" Her face was crimson with rage. Jessica couldn't remember the last time she'd seen her foster mother this angry. "Whose idea was it then? To go horse riding."

She looked at them each in turn. Jessica flinched under her gaze.

"Mine," Alicia said, before Jessica could even open her mouth.

Miss Fairchild raised her eyebrows. "I see."

"Actually," Norah said, "it was mine."

"They're both lying," Jessica broke in, standing taller. "It was my idea."

"Is that right?" Miss Fairchild pursed her lips. Her gaze slid away, as if contemplating something. "All right, since I'm feeling generous, I'll only punish one of you. I'll even let you choose. Who is it going to be?"

She crossed her arms and waited. The savagery of it was breathtaking. Jessica could hardly believe she'd once called this woman "Mummy." She was no longer capable of even a millisecond of kindness.

"Very well," she said, when none of the girls responded. "I'll pick. Eenie, meenie, miney, mo." She was pointing at Norah. "You!"

Jessica was going to interject—volunteer herself for punishment—but Miss Fairchild moved too quickly. She grabbed Norah by the ear, turned on her heel and headed inside and down the hall. Norah, caught unaware, tripped twice in her desperation to keep up. Alicia and Jessica ran after them, all the way to the door under the stairs that led to the basement.

The pitch-black basement.

The moment that Norah realized what was coming would be burned into Jessica's mind forever. Her body went limp. Her eyes became wild. Jessica began screaming. Alicia pleaded. That, of course, was the point.

Miss Fairchild wrenched open the door.

Suddenly Jessica realized how stupid she'd been. She couldn't rebel. She couldn't go horse riding. It wasn't just about her anymore. Alicia and Norah didn't just represent fun, or support, or someone to take risks with. They represented two more ways for Miss Fairchild to hurt her. She should have pushed back against Alicia's idea and kept her sisters safe inside the house.

Miss Fairchild shoved Norah into the pitch darkness, latching the door closed behind her.

The commotion started immediately—Norah kicking the door and hammering it with her hand so hard that the wood around the latch splintered. The worst part, though, was the wail. The wail of a mother who had lost her child or an animal caught in a trap. It was bottomless and aching. After several minutes of it, Miss Fairchild couldn't take any more and walked away. But Jessica and Alicia stayed. They sat on the floor by the door and whispered to Norah. They sang songs and read stories. They stayed for hours, until finally Miss Fairchild permitted them to let her out.

20

JESSICA

Detective Patel held a blue pen in her hand, which she twirled like a fidget toy as Jessica talked. Occasionally she scrawled notes on her yellow legal pad in nearly illegible handwriting. Jessica was curious as to the woman's note-taking system. It seemed to her that it would make far more sense to type the notes and then save the document in a folder labeled by surname and date. The idea of all those little files, neatly organized in folders, brought some much-needed relief to Jessica, after an afternoon spent recalling some of her most difficult memories.

"It sounds like Miss Fairchild really hurt you, Jessica," Patel said evenly.

She wasn't a therapist, Jessica reminded herself, despite her concerned, sympathetic expression.

"You must have wanted to hurt her back."

See? There. Not a therapist—a police officer.

Patel sat back in her chair. She was extremely well-groomed. Her eyebrows were perfect arches, her black hair was shiny and straight. She had a prominent nose, which anchored the rest of the features on her face. Jessica hoped she hadn't considered a nose job. It would be a mistake, taking away her point of interest. She wondered if she should tell her that.

"No," Jessica said. "I only ever wanted to love her."

Jessica was embarrassed to realize that she *still* wanted that. She thought of all the times she'd fantasized about Miss Fairchild hearing about her successful business and showing up on Jessica's doorstep to tell her how proud she was. In the fantasy, Jessica had many different responses—sometimes turning her away, other times hugging her foster mother and inviting her into her beautiful home. They'd share a pot of tea and it would be like old times. The very oldest, before it all went wrong. She felt deeply ashamed of the fantasy; too ashamed to admit it to Alicia or Norah, or even her therapist.

Absently, she reached inside her handbag and wrapped her fingers around the bottle of pills within.

Patel tapped the pen against her chin. "What about your sisters?"

"What about them?" Jessica let go of the pills.

"I understand Norah has issues with aggression. Did she ever hurt Miss Fairchild? Or talk about hurting her?"

"Of course not," she said, instantly defensive. "She was just a child."

Patel looked unconvinced. Jessica understood why. There were probably reams of files detailing Norah's anger issues. She had a criminal record. If it turned out the body had been buried during their time at Wild Meadows, and they started looking for a murderer . . . well, Norah would have to be pretty high on their list.

"From what I've read, she had a fairly colorful history of violent behavior even back then." Patel referred to a document in front of her. "It says here that after you were removed from Wild Meadows, several areas of the home were found to be damaged by your sister." She glanced at the sheet of paper. "The door underneath the stairs was splintered." She looked up.

"Who says Norah did it?" Jessica asked.

Patel gestured to the document. "It says here that Norah admitted to it."

Jessica cocked an eyebrow. "In that case, I imagine you must have been concerned to learn that a child was locked under the stairs?"

"Yes," Patel said, frowning. "Very concerned."

She seemed sincere, but it didn't matter. They weren't investigating child abuse. They were investigating the bones. A violent little girl who'd been locked under the stairs had good reason to lash out, which was why they were interested in Norah, no doubt.

"Look," Jessica said, "you're right. Norah has anger issues. Show me a person who grew up in foster care who doesn't. But she has a good heart. She's as harmless as these big stupid dogs."

She looked at Couch, for the first time feeling something resembling affection.

Patel put down the pen. "Forgive me for asking, but you, Alicia, and Norah aren't biological sisters, are you?"

"No," Jessica said. "But we're sisters in every way that counts."

Patel smiled. "I bet you'd do anything for them."

It was a good try, but Jessica wasn't falling for it. "I wouldn't bury a body for them, if that's what you're asking." She gave an airy, appalled laugh for good measure.

But it was clear from Patel's slow, unblinking nod that she wasn't fooling anyone.

It was nearly 5:00 P.M. and they'd been talking for more than four hours when they were interrupted by a knock.

"Come in," Patel said.

A police officer Jessica didn't recognize stuck his head around the door. He wrinkled his nose; the room smelled rank, thanks in no small part to the so-called "support" dog. "You got a minute?" he said to the detective.

Patel nodded.

"I'll take the dog out for a wee," Jessica said.

"There's a fenced courtyard through the side door," Patel told her as she left the room.

Jessica followed the low-ceilinged corridor toward a glass door, through which she could see Patel with a few other police huddled around a computer screen. Halfway along she saw a brown door and pushed it open. It led to a small, fenced courtyard, bare apart from a lone tree and a ceramic dish full of cigarette butts.

Norah and Alicia were already there.

"There you guys are!" Jessica let Couch off the lead, and the three dogs reunited with jubilant barks and leaps. Jessica and her sisters reunited with similar urgency, less enthusiasm. "How's it going with the detectives? Are you hanging in there?"

Alicia looked tired. She held her phone in one hand and shielded her eyes from the afternoon sun with the other. "I've had better afternoons."

"I'd forgotten how much I hate her." Norah was squatting to let two of the dogs lick her face. The third dog was humping her leg.

"I hadn't," Alicia said. "That part always remains fresh for me."

"Why don't we talk about it on the road," Jessica said. "It's getting late, and we have a long drive ahead. No doggy treats for these guys before we—"

"Actually," Norah said, "Hando said we'd pick it up again

tomorrow, when we were fresh. I guess that means we're staying the night. Maybe even two."

Jessica felt her eyebrows rise. "Did *Hando* say he'd run my business? I don't have a nine-to-five job—most of our jobs are scheduled on the weekends. And is he going to take care of my husband too?"

"It's just one night," Alicia said, yawning and stretching her arms above her head. "Sonja can manage and Phil will be cool. I'm knackered, Jess."

"And I don't think the dogs will tolerate another car trip today," Norah added.

The affection she'd felt for Couch just a short while ago vanished, and Jessica was struck by the panicky feeling that always overcame her when a situation got out of her control.

"But where will we stay?" she said weakly. "Who will have us with these dogs?"

"They're service dogs," Norah replied seriously. "Legally, they can stay anywhere."

Jessica began scrabbling in her bag for her pills. She hated those fucking dogs. Hated the police. Hated Wild Meadows.

"I'll have to check my messages," she said. "Make sure there's nothing urgent."

As she pulled out her phone, she prayed for an organizational emergency that would require her to return to Melbourne that night. She longed to be back in her own home, making dinner before getting into her own bed. She didn't do well out of her routine. She hadn't planned for an overnight stay and hadn't brought the things she needed. The tears that stung her eyes might have been as much to do with that as having to talk about her childhood.

She unlocked her phone and held it to her ear as the voice messages played.

"Jessica, it's Tina Valand here. I just spoke to Debbie."

This was not the sort of organizational emergency Jessica had in mind.

"This is a bit awkward, but Debbie told me there was an issue regarding some medication that went missing from her bathroom cabinet? I feel awful bringing this up, but it has me worried because, well, I noticed that some pills had gone missing from my place too. I'm a big fan of yours, you know that, and I've recommended you to plenty of people—I just hope it won't come back to bite me."

Fuck. This wasn't going away. She needed legal and PR advice. Heck, she might even need rehab advice! Mostly she needed advice on how to make all this exciting on a Saturday while in the middle of a police investigation in Port Agatha.

There were two more messages waiting for her, both from clients. She decided not to listen. Instead, she dropped her phone into her bag and said to her sisters, "I guess we'd better find us somewhere to stay for the night."

THE OFFICE OF DR. WARREN, PSYCHIATRIST

The next time I see Dr. Warren, he is wearing a blue tie, and he only makes me wait for one minute before he looks up from his notes.

"Right," he says. "You were talking about your mother and the parish accountant." He looks at his notes. "John."

"Yes," I say. "So . . . as I feared, my mother soon started spending time with John outside of church. At first, it was ostensibly 'business'—meeting up to look over accounts or to organize the sale of half our land, which was how John suggested we claw our way back to solvency. But before long the meetings became social; they saw each other for coffee, for lunch, and eventually for dinner.

"It took time to adjust to my mother leaving the house again after months of seclusion. When she wasn't with John, she was with the church ladies, sorting secondhand clothes for the jumble sale, or knitting tiny beanies for premature babies. Sometimes she even visited people in need, the way the women had done for her, offering them support and a pathway to God. I was never invited, which was fine by me. I did still have to go to church on Sundays, unfortunately, but other than that I stayed well clear of my mother's new, churchy lifestyle."

"Why?" Dr. Warren asks. "Were you jealous?"

Dr. Warren has a slightly deviant look in his eye. As if he likes the idea. So mother issues are his perversion? Who am I to judge?

"Yes," I say. "Jealous and desperate for attention. When I didn't get it, I had to look for attention elsewhere. So I made friends with the kids at school who scared me: the ones who drank alcohol and went to parties and pierced their own ears at lunchtime with a needle and an ice cube. I stopped handing in my homework so I could hang out with these kids in detention after school rather than going home to a house full of churchy women who tutted every time they saw me—or worse, going home to my mother and John, who was starting to spend more and more time there.

"'Are you and John dating or something?' I remember asking

my mother, when he'd visited for the third time in a week. I'd never witnessed them being openly affectionate but I wasn't naïve.

"'If I were,' my mother said, 'how would you feel about it?'

"'I wouldn't like it,' I told her.

"My mother was quiet for a long time. I assumed she was thinking about how she would break the news to John that it wasn't going to work out between them, so I didn't interrupt. Finally my mother reached for my hands and said: 'John and I are getting married.'

"'Pardon?' I said, even though I'd heard her quite clearly.

"'I know this will be difficult for you to understand, but John has been very good for me. For us. He's got our finances back on track, and he's helped me find the Lord. I know he's quite strict and formal, but he's a good man. He's brought me back from a state of depression that I wasn't sure I'd ever recover from.'

"'Does that mean you have to marry him? Was that part of the deal? You accept the church's money and in exchange John gets you?'

"'Listen—'

"'You can't do this. I am part of this family too, and I don't want to share a house with him. Don't I get a say in it?'

"'No!' my mother snapped. 'You don't get a say. You're a child. John is right—I've given you far too much leeway since your father died. Now you're a disrespectful brat who cares about no one but herself.'

"I was shocked into silence. My mother had never spoken to me like that. I felt my cheeks flush red at the indignity of it. I swore I'd do anything I could to stop their marriage. But, like all the tragedies in my life, I was powerless to do anything to stop it."

"Powerless?" I have Dr. Warren's attention. He is leaning forward. Riveted. "How did that make you feel?"

I can't stop my hands from clenching into fists. Dr. Warren notices. I sense that it pleases him.

21

NORAH

Jessica had found accommodation at Driftwood Cottages, a series of bluestone houses just outside Port Agatha, which had been converted into fairly ordinary B and Bs. Before leaving town, they'd stopped at the general store for toothbrushes, deodorant, and giant pairs of old-lady underwear (chosen from the limited selection of undergarments displayed next to tampons and toilet paper).

Not even Jessica had argued when Norah suggested they walk the dogs. She was probably too wiped from the day to realize she was almost certainly signing up for shoulder surgery from the constant jerking and tugging. As they walked, they fell into companionable silence, each checking their messages before they went out of range. Among Norah's messages was another text from Kevin.

> I've been thinking, I should probably go to the cops about you assaulting me. You know, in case you do it to someone else.

A burst of air expelled from Norah's lungs. She had stopped walking to compose a reply when she saw his next message.

Unless, of course, you wanted to send me a nude?

Wow. Kevin the weasel was wilier than she'd thought.

It wasn't lost on Norah that Kevin was suggesting exactly what Norah herself advocated: a transactional arrangement. If she sent him a nude, he wouldn't go to the cops. Pretty straightforward. But it felt different. Instead of feeling powerful, she felt weak. Instead of feeling like she was in control, she felt trapped. And Norah couldn't think of a worse feeling in the world than that.

As the dogs pulled her forward, an unpleasant sensation built in Norah's chest. She imagined Kevin sitting in his bed with his swollen nose thumbing threats at her. That was the difference, she realized. This wasn't a transaction. This was blackmail.

Motherfucker.

She turned her phone around and opened the camera. She'd send him a photo, if that's what he wanted. A nice close-up. She zoomed in to her hand as she flipped him the bird, making her digit nice and straight. That's what you can do with your threats, Kevin the Weasel. Yes, he might go to the cops, but no one trapped Norah Anderson.

With an angry jab of the thumb, she sent the photo. And just like that, the feeling in her chest subsided.

They'd been walking the dogs along the streets of Port Agatha for nearly an hour when they arrived at the gate of Wild Meadows. It wasn't by chance, nor had they discussed it. It was as if they had made a silent agreement. For some reason or another, they all needed to see it again.

The funny thing was, Norah had been expecting to see the house. But of course it wasn't there. Instead, at the end of the long driveway, was an empty space, a pile of soil and debris, some police tape and what looked to be a large hole.

"I've never been so happy to see something gone," Alicia said quietly.

Norah wasn't sure she agreed. She had never blamed the house for what happened to them. It would be like blaming your bank statement for its shitty balance. But she appeared to be in the minority, because Jessica was nodding.

They started down the driveway. Inside the area surrounded by police tape, men in high-vis vests used an excavator to comb the earth while police stood by, holding red buckets and wheelbarrows. Norah and her sisters weren't the only ones admiring the handiwork. There were several other curious onlookers: a couple in their seventies; a woman with a toddler who was admiring the excavator; and three youngish women, huddled together talking.

As they approached the police tape, the sisters were stopped by a bored-looking policeman.

"This is an active police scene so I'm afraid you can't go any further."

"We grew up here," Jessica said. It was an offhand comment, a statement of fact rather than a request for entry.

At this, the policeman looked less bored. "You lived in the house? You were foster kids?"

They nodded.

He lifted his radio to his mouth. "I've got three more foster kids here," he said.

Norah blinked. Three *more?*

He lowered the handset to speak to them. "Have you spoken to the detectives? Patel, Tucker, and Hando?"

"Yes," Jessica said. "We've just come from the police station. But did you say—"

"I still can't let you on-site, unfortunately. And we're requesting no photographs. But you can walk around the perimeter of the tape. Some of the others are doing that."

"Who are the others?" Norah wanted to know.

Replacing his radio in his belt, he gestured to the trio of women. Norah, Jessica, and Alicia looked at them, then back at him. Their confusion must have been obvious.

"The other foster kids," he said.

Jessica shook her head. "But there weren't any—"

"The babies," Norah said. "Those women must be the babies."

22

JESSICA

In the months that followed the horse-riding day, the girls sank into a sad, new reality. Norah had become different since she'd been locked under the stairs. Angrier. More explosive. At school, she got into fights every other day, over the smallest things. Once, she'd even elbowed Jessica in the ribs, seemingly on impulse, when Jessica approached her quietly and took her by surprise. Jessica knew Norah felt awful about it and she insisted she was fine, though Norah had a very sharp elbow.

The unfortunate consequence of Norah's increasingly violent behavior was that she spent more and more time under the stairs. And the more time she spent under the stairs, the more violent she became. It became routine, coming home from school to find Miss Fairchild waiting on the porch to drag Norah to her punishment. Once, after giving a boy a bloody nose at school, Norah had come home and opened the door under the stairs herself. But her dignity vanished the moment the door closed behind her and she flew into a rage, her body started kicking and screaming as if of its own volition.

Jessica and Alicia pleaded with Norah to stop attacking people, and Norah promised to try. Eventually, after five altercations in five days, she had to concede, "I don't know how."

It was Alicia's idea to hide a flashlight under the stairs. Norah still pretended to kick and punch for a while so Miss Fairchild didn't get suspicious. Once, Jessica even hid a book there, so Norah could read. These small wins kept Jessica going. Unfortunately, every time she came up with a way to make their lives a little more manageable, Miss Fairchild came up with a new way to hurt them.

"Jessica?"

Jessica froze halfway down the stairs. She'd thought she was the first one up, as usual, but not today it seemed.

Miss Fairchild was a woman of fixed habits. At this time of day, she was usually finishing her shower. After that she would dress and wipe down the mirror and benchtop before coming downstairs. Jessica knew her foster mother's morning routine as well as she knew her own. Better.

Jessica glanced to the top of the stairs for Norah or Alicia. Where possible, they tried not to approach Miss Fairchild alone. But though Jessica tried to summon them in a hushed whisper, neither girl materialized.

"Jessica, is that you?" Miss Fairchild sounded impatient now.

"Coming!"

Jessica found Miss Fairchild in the living room. She looked up from the armchair when Jessica entered and *smiled.* A proper smile.

"I had a surprise visitor during the night," Miss Fairchild said.

When Jessica saw what the woman was holding, she gasped.

"Come and see." Miss Fairchild beckoned her closer. "Isn't she beautiful?"

She was a newborn baby. As to whether she was beautiful, it was difficult to say with her all swaddled up like that. All you could see were her closed eyes, a little bit of her hairline, and her mouth, slack with sleep.

"Her name is Rhiannon," Miss Fairchild said, looking down at the baby again. "She was removed from her parents last night. Drug addicts, apparently."

She spoke in an exaggerated singsong voice even when she said *drug addicts*. It was like she'd been sedated or lobotomized or something.

"I told Scott to put my name down for infant respite care," she continued, her eyes fixed on the baby. "Short-term placements for babies who are removed from their parents at short notice. There are so many innocent babies who need homes, and I decided that we should do our part."

Jessica was surprised to hear this. She had assumed Miss Fairchild was prepared to take in only older kids. After all, babies were a lot of work, and Miss Fairchild was so attached to her routines, her clean house, her ability to control everyone and everything. It was hard to imagine how a baby would fit in with the environment she'd created at Wild Meadows.

In other ways, though, it made sense. Above all else, Miss Fairchild demanded utter devotion. She'd made it clear that Jessica had failed to provide it. She wasn't sure Norah and Alicia were ever expected to provide it—their purpose, as far as Jessica could tell, was to help pay the bills. Obviously she'd decided to find someone who would offer the unconditional adoration she craved. Who could be more devoted than a baby!?

Jessica heard muffled voices in the hallway, and a moment later Norah and Alicia peered around the corner.

"Come in, girls," Miss Fairchild said cheerfully.

"It's a baby," Norah said, entering the room then almost immediately taking a step back, as if afraid the baby would leap at her.

"A little girl," Miss Fairchild replied. She cooed softly at the bundle in her arms. "Her name is Rhiannon."

"Are we keeping her?" Alicia asked.

"It's just a respite placement for now, but who knows?"

Norah's lip curled, making it clear what she thought of the idea.

"Anyway, I might put Sleeping Beauty down for a nap, and then I might have a nap myself. Little Miss was quite unsettled last night, and I'm exhausted."

Miss Fairchild heaved herself to her feet, baby still in her arms. Before leaving the room, bizarrely, she kissed each of them on the forehead.

"I think she's gone mad," Norah said, when Miss Fairchild had disappeared upstairs.

"I think she's in love," Alicia said.

The three of them got on with the morning chores, but Alicia's comment reverberated in Jessica's mind for hours. *I think she's in love.* It was distressing how much it hurt.

Rhiannon was an astonishingly unsettled baby. In the three days she'd spent at Wild Meadows, the only time she wasn't crying was when she was asleep, which wasn't very often.

"That baby is broken," Norah said for what felt like the fiftieth time. "It has no off switch."

"*She,*" Jessica corrected. "She has no off switch. She is a human."

"She is a monster," Norah muttered.

Miss Fairchild tried everything she could to soothe her—patting her, singing to her, reading aloud. Nothing seemed to work. For a newborn, she had an impressive set of lungs.

"Norah is right," Miss Fairchild said tersely on the fourth day. "This baby is broken."

Miss Fairchild's buoyant mood had well and truly sunk by then. Jessica wasn't as worried about it as her sisters were. They'd enjoyed her brief period of good cheer, when she'd been far too worried about the baby to bother with persecuting them, but Jessica, to her shame, hadn't enjoyed it all. As far as she was concerned, the less Miss Fairchild liked the child, the better.

On the fifth night, Rhiannon's crying just didn't stop. When Jessica finally peeked into Miss Fairchild's bedroom, she noticed Miss Fairchild hadn't even bothered to pick her up from her crib.

"Want me to have a go?" Jessica said.

"Would you mind?" Miss Fairchild replied with an almost comical level of gratitude.

"Of course not." On the contrary, the idea of feeling needed and appreciated by Miss Fairchild was still like a drug to her. "You go to sleep. I'll take care of everything."

Jessica carried Rhiannon downstairs, where she rocked, soothed, and sang to her. Rhiannon didn't seem to care for Jessica's singing, because she screamed the whole night through. But as the sun rose, she finally drifted off to sleep in Jessica's arms, likely out of sheer exhaustion. And Jessica lowered herself into the armchair and slept too.

When Jessica opened her eyes again, Miss Fairchild was standing in front of her.

"Oh," Jessica said.

Miss Fairchild was showered and dressed in a fresh white top and jeans. Her hair was wet from the shower. She peered down at the baby, who was sleeping peacefully.

"I found the off switch." Jessica smiled. "Took a while, but we got there."

Miss Fairchild didn't return her smile. "Well, well," she said tightly. "Aren't you clever?"

Jessica was still groggy, that was the problem. She hadn't meant to offend Miss Fairchild. And yet, somehow she'd unwittingly suggested that she had a skill that Miss Fairchild lacked, or that she was better with the baby. But it was too late to correct her mistake; the damage was done.

"I think she just got worn out from all the crying," Jessica said desperately. She felt like she might cry herself.

Miss Fairchild glared at her. She was still a young woman, but faint lines had started to appear in her cheeks, slanting downward. They looked especially pronounced today. "Or maybe perfect Jessica just had the magic touch? Why not? Jessica is perfect at everything."

Jessica struggled for something to say, but nothing occurred to her.

"Since you're so perfect," Miss Fairchild said, "why don't you look after Rhiannon from now on?"

"But I have school," Jessica reminded her.

"Not anymore," Miss Fairchild said, and she stalked out of the room.

"How do you make a baby alien go to sleep?" Alicia said.

It had been a week since Rhiannon became Jessica's full-time responsibility. Feeding, burping, bathing, soothing, all of it. Miss Fairchild didn't even reach for her anymore. It was as if the baby had been sullied. As if she didn't exist. Luckily, Norah and Alicia were willing to share the burden.

"You rocket."

Jessica and Norah were too tired even to laugh. They hadn't been to school in a week, instead working in shifts, pacing the floor with Rhiannon as she howled. Norah was unexpectedly good with her. She'd borrowed a book about babies from the local library and they'd tried tilting her crib at a slight angle, to help with reflux. If they got it exactly right, occasionally she stopped crying long enough to sleep.

Every now and then, Miss Fairchild stuck her head in the room to glare at them, as if the baby's presence was their fault instead of hers. After a while, Jessica became too tired even to feel hurt by it.

They all developed a ringing in their ears from the crying. They started walking with a bounce in their step, whether they were holding the baby or not. The house went to hell. Chores didn't get done and the laundry piled up. Miss Fairchild let it go, perhaps aware that they had nothing left to give.

The following week, when Scott arrived to take Rhiannon home, no one was upset.

"Bye," they called from the door, while Miss Fairchild walked Scott and Rhiannon to the car.

They'd just fallen onto the couch, fantasizing about the full night of sleep that awaited them, when Miss Fairchild returned.

"This place is a pigsty," she said. "No one sleeps until it's spick-and-span."

Two weeks later, when they came downstairs for breakfast, there was another baby in Miss Fairchild's arms.

"Shh," Miss Fairchild said. "She's sleeping."

"Am I having a déjà vu?" Norah muttered. "Or is this a nightmare?"

This baby was older than Rhiannon, maybe a year old, with masses of dark brown hair. One of her eyes was covered with a white surgical patch.

"Her name is Bianca."

"What happened to her eye?" Jessica asked.

"Her stepfather happened." A muscle tightened in Miss Fairchild's jaw. For a moment they were all silent, watching the poor baby sleep.

"I need one of you girls to get the bus to the pharmacist for fresh gauze and bandages for her eye. Then head to the thrift shop and buy whatever you can find in her size. I have a voucher for formula and nappies over there on the dining table."

"I'll do it," Jessica said. She was still wary of Miss Fairchild after what happened with Rhiannon, but there was also something about being needed that she was helpless to resist.

"It's unimaginable, isn't it?" Miss Fairchild said, looking from Jessica to Norah to Alicia. "To think that someone would hurt a child." She shook her head, lowering her gaze back to the baby.

None of them replied.

At first, just like with the first baby, Miss Fairchild spent every waking moment with Bianca. Unlike Rhiannon, Bianca was a placid baby. She ate and slept and was content to sit and play. At night, if she woke, she could be settled with a pat on the back. The problem with Bianca was that she didn't like to be touched. If you tried to show her affection, she flinched or cried.

In response, Miss Fairchild showered her in kisses and hugs that were clearly unwanted. After a week of being rebuffed, Miss Fairchild started to get annoyed.

"What's wrong with her?" Miss Fairchild asked. "Why doesn't she like cuddles?"

There were just so many ways a person could fail her, Jessica realized. Rhiannon cried too much. Bianca didn't want cuddles. How could a foster child, who already carried his or her own trauma, ever have room in their little hearts to love Miss Fairchild the way she needed to be loved?

Five days into her stay, Miss Fairchild relinquished responsibility for Bianca like she'd done with Rhiannon. This time, Jessica, Norah, and Alicia hit their stride quickly, establishing a routine for Bianca and divvying up the duties.

Bianca was collected a few days later. They all stood on the porch and waved her off as she left. This time they didn't need to be told that there'd be no rest until they'd restored the house to order.

More babies came. They were always girls and they all arrived in the dead of the night. Some stayed for a day or two, some for a week or more, but the pattern was the same. Miss Fairchild started out caring for the child enthusiastically before becoming disenchanted. One had crossed eyes. One was overweight. One had fetal alcohol syndrome. Each time a baby came and went, Miss Fairchild became more irritated, and the girls became more tired.

"I have been trying to figure out why I haven't been sleeping at night," Alicia said as she paced the floor with a baby in arms. "And then it dawned on me."

"That's funny," Norah said, stony-faced.

If it was just the fatigue they had to deal with, they might have been able to cope. Unfortunately, to add to their fun, Miss Fairchild was becoming impossible to live with. During the day she was mean, always finding ways to criticize or obstruct them. At night, she drank. Often when they were up feeding a baby they could hear her rattling around downstairs, muttering as she threw an empty bottle into the rubbish bin.

When a baby stayed longer than a week, a social worker came to visit, usually Scott. The girls always knew when he was due, because Miss Fairchild would instruct them to clean the house from top to bottom and then stage some sort of ridiculous activity—a puzzle or a board game that they'd be playing "spontaneously" when Scott arrived. Jessica didn't know why she bothered; Scott didn't pay any attention to them anyway. He seemed far more interested in Miss Fairchild's well-being, making sure she was "coping." Which would have been fine and well, except he didn't seem to notice that she wasn't.

23

NORAH

After briefly introducing themselves to the "babies," all the women adjourned to the Port Agatha pub, which was deserted apart from the bartender and a guy at the bar watching the footy in his Richmond scarf. Despite its impressive external appearance, this was not one of those fancy, renovated pubs with fancy food to match. It was a sticky, smoky drunk-old-man pub, the kind with a dartboard, brawls and alcoholics, serving breaded meat of obscure origins.

"Why don't we introduce ourselves?" Jessica said. She sat at the head of the long table of women as if she were conducting a board meeting. "I'm Jessica, I lived at Wild Meadows from when I was four until I was fourteen. This is Norah, she lived there from ten to thirteen. And Alicia lived there from when she was twelve to thirteen."

"I thought we were introducing *ourselves*," Alicia said.

Jessica ignored her.

"I'm Rhiannon," said the woman with the dreadlocks and fingerless gloves. "I was at Wild Meadows for two weeks when I was an infant."

Norah blinked. "I remember you. You cried all the time. I've never heard anything like it."

"Norah!" Jessica admonished her.

Rhiannon just laughed. "That'd be right. In fact, the story goes that the whole reason I went into foster care at all was because I cried so much my mum went to the neighbors' place to have a beer and left me alone to cry it out. She came back an hour later and the police were there. A delivery person had showed up and heard me crying, and when no one came to the door he called the cops." She sipped her beer. "The police took me to Wild Meadows and Mum had to do a parenting course. She still maintains that *I* should have been forced to take a sleeping course."

"I'm with your mum," Norah muttered, reaching for the bowl of nuts on the table.

"So after two weeks you went home?" Alicia said.

Rhiannon nodded. "They were the only two weeks I ever spent in foster care. I grew up in the next town, so we often drove past Wild Meadows when I was a kid, and Mum would threaten me and my sisters, saying that's where we'd go if we didn't behave." She laughed fondly. "A detective rang me yesterday. It was a courtesy call to let me know what was happening before it hit the news, because obviously I can't remember anything about my time there. But I thought I'd come anyway, see what I could find out."

"I'm Zara," the next girl said. She was petite with pale skin, blue eyes and mousy brown hair wrapped around her head like a headband. "At least, that's the name my mum and dad gave me; they don't know what I was called in foster care. My parents were told nothing about my previous life other than that I'd been living at a foster home in Port Agatha. Then last night I saw the newspaper article and I came straightaway. I don't suppose you guys recognize *me?*" She looked at them hopefully. "I mean, you probably don't, but I'd love to know anything about my life before."

"There's something familiar about you," Alicia said.

Norah agreed. But she couldn't place her. And when the bartender approached, Norah stopped trying and decided to look at him instead. He had brown skin, a mop of back curls, and—Norah felt faint at this—a *mustache.*

"Are these your dogs?" he said to Norah as he put their drinks down on the wooden table. A gin and tonic for Alicia, a lemonade for Norah, a soda water for Jessica. The other three women were all drinking beer.

Automatically, Norah rose up to her full indignant, defensive self. She was preparing to trot out her service-dog spiel when he squatted down and began petting them all vigorously.

"They're gorgeous," he said. "My Australian shepherd is out back. Maybe I could take these guys out to have a play with him? It'd be good for him to have some company."

The bartender grinned at her, revealing a slight gap between his front teeth. Norah was so busy ogling him, she failed to register his question.

"So? Can I take them outside to play?" he repeated.

"Oh," Norah said. "Sure. Thanks. Okay. I love your mustache."

She felt . . . flustered. Norah couldn't remember the last time she'd felt flustered.

"What's wrong with you?" Alicia asked.

"Shut up," Norah replied.

"Shh," Jessica hissed, as the last girl began to speak.

"I'm Bianca," she said. "I got a list of all my foster-care placements recently—all sixteen of them—and Wild Meadows was one of them. I don't remember it, though. I also had a call from the cops yesterday."

Bianca. With the eye injury, courtesy of her stepfather.

Bianca didn't ask if they remembered her. Norah was glad. She gulped her lemonade.

"So," Zara said, when the introductions were complete, "any idea who the bones belong to?"

"I spoke to the cops this morning," Rhiannon said, "and they were still waiting for forensics to give them more info about the body. Apparently when the bones are old it can take a while."

"Do you think one of the foster kids did it?" Bianca asked.

"There wasn't anyone else," Norah said. "Just us—and the babies."

"Well, did you guys kill anyone?" Zara asked, looking from Jessica to Norah to Alicia.

Everyone laughed. Except Zara, who was looking at them expectantly, waiting for an answer.

"I'll get another round," Norah said.

She put her hand out for Jessica's credit card. It was getting late. Their dinner plates had been finished and collected.

Zara was like a TV-show detective looking desperately for answers in the plainly obvious. Rhiannon and Bianca were less intense, but still curious. Unfortunately, there was no information to share. Nothing to know.

The only thing Norah was curious about was the bartender.

"This round's on me," Alicia said, intercepting Jessica's card and placing her own card in Norah's hand. She leaned closer to Norah. "The bartender keeps looking at you."

"Shut *up*."

"He looks familiar," Alicia said. "I think we went to school with him? Avish or—"

"Ishir!" Norah cried, slapping the table so hard that Jessica's drink tipped over and spilled on her lap.

"Norah!" she cried. "For God's sake!"

But Norah was already beelining for the bar. "Ishir!"

Ishir, who'd been bent over looking for something in the fridge, stood up straight upon hearing his name. A tea towel was slung over his shoulder.

"I know you," Norah said triumphantly.

It took a minute, but recognition finally dawned in Ishir's eyes. "Oh yeah . . . I know you too." He grinned. "Nerida, right?"

"Norah," she corrected. "With an *h*."

But even as she said it, a memory was coming at her. "Wait . . . did you work at the grocery store?"

"That's me. My parents owned it. They still do. And this pub."

"You probably won't remember this," Norah started, and to her delight, he rested his elbows on the bar, listening eagerly.

Miss Fairchild had dispatched Norah to the shop to collect her face cream and a few other things. It was miraculous, really, how she always had enough money for such things when so much else—like fruit for their lunch boxes—wasn't in the budget.

It was no surprise she'd asked Norah to go; Norah was the fastest of the three girls. For a while Norah had made a game of seeing how fast she could be—timing herself as she ran all the way there and back. It had been fun, until Miss Fairchild got wind of it and started using her best times to shame Jessica and Alicia when they weren't as fast.

For this reason, Norah was taking her time and didn't bother ringing the bell to get the attention of the cashier. She was about to shoplift a Caramello Koala when he finally made an appearance.

"Sorry, I didn't see you there." He grinned, revealing a slight gap in his teeth. "Hey," he said. "You're Nerida, right?"

"Norah," she replied. "With an *h*."

Ishir gestured to the chocolate in her hand. "Caramello Koala—my personal favorite."

She put it back on the shelf and pushed Miss Fairchild's items forward. "I'm not allowed, unfortunately. The foster mother will lock me in the basement for buying chocolate." She laughed as if it were a joke. Telling the truth as if it were a joke was one of many ways she amused herself. "Anyhoo," she continued, "can you put this on the Wild Meadows account, please?"

Ishir wrote the total in the account book and put the face cream in a bag. As he handed over the bag, he took the chocolate off the shelf and dropped it in. "You know you want it."

Norah shook her head. "I said—"

"It's on me," he said in a magnanimous tone that was perhaps supposed to make him sound like a wealthy person. It came out a bit weird, and he seemed to realize this because he immediately dropped his gaze. "I won't put it on the account," he explained in a normal voice. "It's a gift."

"Why would you give me a gift?" Norah frowned. "What do you want?"

"Nothing." He looked offended.

"You must want something."

"No. Just to do a good deed." He looked like he was regretting it.

"Oh."

"It's no big deal. Really."

But it was a big deal. Norah thought about it for ages afterward, wondering if he'd come and ask her for something in return. He never did. It was the only time anyone other than her sisters had done something for her without wanting anything in return.

"I gave chocolate to all the pretty girls," Ishir said, when Norah told him the story.

"Oh."

"But you were the prettiest," he said, catching himself. "You were the most beautiful girl in our entire school. I would have given you the entire stash of Caramello Koalas if you'd wanted them."

Norah couldn't tell if he was serious. She decided to test him on it. "So, if I wanted a round of drinks for my friends?"

"Then I'd tell you to put that credit card away."

He grinned, and Norah got the same giddy feeling as when she arrived home to the dogs at the end of the day.

"So you're back here because of the bones?" he asked, turning to reach for a glass. The tea towel hung from his back pocket now. Norah hadn't known how sexy a tea towel could be.

"Yep."

"And these guys too?" He glanced over at the table.

She nodded. "What about you? Why are you still in Port Agatha?"

He grimaced. "*Back* here, not *still* here." He started pulling their beers. "It's an important distinction."

"If you say so."

"It is," he said. "My dad passed away six months ago so I came back to help out my mum. I'm recently divorced, so it was a good excuse to get away." He put two beers on the counter and started pulling two more. "The pub's on the market now, but we haven't had a lot of interest, if you can believe it." He nodded at the drunk at the bar. "I keep trying to convince Larry to make me an offer, but no luck so far."

"Kids?" Norah asked.

"Dog," he replied.

Norah made a low, involuntary noise.

She wasn't stupid. He was a divorced man in a small town. He'd likely worked his way through the eligible women and was just looking for some fresh meat. Norah wasn't offended. On the contrary, she was delighted.

He finished pulling the beers, then lifted the hatch on the bar. He picked up the tray of drinks, but didn't move for a moment. He seemed to be surveying her.

"I can't believe I gave you a Caramello Koala." He shook his head and sighed, as if really disappointed in himself. "A girl like you deserves a Toblerone at the very least."

Norah beamed. It was perhaps the nicest thing anyone had ever said to her.

24

JESSICA

BEFORE

Miss Fairchild's behavior became intolerable.

"You didn't give her *those* crackers, did you?" she shrieked one evening after Alicia had managed to get the most recent foster baby to eat some rice crackers. The baby had refused everything but formula for three days. The irony was, Miss Fairchild had *given* Alicia the crackers and pressured her to feed them to the baby. After all, it wouldn't look good if babies lost weight on her watch.

"You stupid girl! Babies can't eat *those*. Are you trying to kill her?"

There was no point in arguing with her, or defending themselves; it only made things worse. After a while they'd learned just to lower their gaze as if she were an aggressive stray dog.

"We've had a lot of these crying babies," she snarled another time, after they'd cheered upon getting a burp out of a particularly colicky newborn. "You three are the common link. Don't think I haven't noticed."

That day, it was noon and she was still in her pajamas, her greasy hair in a ponytail. As she watched them suspiciously, Jessica found herself wondering if she'd been drinking. It worried her. She'd always been unpredictable, but this was something else.

The first night-time rampage happened on a Monday.

It was after midnight. Jessica had just finished settling a nine-month-old girl called Suzy who'd arrived with insect bites all over her body. Suzy was (quite rightly) incensed by the itch. It had taken an insane amount of rocking, shushing, singing, and calamine lotion to get her to drop off in her crib. When at last she did, Jessica thought she would cry with relief.

Then Miss Fairchild burst into the room.

"Girls!" she cried, switching on the light.

Alicia and Norah sat up in bed sleepily, shielding their eyes.

"I've been rocking the baby for two hours and she's just gone down," Jessica whispered, holding her fingers to her lips. "Can you turn off the light, please?"

"Can I *turn off the light*?" It was clear from her slurring that Miss Fairchild had had a lot to drink. "Well, that's lovely, isn't it? I'm the one who feeds you, puts a roof over your head . . ."

Jessica was too concerned about waking the baby to even absorb Miss Fairchild's sloppy rage. She glanced down into the crib and saw that, of course, the baby was stirring.

"She's awake!" Jessica said, her heart sinking.

"Whose fault is that?" Miss Fairchild retorted, and she flounced from the room. She never explained what had brought her into the room in the first place, yet Jessica had a feeling she'd got exactly what she came for.

The next night, she burst in at 2:00 A.M.

"What's going on in here?" she demanded, fumbling for the light switch.

Jessica and Alicia sat up in alarm. Norah buried her face under a pillow.

Jessica didn't know what to say. What was *going on*? Up until that moment they'd been fast asleep. Luckily Miss Fairchild didn't require an answer. The purpose of her visit was to shout about how ungrateful they were until the baby woke. Then she disappeared, leaving them to deal with it.

"I'm so tired I think I might die," Alicia said the next day at breakfast. "Can you die from being tired?"

"You can," Norah said. "I read it in a book."

"We can't go on like this," Jessica agreed. Her eyes were closed, even as she ate.

Suzy was due to be collected by Scott at 9:00 A.M. The girls dared to hope that, without a baby to wake, Miss Fairchild wouldn't barge into their room that night.

But just after midnight, they heard her footsteps thundering up the stairs.

"Block the door!" Norah cried.

Jessica assumed she was joking, but Norah leaped out of bed and began heaving the freestanding wardrobe toward the door.

"Are you mad?" Jessica said. "We can't do that!"

But Norah looked so resolute, so determined, that first Alicia then Jessica climbed out of bed to help her. One in, all in.

They got the wardrobe in position mere seconds before Miss Fairchild turned the door handle.

Jessica held her breath.

The handle twisted back and forth uselessly. Finally, their foster mother pounded on the door.

"Girls! Open up right now!" The handle twisted again, and this time the door opened a crack.

The sisters looked at each other.

"Push against it," Norah instructed, and so the girls pressed their backs against the wardrobe until the door slammed shut again. *Dear God, what were they doing?* Miss Fairchild was easily provoked, even when they did nothing to aggravate her. They were going to pay dearly for this.

"Open the door this second or heaven help you!" she screeched as the three of them continued to press their weight against the wardrobe. Jessica started to worry that she might get an axe and break down the door.

The stand-off seemed to go on forever. Miss Fairchild banged and screamed and cursed until she was hoarse. She flung words at them Jessica had never heard her use before—terrible words that sounded frightening coming from her mouth.

When she didn't let up, Norah shouted in exasperation. "Go away, you psycho bitch!"

To everyone's surprise, the banging stopped. After all the commotion, the silence was even more worrying. Jessica could hear her heartbeat thudding in her ears.

Finally they heard her footsteps recede.

Half an hour later, when it seemed safe to assume that she wasn't coming back, they stepped away from the door and lay on Norah's bed, leaving the wardrobe blocking the door.

"This can't continue," Alicia said into the darkness.

"Maybe it won't," Jessica replied. "Maybe after tonight, she'll get rid of us."

"She won't," Alicia said with a mirthless laugh. "She needs us to look after the babies."

The moonlight streamed in through the dormer window, and Jessica noticed that Norah's expression was somber.

"What if she *does* get rid of us?" Norah said. "What if we're split up?"

There was a tremor in Norah's voice. Jessica stole a look at Alicia and saw that she'd registered it too.

"Then I'll track you down," Jessica said. "Both of you. I'll climb in your window and we'll pack a bag and steal away into the night."

"Jessica will pack the bags, of course," Alicia said.

Jessica forced a smile. "Naturally."

"You promise?" Norah looked at her with an unusual amount of emotion. "You promise you'll come for me?"

Jessica extended her pinkie. "Pinkie promise."

There'd never been a promise that Jessica was more determined to keep.

Jessica barely slept. Judging by the way Norah and Alicia tossed and turned, they didn't either. The uncertainty of what awaited them made it impossible.

They'd witnessed Miss Fairchild's wrath when they'd said or done the wrong thing unwittingly—but this time they'd *deliberately* gone against her. Worse, they'd joined forces to do it. She'd probably been awake all night dreaming up new ways to make them suffer.

When the sun rose, they dressed in silence, and waited until the last possible moment before they removed the wardrobe from in front of the door. Then they marched down the stairs in gloomy silence, like soldiers going to war.

Jessica expected to find Miss Fairchild sitting at the breakfast table, straight-backed and furious, but she wasn't, though the table was already laid.

Norah sat. "Shall we eat?"

"Where is she?" Alicia asked.

Jessica checked the laundry and the bathroom. Miss Fairchild wasn't in either. After that, the girls went from room to room. But there was no sign of her. It was as if Miss Fairchild had vanished into thin air.

25

JESSICA

It was nearly 9:00 P.M. Norah had spent the majority of the evening at the bar, insisting on getting every round (with the help of Jessica's credit card, of course). The bartender was not complaining. Jessica imagined it wasn't every day that someone who looked like Norah showed up at the Port Agatha pub.

Alicia was filling the "babies" in on their upbringing at Wild Meadows—being honest but not brutal in the retelling—and the girls were all leaning forward, elbows on the table, enraptured. Jessica was enraptured too . . . but not by Alicia. She was mesmerized by what was happening at the bar.

Norah was *flirting*.

Jessica wasn't sure she'd seen Norah flirt with anyone before, but it was undeniable. She moved her body differently—shoulders back, hips all slidey, head cocked. She *giggled*. Jessica practically felt the heat in her cheeks right along with her sister.

Had she ever flirted with Phil? She supposed she must have. But it had been a while. Perhaps she needed to start? She glanced at her phone. She'd had two text messages from Phil today. The first: Did you water the maidenhair fern? (Naturally she had.) The second: Thinking of you today. (He'd sent a variation of the second message to Norah and Alicia too; Jessica knew because Norah had asked how to send back a GIF of someone trying to kill themselves.) Sweet, really.

She'd responded to the first message: Yep. As for the second, she still hadn't responded. What could she say? She really wasn't good at that sort of thing. At the same time, shouldn't she try?

Lately, Jessica had been harboring a secret fear that Phil was going to leave her. He'd have no trouble finding someone else. A younger, sportier woman who enjoyed things like canoeing and stand-up paddleboarding. After a day out with the young sporty woman, Phil would post photos of them on social media and the sporty woman would comment "BEST day" with three heart emojis. The worst part was that if it happened, Jessica would have no one to blame but herself.

She quickly thumbed in a response to his last message.

Thanks, Phil.

Three heart emojis. She pressed send as Norah returned from the bar and put down drinks no one had asked for. Then, just as Jessica was about to ask her about the barman, the pub door opened and Detective Patel walked in.

The chatter at the table stopped immediately.

Patel's expression was grave. Her white shirt was rumpled and the sleeves were rolled up. Her severe ponytail was now not so severe. The change in appearance made Jessica anxious.

"She doesn't look happy," Bianca muttered.

Jessica's heart rate kicked up a gear.

"I thought I'd find you here," Patel said.

"Why?" Norah said.

"Because there's nowhere else open past five P.M. in this town." She gave them a tight-lipped smile. "And I saw the lights were on when I left the police station."

She pointed across the road.

"Do you want to join us?" Bianca asked, but Patel shook her head. She hesitated a moment, clasping the back of the wooden chair in front of her as if steeling herself for something.

"It's good that you're together. We received some information from the medical examiner tonight and I wanted to let you know before the media got wind of it."

"About the bones?" Jessica asked.

"Yes. There's more analysis to be done—the forensic anthropologist is yet to determine the cause of death and time of death—but we do know that the body belonged to a female child. A young child. Possibly an infant."

"*An infant?*" Zara said. "Like a foster child?"

"What does this mean for the investigation?" Bianca asked.

"Do you have any suspects?" Zara chimed in.

"I bet it was one of the foster mother's boyfriends," Rhiannon said. "It's always the boyfriend."

Jessica stole a glance at her sisters. Norah's brow had settled into a deep frown. Alicia's face was drained of color, and she was gripping the greasy table in front of them, as if it were a life raft.

"But if someone killed a foster kid," Zara said, "why weren't they reported missing? Foster kids have a paper trail, don't they? A social worker? Surely a child can't just disappear without anyone asking any questions."

Normally this was where Alicia would jump in. She'd told Norah and Jessica of the sobering reality many times: foster children went missing with frightening regularity. That said, the children Alicia described were typically teens. It would be hard for an infant to go missing without anyone asking questions. Practically impossible.

"We're looking into all of this now we know that the bones were those of a child," Patel said. "I'm sorry—I know this is upsetting."

Patel was looking at Alicia. When Jessica followed her gaze, her heart gave a tiny lurch. Alicia was *crying*.

Jessica went to Alicia's side and kneeled beside her. She placed what she hoped was a comforting hand on her sister's thigh.

"It's okay," Jessica said to her quietly. "You're okay."

Norah stood on Alicia's other side, a hand on her shoulder.

Jessica felt the eyes of the detective and the other women on them, even though they could have no idea how momentous the occasion was. They didn't know that Alicia hadn't cried a single tear since the day Grammy died.

Then, just when Jessica thought things couldn't get any more momentous, Miss Fairchild walked into the pub.

THE OFFICE OF DR. WARREN, PSYCHIATRIST

Today when I arrive to see Dr. Warren, he meets my eye and doesn't make me wait at all. He seems *excited*. And I am excited that he is finally listening.

"The moment John moved into Wild Meadows he became master of the house," I say to him. "It was so different from when my father was around. Even though my mother's financial troubles had been rectified by selling off land, he was obsessed with money, scrimping and saving and watching every penny. Our meals became smaller, we stopped buying new clothes. John hid a tin of cash that he hid in a sack of rice, and occasionally, he would get it out and count the contents. If he ever saw me watching, he said, 'Don't get any ideas, I know how much money is here to the cent.'

"The other difference was the change in my mother. When my father was alive, she'd lie around in bed in the morning while my father got up and did the chores. Now my mother was up at dawn, cleaning the house from top to bottom. John was fastidious, pointing out even the smallest skerrick of dust or dirt. When she was done cleaning, Mum cooked breakfast for John, then she did all the dishes and put them away before wiping down the table and counters and mopping the floor. I would have been appalled even if I hadn't been required to help. But John insisted that I pull my weight.

"'But *he's* not pulling *his* weight!' I cried when my mother gave me my new list of chores.

"'He works.'

"'So did Dad, and he didn't expect you to run yourself ragged all day cleaning a perfectly clean house!'

"I didn't see John standing in the doorway, so when he grabbed my ear, the surprise was nearly as shocking as the pain.

"'You will not disrespect me!' John screamed at me. He pulled me close enough that I could smell his breath. 'And you will not talk back to your mother.'

"My feet barely touched the floor as he dragged me out of the room and into the kitchen. I didn't know what to think when he reached for the bar of soap. I was silent and perplexed until the moment he shoved it into my mouth so far I retched.

"'This is what happens to people who talk back.' He clamped his hand over my mouth.

"I had heard of this happening to other kids, but it was not at all how I imagined it. I'd thought that at worst there would be an irritating soapy taste. Instead, it was an assault. Every time I sucked in a breath I inhaled bubbles instead of air. I couldn't cough. My body became drenched with panicked sweat. I thought my mother would tell him to stop, that she would be horrified. But other than an initial 'John . . .' she said nothing.

"When he finally pulled his hand away, I ran to the sink and began rinsing my mouth.

"'I trust we won't hear more backchat from you,' John said before storming from the room. When he was gone, I thought my mother would apologize for what her husband had done. But she didn't. And I realized that my mother was every bit as lost to me as my father was."

Dr. Warren shakes his head, aghast.

"John punished me often after that," I continue. "Usually when I failed to do my chores. He was militant about chores, and I was always falling short. Mind you, I don't think it was possible to meet his standards. Even on days I'd double- or triple-checked, he'd always find fault."

"And then he'd wash your mouth out?" Dr. Warren asks, slightly breathless.

"No. That was reserved for talking back. He had different punishments for cleaning infractions. One time, when he decided I'd failed to clean the kitchen adequately, he grabbed me by the ear and dragged me to the doorway under the stairs, opened it, pushed me inside and latched it shut. I contemplated screaming, but I decided it was better to remain quiet as I waited for what came next. Stupidly, I hadn't given up hope that my mother would save me. Needless to say, that didn't happen."

"What did happen?" I may be imagining it, but it looks like Dr. Warren's pupils are dilated.

"Nothing. I kept waiting for someone to open the door, but no one did. They left me there. When I was finally let out, I'd been in the basement for *twenty-four hours*."

"No," Dr. Warren exclaims.

I nod. "I was lying on the floor, weak with hunger and thirst, my face dirty from licking the floor to wet my lips. In the stream of light that flooded in from upstairs, I saw John descending the stairs, followed by my mother. John came to a stop by my feet.

"'Have you learned your lesson?' he asked.

"When I didn't respond, he kicked my foot. It wasn't especially hard, but this time my mother dropped to her knees by my side. 'Give her a minute,' she begged.

"'I have . . . learned,' I managed to croak.

"'Will you be respectful from now on?'

"'Yes.'

"'Whose house is this?'

"My gaze darted to my mother.

"'Don't look at her,' John bellowed. 'Look at *me*. Whose house is it?'

"'Yours.'

"'Whose rules must you follow?'

"'Yours.'

"At this, he nodded. It took me a moment to realize he was waiting for me to stand. I hauled myself to my feet, but was so weak I nearly fell down again. My mother reached for me then stopped short, glancing at John as if this might not be allowed. Apparently it wasn't.

"John led the way up the stairs. As he did, I looked at my mother.

Later I consoled myself with the fact that at least my mother was too ashamed to meet my eye."

"So you blamed your mother for that?" Dr. Warren asks. "Even though John was the one who threw you in the basement?"

He is watching me avidly.

"Yes."

He cocks his bald, shiny head. "Doesn't seem fair."

"No," I say, matching his smile. "But then no one ever said motherhood was fair, Dr. Warren."

26

JESSICA

Miss Fairchild was attired in her finest designer country-dweller clothes—jeans, checked shirt, riding boots, a soft cream jumper tied around her shoulders. Her hair was bobbed, and leaning more toward silver than blond, but otherwise she looked the same, which was impressive given that she must have been close to sixty. From the doorway she gave them a polite, uncomfortable wave. She looked hesitant, as if she wasn't sure whether to approach, as if she didn't know exactly what she was doing. Finally she nodded, as if to herself.

As she walked toward them, Jessica found herself pushing her hair back over her shoulders and standing up straight, even as her heart began to beat so loudly she felt like the whole pub could hear it.

"Hello," Miss Fairchild said. "I thought I might bump into you three this week."

Up close, her face had that slightly airbrushed look of middle-aged women who had conservative levels of Botox coupled with the odd cosmetic peel. Clearly, Miss Fairchild had the money to do that sort of thing since selling Wild Meadows.

"How are you, Jessica?" Miss Fairchild asked, when no one spoke. "You look great."

Jessica sensed the other women watching the pair of them with interest. Miss Fairchild, Jessica could tell, was aware of her audience. She reached out and touched Jessica's arm. "Jessica?"

Jessica's head swam; she felt like she might faint.

"How do you *think* she's doing?" Norah said. "A child's bones have been found under the house where we grew up, in case you hadn't heard."

Miss Fairchild's gaze moved to Norah. "I know. It's terrible what they've discovered. I'm going to assist the police investigations in any way I can."

Norah's hands were clenched and her face was flushed. Jessica felt uneasy watching her. You could practically see the blood pulsing under her skin.

"What are you doing here?" Alicia asked, stepping forward and slightly in front of Norah. Jessica moved to the other side of her.

"It's a small town," Miss Fairchild said, somewhat defensively. "I was driving past the pub and I saw it was still open. I don't need to tell you that there are not a lot of places to go around here, so I thought this is where I'd find you." Miss Fairchild smiled, as if this were a happy reunion, as if they were old family friends.

"And you wanted to find us . . . *why*?" Alicia said.

"Because I care about you girls. I've thought about you a lot over the years. I've worried about you. You had such a rough start to life. You probably won't believe this, but I really did try to help you."

"We know you tried," Norah said, stepping forward. "You tried isolating us, humiliating us, terrifying us . . ."

Alicia's and Jessica's shoulders were touching now, preventing Norah from coming closer to Miss Fairchild; her sister reminded

Jessica of an angry dog being restrained by a lead. Jessica wasn't sure how long they would have succeeded in holding her back had Patel not stepped in.

"I'm Detective Patel," she said, extending her hand to Miss Fairchild. "We spoke on the phone."

"Of course," Miss Fairchild said. "Nice to meet you, Detective."

"Why don't I walk you out?" Patel said to Miss Fairchild. "What time are you coming in tomorrow?"

They all watched as Patel guided Miss Fairchild toward the door. It was a smooth maneuver on Patel's behalf, but Jessica could tell Miss Fairchild wasn't happy to be ushered away. Even after twenty-five years, Jessica still knew how to read her.

As Jessica watched them go, many things ran through her mind. Foremost was Miss Fairchild's comment to her: *You look great.* She was ashamed to realize how much it had pleased her.

27

ALICIA

That was . . . intense," Norah said, as they walked back to the car.

It was indeed intense. So intense that Alicia still couldn't find words. Even seeing Miss Fairchild's face after all these years—trying to match it with the face she'd once known—was enough to make Alicia feel depleted and furious all at once.

Jessica, perhaps feeling the same, slid into the driver's seat in silence.

"I don't get it," Norah was saying. "Why is Miss Fairchild cooperating with police?"

"She's not cooperating," Alicia muttered. "She's trying to bury us."

Norah opened the back door of the car, and the dogs leaped inside.

"How are you doing, Alicia?" Jessica asked, when Alicia climbed into the passenger seat. She was clearly referring to the fact that Alicia had cried.

"I'm fine," she said automatically. Then she shook her head. "I'm not fine. The bones they found are from a child."

"I—" Jessica started.

But Alicia wasn't finished. "It changes everything, doesn't it?"

Jessica, who still hadn't started the engine, rested her head against the steering wheel. "I don't know about *that*."

It was true that they didn't know anything for sure. And yet, Alicia couldn't shake the feeling that in discovering the body was that of a child, they'd discovered a missing piece to an otherwise completed puzzle. Now they had to pull the puzzle apart and start over, putting it back together piece by piece. Only then would they figure out *exactly* where they'd gone wrong.

The accommodation at Driftwood Cottages was set around a central grassy car park, the units connected to each other by a pebbled walkway. The inside of their three-bedroom cottage was as you'd expect—blue-and-white 1980s bathrooms with plastic-wrapped soap and water glasses. Beds with worn, frilly linen, gauzy sheer curtains and framed prints that Alicia had seen on special at the general store.

As each cottage had its own entrance, Norah wasn't required to give her service-dog spiel to anyone at reception—a fact that seemed to disappoint her no end.

"Those dogs had better stay in your room," Jessica said when they were inside, collapsed on couches, staring at their phones. Jessica was sitting up straight, her posture stiff. Converse tried to climb onto her lap at one point, and Alicia decided that if Jessica allowed it she'd call an ambulance, but thankfully Jessica shoved him off.

"If I wake up with a dog beside me, Norah, I swear to God . . ."

"*Of course* they'll stay in my room," Norah said, with a notable lack of confidence. Then she chuckled a little.

Jessica looked like she was about to say more, perhaps even issue a threat, but Alicia was distracted by her ringing phone.

"Sorry, I have to take this," she said. She walked to the corner of the room and lifted it to her ear. "Hey, Aaron. Theo giving you grief?"

"Twenty-four hours a day." Alicia heard the affection in his voice. "One upside of aging out will be getting a little piece and quiet."

Alicia had received official confirmation this afternoon that Theo's parents had relinquished their parental rights, which meant he'd soon be moved to a permanent placement—leaving Trish and Aaron, whom he clearly felt safe with. It broke Alicia's heart.

"By the way, Trish said I can stay with her until the end of the school year, even after I turn eighteen."

"That's great," Alicia said.

"Yeah," Aaron said. "I'm pretty lucky."

Alicia felt something twist inside. "No you're not."

Aaron was quiet, likely confused by her comment.

"Trish is a wonderful foster mother, and it's very generous of her to keep you on, but you're not *lucky*. You lost your parents. You lost your grandmother. You've spent the last few years living in uncertainty. Having a stable home until you finish school is actually a lot less than you deserve. I want you to remember that, okay?"

Alicia felt her sisters looking at her, which meant she'd probably been a little too strident in her delivery. But so what if she had? Love and security were the most basic of rights. Forcing these kids to believe they were lucky to have that was even more damaging than what some of them experienced in care, Alicia thought.

"O-*kay*," Aaron said, sounding amused. "I'm not lucky. Poor me."

Alicia smiled. She knew he'd understood her point.

"So the reason I called," Aaron went on, "is that I was wondering what was going to happen to Theo after he leaves here."

Alicia sighed. "I don't know yet, mate."

"It's just that . . . I was wondering . . . if I applied to be a foster parent, once I turned eighteen, could—could I take him?"

A lump formed in Alicia's throat. She realized she was in danger of crying for the second time that night. "That's sweet of you. But what about uni?"

"I don't know. I guess I thought that if I did foster him I could get a job instead. Then I could rent an apartment for us. I know you get some money if you're a foster parent—maybe that could help with the rent?"

"Aaron, listen . . ."

"I know. I know. I just want to know if it's possible," he said.

He sounded resolute. Which meant Alicia owed him a straight answer. "All right. In theory, yes, it's possible. But it would take time to be approved as a foster parent. And by the time that happened, in all likelihood Theo would already have been placed somewhere else."

"Oh." Aaron sounded both disappointed and relieved.

"Listen," Alicia said, "I'm his caseworker, and I'm not going to let him go to just any family, all right? If he's moved to a new placement, I'll make sure he gets the best family possible, okay. I promise."

Aaron didn't respond. Through the phone she heard him swallow.

"You're a sweet kid, you know that?"

"Whatever," he said, his adolescent voice back again. "I was just wondering, that's all."

"Call me if you wonder anything else," Alicia said.

When she ended the call, she saw that Jessica and Norah were still looking at her. Jessica was leaning back against the pillows, almost reclining. Two dogs sat on top of Norah, making her look like a three-headed beast.

"That was nice, what you said," Norah told her. Alicia couldn't see her face, behind the dogs. "About what a child deserves."

"Well," Alicia said, "it's the truth."

"For what it's worth, I think a child would be lucky to have you as their foster mother."

It sounded like the dog had said it. Which was odd, but still nice. Perhaps this was why Alicia didn't respond with her usual spiel about how the best way for her to help kids was to be a social worker. Instead, she merely said, "Thanks, Norah. That means a lot."

In her bedroom, Alicia folded one of the thin pillows in half and lay down on the bed. She'd been waiting all day to listen to Meera's message. It felt like an indulgent treat, after the day they'd had.

"Hey," the message said. "Not urgent but I received a petition to terminate parental rights today for Theo Moretti. Give me a call Monday and I can talk you through the timeline and next steps."

It was an entirely businesslike message, but Alicia closed her eyes as she listened. There was something about Meera's voice—calm, clear, and intelligent—that soothed Alicia. For this reason, she listened to the message twice more before she returned the call.

Meera answered after just one ring. "There you are."

"Here I am."

If listening to Meera's voicemail had been soothing, having her on the phone in real time was a trip to a day spa. Alicia imagined her in front of the television, her laptop on her knees, propping the phone between her shoulder and ear. It was possible she had a pencil in her hair.

In the next room, the dogs started barking.

"Is Norah there?" Meera asked. She'd met both Jessica and Norah one day at a small gathering for Alicia's birthday—and Alicia had talked about them both enough for her to know about Norah's dogs and Jessica's neuroses. Still, Alicia found it touching that she remembered these details.

"No. Well, yes. We're away. Jessica too."

"Oh, tell them I said hi," Meera said. "Where are you guys?"

"Port Agatha."

A pause. Meera knew very little about Alicia's upbringing, but she *did* know that Alicia had grown up in foster care—and where. As for the rest, she'd had enough experience with child protection to be able to fill in the gaps. "Hey, look, we can talk about this on Monday. I just thought that maybe you were as sad as me, working on a Saturday night . . ."

"I am definitely as sad as you," Alicia said. She pushed herself up into a sitting position and grabbed another pillow. "In fact, I was going to call you too."

"About Theo?"

"No, about another kid. His name is Aaron and he's aging out soon." Alicia felt weirdly emotional. "He's a good kid. And it got me thinking . . . Hypothetically speaking, if I wanted to foster him . . . could I?"

Several beats passed. Alicia could practically *see* Meera's eyebrows rise.

"Hypothetically," she repeated. "I *said* hypothetically."

"Okay," Meera said, clearly not believing her. "Well, in that case, no. You can't foster a kid once they turn eighteen."

Alicia sighed. It was what she'd expected. In a way she was relieved to hear it. Relieved and also . . . bitterly disappointed.

"But you could adopt him."

Alicia blinked. "I could? Even if he's eighteen?"

"There's no age restriction on adoption," Meera said. "It's unusual to adopt an adult, but it happens—for sentimental or financial reasons, or occasionally if there is an adult with additional needs. Sometimes it's for inheritance purposes. The adoptee would have to agree to it, obviously."

"Obviously," Alicia said, wondering if Aaron would. Then she couldn't believe she was wondering. It was *hypothetical*.

"Does an eighteen-year-old even need a mum?" Alicia mused aloud. But it was a silly question. She knew they did. Even at thirty-eight, Alicia would have killed for a mum.

Meera must have thought it was silly, too, because she didn't respond. Instead, she said, "Tell me more about Aaron."

Alicia shrugged. "Honestly I don't know much, other than that he was raised by his gran. We've only met a few times."

"It's not always the length of time that's important," Meera said. "Sometimes you just know."

As the silence settled between them, Alicia wondered if they were still talking about Aaron. She found herself wishing they weren't. But that was stupid. A waste of a wish.

"Right," Meera said. "Shall I go do a little research into adult adoption?"

"No," Alicia said quickly. "It was hypothetical."

But Alicia knew Meera was probably looking into it as they spoke. It was just the kind of thing Meera did.

"Meera," she heard herself say.

"Yeah?"

She wanted to say, *I love you. I want to be with you. I want to feel worthy of love, and unafraid to love someone in return. I want that with you.* But instead she said, "I'll speak to you Monday." Then she ended the call and banged her head repeatedly against the head-board.

28

NORAH

Couch, Converse, and Thong were already asleep on her bed, but Norah was wide awake. As if today hadn't been stressful enough, she'd just checked her voicemail—bastard that it was—and found a message from a police officer in Melbourne.

"Miss Anderson, it's Constable Perkins from Victoria Police. We'd like to talk to you at your earliest convenience about a complaint we've had regarding an assault that occurred in Melbourne yesterday. When you get this message can you please give me a call on . . ."

"Kevin, you son of a bitch," she said out loud.

The unpleasant sensation she'd felt after receiving his earlier message returned with a vengeance. He'd done it. He'd fucking done it. He'd actually gone to the *cops*. She hadn't thought the weasel had it in him.

Her face became hot, her heart started pounding loudly enough to make her aware of each individual beat. She wanted to hit something . . . preferably Kevin's face . . . but she had to make do with punching the mattress insetad as she tried to corral her thoughts.

The ramifications came to Norah in layers. Not only would she likely be charged with assault, there was also her community corrections order to think about, and the fact that this offense might well send her to jail. As if that wasn't bad enough, the cops wanted to talk to her and her sisters about a *dead child*, found buried under the home they'd grown up in! With her criminal record, an active assault charge, and a community corrections order . . . this could look very bad for her indeed.

She took a deep breath. Jessica was forever taking deep breaths. It never seemed to help her, but given the lack of other options Norah decided to try it herself. It proved surprisingly effective. As she sucked in air, everything suddenly became clear. She'd just have to deal with it. She'd have liked to deal with it by giving Kevin a swift kick in the balls, of course, but fighting wasn't going to help her this time. She needed to be more resourceful. The priority was making this go away, and fast. And as Norah had learned when she was young, sometimes that meant gritting your teeth and doing what you had to do.

She glanced around the room. There was a full-length mirror in one corner of her room that would do nicely, she decided. The lighting in the room wasn't great, but she had to work with what was on hand. She stripped off her clothes, and arranged herself on the floor with her knees angled just so. It was quite arty, really. She probably could have submitted it to a magazine. It was certainly good enough to get an assault complaint dropped.

She attached the photo to a text and wrote:

> I made my clothes go away. Now make the charges do the
> same.

She pressed send, then threw the phone across the room, knocking a lamp off the bedside table and sending it crashing to the floor. *Fuck you, Kevin,* she thought.

"Everything okay?" Alicia called from the next room.

"Fine," she called back.

She didn't see the point of involving her sisters in this. They had enough to worry about.

29

JESSICA

Even before she got into bed, Jessica knew she wouldn't fall asleep that night. The bones belonged to a child. Maybe even a baby. A *baby*.

This changes everything, Alicia had said. Jessica had always found it difficult to think about her upbringing at Wild Meadows, and there was no question that this new piece of information—that a baby had been buried under the house—made it infinitely more difficult. But Alicia was wrong when she said it changed everything. It wasn't possible. There had to be another explanation for what happened to this child or baby. One that had nothing to do with them.

Jessica pottered about the bedroom, trying her best to re-create her home routine—showering, brushing her teeth, taking her Lexapro and melatonin, washing her face—hoping to convince her body that it was time to sleep. But of course, her body was too clever. If anything, it was insulted by her pathetic attempts and more determined to stay awake. Norah, judging by the snoring sound that traveled through the wall, wasn't having the same trouble. As for Alicia, who knew?

Jessica was concerned about her. It had been so shocking seeing her crying. For as long as Jessica had known her—or at least since her grandmother had died—Alicia had kept her emotions so tightly contained that even she couldn't access them, let alone express them outwardly. It had always troubled Jessica. Norah's troubles were right out there for everyone to see. Alicia's troubles were better hidden but just as serious. Jessica needed to keep an eye on her. If she started to spiral, Jessica wanted to be on hand.

On the bedside table, her phone lit up with a voicemail message and Jessica lunged for it, desperate for something to distract her from her worries.

But sadly, the message just brought more worries.

"Jessica, it's Cate McDonald. Can you call me ASAP? I've just had a conversation with Debbie Montgomery-Squires and—"

Jessica ended the message and swore out loud. Could she sue Debbie for defamation? Although Jessica was pretty sure you had to prove the person was spreading lies about you and she wasn't sure she'd be able to do that. She scrolled through her phone in search of her lawyer's details and fired off an email, cc-ing Sonja. As soon as she heard back, she'd decide how to handle this.

Until then, she was alone with her shame.

Jessica was no stranger to pain, but shame was its own specific brand of agony. Something about its assertion that all of your worst fears about yourself were true, its unrelenting focus on your negative qualities. Thankfully, Jessica had ways of dealing with shame. She tipped two of them out of a bottle and into her hand,

and then, after a moment's consideration, she tipped out another two. Everything would be better after a good night's sleep, she reminded herself. She swallowed the pills and waited for peace to descend.

30

NORAH

Norah stood outside the cottage watching the dogs bound across the grass, pissing on cars, and digging up garden beds. She hadn't heard back from Kevin since sending the photo—he hadn't even double-tapped on it. She assumed this was a good thing; perhaps he was going to wait until he'd spoken to the cops and got the complaint dropped before replying? Still, she would have preferred it if he'd confirmed receipt.

"Is Jessica still not ready?" Alicia called. She was standing by the car, having already been to reception to check them out.

"Nope," Norah replied.

Alicia looked perplexed. "Is she ill?"

"That's what *I* said!"

Jessica had slept through her alarm, which never happened. Usually, she and Alicia gave her hell for even *setting* an alarm, since her body clock was more reliable than anything Steve Jobs could create, but this morning, after listening to her alarm beeping for several minutes from the next room, Norah sent the dogs in to rouse her.

Jessica had complained bitterly about Thong's morning breath, but then a few seconds later she'd gone back to sleep.

"Are you ill?" Norah had demanded when she went in herself a few minutes later.

Jessica didn't have a fever, or a cough, or sore throat. She was just tired, she said. A reasonable excuse, and one Norah might have accepted from anyone else, but Jessica didn't get tired. She was wound up too tight to get tired.

"Sorry!" Jessica said breathlessly, stumbling out of the cottage. She unlocked the car. "What did I miss?"

"Us talking about you sleeping in," Norah said. "I feel like I'm in an alternative universe."

Norah rounded up the dogs and then they all got into the car. As Jessica slipped into the driver's seat, she threw her phone into the center console. "You're always telling me to chill out," she said, starting the car. "Now I do and you both freak out."

"We assumed you *couldn't* chill," Norah explained. "Like a penguin can't fly. I imagine you'd freak out too if penguins suddenly started flying."

Jessica frowned, contemplating that as she turned out of the parking lot onto the highway. Norah was disappointed when Jessica's phone started to ring. She'd been hoping for a compliment on her clever penguin analogy.

"Leave it!" Jessica cried, when Alicia reached for Jessica's phone. Her voice was so loud and abrupt that even the dogs startled. Alicia raised her hands as if in surrender. "I can't deal with work right now, okay?" Jessica added. "I need coffee first."

A few beats passed as they listened to the insistent ringtone. Norah and Alicia's eyes met in the mirror.

"Are you okay, Jess?" Alicia asked when the phone was silent.

"Of course I am. Why?"

"You're acting weird," Norah said.

"In case you hadn't noticed," she said, as her phone started to ring again, "the circumstances are pretty weird."

She pressed a button to decline the call. Immediately it rang again. The moment it stopped, Jessica turned off the phone and put it into the glove box.

Norah and Alicia's eyes met in the mirror again.

"Shut *up!*" Jessica said, even though neither of them had spoken.

As they pulled up in front of the police station, Norah received a message from Kevin.

Nice, but not exactly what I had in mind.

Norah stared at the message. What the actual fuck? She inhaled deeply and wrote: What did you have in mind?

Three dots appeared immediately.

Norah clenched her teeth as she imagined his delighted weaselly smile, his revolting weaselly hard-on.

I was thinking video.

Perhaps it was the thought of the weaselly hard-on, but Norah gagged. Seriously? This guy, who didn't even deserve her boob pic, wanted a *video*? Every instinct urged Norah to tell him to take his weaselly hard-on and go fuck himself. But she couldn't. She couldn't even tell her sisters what was happening. She felt like she was being squeezed. Like she was back in that space under the stairs where Miss Fairchild used to lock her.

What kind of video?

He was clearly prepared for this, because his long response appeared only seconds later. Norah considered herself to be sexually liberated. She understood fetishes and role-play and BDSM. Even so, reading the message, she gasped.

"What is it?" Alicia asked from the front seat.

"Nothing. Just . . . a funny TikTok."

Norah read the message again. Judging by what he was suggesting, he watched a lot of very intense porn. For the first time in a long time, she felt tears—angry tears—stinging her eyes.

She took a deep breath.

Have you spoken to the police about the assault? Told them I didn't do it?

His reply was swift.

Not yet.

Mother fucker. How do I know you'll do it after this?

Another swift reply.

You have my word.

His *word*? Norah wanted to reply and tell him exactly what she thought of his word. But what choice did she have other than to trust him?

They pulled into the parking lot of the police station. As they got out of the car, Norah noticed that Patel and Hando were crossing the street, holding takeaway coffees. Hando had spilled his and was wiping uselessly at a coffee stain on his white shirt.

"Stupid lids," Hando said to them as they emerged from the car. "Don't get coffee from that place. This is the second time it's happened!"

Patel had also spilled her coffee, Norah noticed, but she didn't mention it. She avoided looking at them as they made their way toward the doors of the station. Norah wondered what was eating her. She'd seemed fine last night when she'd escorted Miss Fairchild out of the pub. Perhaps, like Jessica, she was just tired.

Tucker, who must have been waiting in reception, opened the door as they approached and filed in with the dogs at their heels. For a moment, they stood in the foyer while Hando and Patel attempted to clean themselves up.

"How is everyone this morning?" Hando asked, grabbing some tissues from the front desk.

"Tired," Jessica said.

Hando dabbed at his shirt with the tissues, nodding. "It's always hard to sleep after hearing confronting news."

"I didn't sleep well either," Patel said, accepting the box of tissues Hando held out to her. "I lay awake for ages. I just kept asking myself why you guys wouldn't be honest with us."

It was as if someone had entered the room carrying a machine gun. They all went silent. Movements became cautious and slow and wide-eyed.

"What do you mean?" Jessica said.

"I mean," Patel said, "the fact that not one of you have mentioned her."

In the silence, the dogs began circling uneasily, clearly noticing the change in energy. Norah shot a look at her sisters, who looked equally uncomfortable. "Mentioned who?"

Patel glanced from one of them to the other like a disappointed school principal. Finally she lifted her hands, then dropped them with a soft, disappointed exhale. "The fourth sister? The other girl living at Wild Meadows with you? The one we just learned about in this police report?" Patel gestured to her laptop.

Silence. Alicia, Norah, and Jessica exchanged a look.

The police were looking at them as if they were criminals. As if they'd been deceptive, or withheld something relevant, which they most certainly had *not*.

"But why *would* we mention her?" Norah asked.

Patel blinked dramatically. "Seriously?"

Norah blinked back, indignant. "If you'd done your job properly, you would have found this report days ago."

"And if you'd read the report," Alicia added, "you'd know exactly why we didn't mention her."

Patel exhaled. They had her there.

Finally Jessica stepped forward, her inner boss-lady turned up to high gear. "And if you have any other questions, you'll have to speak to our lawyer."

31

NORAH

It had seemed like such a promising day. They'd trooped downstairs to find that Miss Fairchild had vanished into thin air. It was like a miracle. Norah felt like Kevin from *Home Alone*. As they dressed for school, Norah was already fantasizing about how life might be if it was just the three of them. She would take the master bedroom, she told her sisters. She was even prepared to go out and get a job.

Jessica, of course, was the one who warned her not to get too far ahead of herself. It was good advice, as it turned out, because by the time they got home from school that afternoon, not only was Miss Fairchild back, but there was someone with her.

"Girls," Miss Fairchild called from the living room. "Can you come in here, please?"

In many ways, it was your classic déjà vu. In other ways, not so much. Because there were a few distinct differences from the other times. For one, instead of sitting in the armchair, Miss Fairchild sat cross-legged on the floor. For another, where the other babies had been a year at most, this child was a fully-fledged toddler with masses of blond hair and a mouth full of tiny white teeth.

"There's someone I want you to meet." Miss Fairchild beamed at them, showing no evidence of their unpleasant interaction the evening before. "This is *Amy*."

They all stared at the child. Amy blinked back at them, looking as shocked and confused as they were. She held a worn-looking Barbie doll in one hand and with the other clutched a stuffed bear to her chest.

"Amy is nearly two," Miss Fairchild said, her smile growing. "And here's the best bit. Amy isn't a respite baby. I'm adopting her!"

She said it with such delight it was hard to believe she was the same woman who'd been terrorizing them for months. Who just last night had screamed obscenities at them while trying to force her way into their bedroom.

Alicia appeared as disturbed as Norah felt. "But . . . where are her parents?"

"Her *birth* parents didn't want her." Miss Fairchild's made an expression of disgust. It was more familiar than the grotesque smile, at least. "Some people only want perfect children."

Norah looked at Amy again, clasping her teddy. She didn't have crossed eyes, or insect bites, or obvious special needs. As far as babies went, she looked pretty perfect.

"Amy was born with a slight defect," Miss Fairchild said, answering their unspoken question. "It's ridiculous really; it's not anything anyone would notice."

She removed one of Amy's socks, and the girls leaned forward. The girl's little foot was pink and plump: perfect apart from the tiny extra pinkie toe nestled against the others.

"Her parents didn't want her because she has an extra *toe*?" Norah said.

"Some people are so busy chasing perfection they don't appreciate the wonders right in front of them," Miss Fairchild replied. "Can you imagine? Having a child this beautiful and not appreciating her?" She shook her head and tutted. "Some people don't deserve children, they really don't."

Miss Fairchild didn't let Amy out of her sight. During the day, she carried her around in a wrap on her chest, and if she had any errands to run, she sent the girls out so she didn't have to leave Amy for a single second. At night, Amy slept in her room, and Miss Fairchild got up to settle her if she woke.

"I am the only one who's allowed to care for her," she said, if she ever caught them interacting with Amy. "It's important for bonding. So she knows I'm her mother."

There was rarely a moment when Miss Fairchild wasn't singing or bouncing Amy. Norah assumed that eventually she would tire of round-the-clock caring the way she had with the other babies, but weeks went by and Miss Fairchild remained devoted. It was wonderful as far as Norah and Alicia were concerned, because it meant she left them alone. It was as close to Norah's fantasy of being Kevin from *Home Alone* as she could have realistically hoped for. But Jessica didn't seem to share Norah and Alicia's enthusiasm for the new Miss Fairchild.

"I'm happy she's taking such good care of Amy," she would say when her sisters asked if she was all right. "It makes life easier for us!"

But her smile didn't reach her eyes. It reminded Norah that, unlike she and Alicia, who felt nothing but hatred for Miss Fairchild, Jessica's feelings for their foster mother were complicated.

A few times, Norah caught Jessica staring as Miss Fairchild played with Amy. The look on Jessica's face worried her. There was something possessive about it. If Jessica noticed Norah watching her, she rolled her eyes and made a joke of it, which worried Norah more. Jessica had never been much of a joker.

"Happy birthday, Amy!" Miss Fairchild cried, cracking a party popper and cheering like a deranged lunatic.

Norah stood by the pool, wearing a party hat, eating a cold sausage roll and feeling significantly better about the fact that she'd never had a party of her own. Alicia, by the look of her, was equally appalled.

The party, it had to be said, was a fizzer. Amy appeared to agree. They'd played party games that Amy was too young for, opened gifts that she didn't seem interested in. The only part that had been somewhat enjoyable was the piñata—enjoyable for Norah, because she'd been allowed to smash it with the broom until it broke into a million pieces.

Now they stood around wondering what to do next.

A few days earlier, when they'd come downstairs for breakfast, Miss Fairchild had been bent over the sewing machine surrounded by pink fabric.

"What's going on?" Jessica asked, taking it all in.

"It's Amy's birthday on Friday," Miss Fairchild said cheerily. "She'll be two. We're having a party."

Norah, who was loath to show enthusiasm for anything Miss Fairchild did, couldn't deny she'd felt a pulse of excitement. A *party*. Apart from the silent dance party that Alicia had thrown her, it would be the first party she'd ever attended. Or at least the first one she *remembered* attending.

"Will there be cake?" she asked.

"Of course!" Miss Fairchild beamed. "Only the best for my darling girl."

Despite Miss Fairchild's efforts, though, Amy looked miserable. She often did, now that Norah thought about it. She wondered suddenly if the point of this party had been to lift the child's spirits.

"Why isn't she having fun?" Miss Fairchild said eventually, with a hint of irritation.

Several possible reasons sprang to mind for Norah—the most obvious being the proximity of Miss Fairchild, and her maniacal party popping. Beyond that, there was the fact that, bizarrely, a Barbie had been shoved into her birthday cake, and that she'd been forced to wear a pink dress matching the one Miss Fairchild was wearing.

"Maybe's she's bored?" Norah suggested.

"Bored?" Miss Fairchild seemed perplexed by the idea. "Well . . . what shall we do?"

Norah shrugged. "Pony rides?"

She didn't expect Miss Fairchild to agree, so she was shocked when their foster mother glanced down the hill toward the stable, then nodded at Norah.

Wow. She *must* be desperate, Norah thought.

It took Norah only a couple of minutes to steal down to the stables. Trying to get Bertha back up the hill took longer.

"Ta-da!" Norah announced breathlessly when she finally got the stubborn horse to the top.

Amy pointed a chubby finger at Bertha. "Horsey!"

Her expression was cautious, well short of a smile, but Miss Fairchild's face lit up. She even shot Norah a grateful look.

For the next half hour, Amy sat on Bertha's back while Miss Fairchild led the pony in circles around the pool, and Norah, Alicia, and Jessica demolished the sausage rolls. Amy was still perched on Bertha when Norah noticed the figure loping up the hill. He wore a baseball cap and had a funny way of walking, more of a shuffle really, his feet barely leaving the ground.

Dirk came to a stop several meters away, and assessed the scene: Amy on Bertha, the party decorations.

"Shit," Norah said.

Alicia and Jessica looked at her, and she gestured at Dirk. They both blanched.

Norah gave the stable hand a beseeching look.

He rolled his eyes. "Bring her back when you're done," he said, and turned and walked back down the hill. Miss Fairchild was so busy with Amy that she missed the whole thing.

"Look. She's asleep."

It was one of the rare moments they'd been left alone with Amy. A few minutes earlier, Amy had been still picking at her dinner when Miss Fairchild had taken advantage of the distraction to run upstairs and run the bath. They'd just finished dinner, and were doing the dishes when Jessica noticed that Amy had fallen asleep in her high chair.

"Aw," Alicia said. "She *is* pretty adorable."

"I think she's snoring," Norah said.

They watched her a moment, her body lolling forward, her little cheek squashed against the tray. They knew not to pick her up—Miss Fairchild could be so weird about that—but Jessica and Alicia edged forward to take a closer look.

They were inches away when Amy sat up, grinned, and said, "Boo!"

Jessica and Alicia screamed.

"You little trickster!" Jessica cried.

Amy squealed in delight, then immediately closed her eyes and lay down again. Even Norah could agree, albeit begrudgingly, that was pretty cute.

"All right," Jessica said, with a wink at the others, "she's asleep. Better pick her up and take her to bed."

"Boo!" Amy cried, sitting up again. She lifted her arms up, then opened them wide like a starburst.

This time, when they all squealed, Amy giggled. *Giggled.* It was so unexpected after months of sadness that they stood still for a moment, appreciating it.

Amy rested her head on the tray again, still giggling.

"You pick her up, Norah," Jessica said.

"Why? She's not asleep. She's laughing." But Norah squatted down beside the high chair, so her face was right up next to Amy's. When Amy opened her eyes, Norah beat her to it. "Boo!"

Amy's laugh reverberated through the house. It sounded like wind chimes. Like joy.

"Right then," Miss Fairchild said, entering the room like a rain cloud. "Bath time." With no regard for the fun they'd been having, she scooped Amy up and carried her away, despite the child's protests. No wonder the kid was always so sad.

When she was gone, the three sisters remained in the kitchen for ages, trying to hold on to the moment. But without Amy, it almost felt as though it had never happened. As though it had been just a figment of their imagination.

32

JESSICA

BEFORE

"Huwo."

Jessica was in the lounge room reading her book when she heard the greeting.

It was Saturday afternoon. Miss Fairchild had put Amy down for a nap and then ducked down the street to do some errands. Norah and Alicia were doing homework in the kitchen.

"Well . . . hello." Jessica lowered her book. Amy stood in the doorway, wearing a nappy and a guilty expression. The teddy she carried everywhere dangled from her hand by a paw. "Aren't you supposed to be napping?"

Amy rubbed her eyes sleepily as she toddled over to Jessica. When she extended her arms, it felt so instinctual to pull the girl into her lap.

"Aw," Jessica said, even as she glanced toward the window to check for Miss Fairchild. But the coast was clear. All she saw was a blue-sky, sunshiny day. "That's a nice cuddle. Thank you very much."

Amy rested her cheek against Jessica's chest and stuck her thumb in her mouth. Even though Jessica was the one holding Amy, she had an overwhelming feeling of being warm and held. Safe.

As Amy snuggled closer, Jessica found herself afraid to breathe, in case the moment dissipated. It was as though the child was a part of her. It was as though she *was* her.

The arrival of Amy prized open wounds for Jessica, picking open scabs of rejection she'd thought had long healed. The cocktails of emotions Jessica experienced when she saw Amy and Miss Fairchild together was overwhelming. Hot, spiky jealousy, followed by all-consuming guilt. Burning shame. Black resentment. Ice-cold melancholy.

She didn't talk to Alicia and Norah about it because she knew they didn't feel the same way. Perhaps that was what made the pain so personal? They had never been Amy, after all. They had failed to live up to Miss Fairchild's expectations, failed to be her everything. And so, they'd never understand.

The pain was hers and hers alone.

"I sleep here," Amy said.

Jessica was putting on her pajamas when Amy ran into the sisters' room and climbed onto her bed. Immediately the girl crawled under the covers and pretended to snore. "Night, night."

Jessica glanced toward the door anxiously. It wasn't the first time Amy had requested to sleep with Jessica, and Miss Fairchild had made it clear she wasn't happy about it. Unfortunately, Amy was persistent.

"Amy!" Miss Fairchild called. She was still speaking in a bizarre singsong voice, but it was laced with irritation. "Where did you go?"

Miss Fairchild stuck her head into the bedroom. She had already narrowed her eyes, knowing what she would find.

"Amy—" she started, but Amy got in first.

"I. Sleep. Here." She wrapped her arms around Jessica and looked up at Miss Fairchild defiantly.

Miss Fairchild glared at Jessica.

"No, Amy." Miss Fairchild smiled but her eyes were cool. "You sleep with Mummy."

"No!" Amy cried. "I sleep *here*!"

Jessica had to admit, her determination was impressive. She wondered if things would have been different if she'd defied Miss Fairchild rather than bending to her every whim in an attempt to win her love.

It was the humiliation, Jessica knew, that would upset Miss Fairchild the most. She'd always been so aware of how things looked. Jessica was much more interested in how they felt. And she knew this interaction did not feel good.

"Okay," Miss Fairchild said, advancing on Jessica and Amy in a way that made Amy cower. Her little fingers gripped the back of Jessica's neck. "Enough of this silliness. Let's go."

Amy flailed and kicked and cried as Miss Fairchild pried her away from Jessica. Jessica suffered the brunt of it, receiving several kicks, but she didn't mind. It wasn't Amy's fault. Miss Fairchild wasn't as forgiving when she was kicked.

"Amy," Miss Fairchild said sharply. "That's *very naughty*."

It was the closest to angry she'd been with Amy since the girl had arrived. A bead of worry formed in Jessica's chest—one that never truly went away.

• • •

Amy had been with them for six months when a car pulled into the driveway unexpectedly. Jessica and Alicia were sweeping the porch at the time.

"Who is that?" Jessica asked, squinting.

"I think it's Sandi," Alicia said. "My social worker."

She sounded mystified. This was justified, as it had been more than a year since they'd had a visit from a social worker other than Scott. Miss Fairchild seemed similarly mystified when Jessica slipped inside to give their foster mother the heads-up.

"But the place isn't clean!" she cried.

"It is," Jessica said, unable to repress the urge to reassure her. "It's fine."

Miss Fairchild hesitated. "Not the basement."

It was an odd comment. The social workers had never looked in the basement—at least, Scott never had.

"You need to go down there," she said to Jessica. "Take the broom. It's probably covered in dust."

Jessica stared at her. "What?"

"Go on. You can take Amy for company, since she loves you so much. Don't come up until it's spick-and-span."

She dragged Jessica down the hallway and pushed her through the door leading to the basement. "There's a light on a chain at the bottom of the stairs," she said, thrusting Amy into her arms. "Have fun, my darling girls."

The door closed, plunging them into absolute darkness. Jessica was still reeling as she heard the latch. They were locked in.

Amy began to cry.

"It's okay," Jessica said, reaching for the handrail. "We're playing hide-and-seek."

Amy clung to her as Jessica made her way carefully down the stairs. She was warm and sweet-smelling and comforting in the dark. At the bottom, as Miss Fairchild promised, she found a chain, and pulled it. The light was a single globe, only slightly better than nothing. Only then did Jessica realize Miss Fairchild had forgotten to give her the broom.

What the hell are we doing down here? Jessica wondered. It didn't make sense. She didn't really believe that Miss Fairchild wanted her to clean the basement. Even given the surprise nature of the visit, the social worker would have found a clean house, well-looked-after kids—a vision of happiness, at least from the outside. Instead, she'd find two children unaccounted for.

"Down," Amy said, wriggling to get out of Jessica's grasp.

Jessica looked at the floor, trying to assess whether it was suitable for a toddler. As Miss Fairchild had said, it *was* dusty. It was also cold. And mostly empty other than a pile of boxes beside an old bicycle. At the far end of the room was a single window that faced a brick wall, and a mattress turned on its side.

"Down!" Amy said, louder now, and Jessica had no choice but to let her slide off her hip to the ground.

"All right," she said. "But don't sit, okay? We have to stand."

Amy showed no indication she'd heard or understood as she toddled toward the bicycle. Overhead, Jessica could hear footsteps and the murmur of voices. Amy spun the wheel on the bicycle and rummaged in the boxes. Unlike Jessica, who was quite unnerved by being plunged into darkness, Amy now seemed quite relaxed and happy.

"Raaaaa," she said into the darkness.

She was holding a knitted lion she'd retrieved from a box. It was scrappily knitted—obviously homemade.

"Lion," Jessica said. "Can you say 'lion'?"

Amy dropped the lion and dug into another box, this time pulling out a toy duck. "Kack kack," she said.

"Quack quack." Jessica peered at the toys. She didn't recognize them. Perhaps they were from Miss Fairchild's own childhood.

Amy pulled out a knitted doll. It was bigger than the duck and the lion, almost as big as a newborn. Amy settled down and started to play with it, making adorable crying sounds and then patting it on the back, while Jessica listened for what was happening above.

They'd been down there about half an hour when a shaft of light finally broke into the space.

"Jessica?" It was Miss Fairchild. "You can come up now."

"Let's go, Amy," Jessica said, eager to get out of there. As she took the doll from the girl to return it to the box, she noticed it had blond curls, blue eyes, a blue dress, frilly socks, and black Mary Janes. Across its chest a name had been sewn into it in block letters.

Jessica blinked as she read it.

AMY.

33

JESSICA

"Can you all hear me?"

It was the universal greeting of a Zoom call. Alicia, Jessica, and Norah responded by saying yes, they could hear their lawyer, but unfortunately their microphone was on mute.

Alicia had called Meera after they left the police station. Meera had managed to find them a lawyer so quickly they didn't even have time to get back to the city. Instead, they'd had to check back into Driftwood Cottages and meet with their legal counsel via Zoom. Now they sat in a row on the same couch, with Jessica's laptop in front of them on the glass coffee table.

Their lawyer's name was Anna Ross. She looked to be in her mid-fifties, with short gray hair and, somewhat unexpectedly, a small silver nose ring. She wore reading glasses, under which her piercing eyes had no eye shadow or mascara. The absence of makeup screamed, *I have more important things to care about than my eyelashes!* Jessica felt intimidated by her confidence, even though Anna was on her side.

"All right," Anna said, once they'd unmuted themselves. "I think I'm up to speed on the particulars." She removed her glasses and looked straight into the camera lens. It was clear she was a commanding lawyer. "Tell me about the doll."

Jessica shrugged. "What do you want to know? It had blond curls, blue eyes, and 'Amy' written across its chest."

Anna pinned her with a makeup-free stare. "And you just stumbled across it in the basement?"

"Yes," Jessica said. "It seemed old. Like it had been there awhile."

"Bizarre," Anna said. "What did you make of it?"

"We thought it was strange," she said. "But what were we supposed to do? It wasn't like Miss Fairchild was going to give us any answers."

"But you must have wondered about it?"

"At first. Then . . . I don't know." Jessica looked at her sisters. "We kind of forgot about it."

Anna raised her eyebrows. "You *forgot*?"

Jessica had known this meeting was going to be intense, so she had taken two pills before they started, yet she could already feel their effect draining from her bloodstream. She started to stammer. "I—I know it seems strange. But we could only focus on so much. In the scheme of things, the doll just wasn't very important."

Anna nodded, replacing her glasses and looking at the file in front of her. "But according to my notes," she said, "the doll would later become very important indeed . . ."

34

ALICIA

BEFORE

The doll had the name Amy written on it?"

Alicia and Norah sat on their beds staring at Jessica. It was the first chance they'd had a chance to talk alone since Sandi left, because her visit had put them behind with their chores. It wasn't until bedtime that they were able to discuss what happened.

"Yes. It was written across her chest."

The visit had been routine. Apparently, Scott was on sick leave and so Sandi had stepped in. She'd asked about Jessica, but she'd been unconcerned when Miss Farichild explained that she was at a friend's place. The social worker hadn't asked about Amy at all.

"Maybe Miss Fairchild bought the doll for Amy?" Alicia suggested.

"But it was old and dusty," Jessica said. "It looked handmade. Like something you'd find at an old lady's house."

"Amy is a common name," Norah said, after taking a moment's consideration. "Maybe she had a doll called Amy when she was a child?"

"Probably," Alicia agreed.

But as they all fell silent, Alicia had a feeling she wasn't the only one searching for another explanation.

"Hello, Barbie," Alicia said. "I'm Mr. Teddy."

Alicia kneeled in front of Amy, the girl's teddy in her hand. They had just arrived home from school to find Amy sitting on the living room floor, clutching a bald Barbie doll. Miss Fairchild was nowhere to be seen.

Alicia bounced the teddy up and down. "Uh-oh." She threw the bear up in the air and let it drop to the floor. "I fell down."

It was a pathetic attempt at play, but Alicia was rewarded with one of Amy's magic giggles. Alicia would have thrown the teddy a million times for that giggle.

It was unusual for Alicia to seek out a moment of joy like this. In the period following Grammy's death, Alicia had noticed that on the rare occasion when someone showed her kindness—letting her cut in front of them at the shop, a teacher commenting on work well done, someone paying her a compliment—it pushed her to the verge of tears. Her vulnerability had become so embarrassing that instead of seeking kind people she sought out those who disliked her—like Edwina Wooldridge, the mean girl at school who always seemed revolted by Alicia's very existence. Something about her cruelty fortified Alicia. The certainty and security of what she was getting became like a drug. A much more powerful drug than the agony caused by a desire for love and warmth.

But it was different with Amy. Perhaps it was the darling little face that transformed with her moods, from puzzled to delighted to angry as if at the flick of a switch. Or maybe it was her theatrical gestures—the way she tapped her toe when she was impatient, or cupped her chin to think. Or maybe it was the comfort she brought. It was astonishing how much comfort one chubby little hand on your thigh could provide. Alicia became hungry for it.

"Wheeeeee!" Alicia cried, tossing the teddy in the air.

Of course, Miss Fairchild materialized to quash her joy. "Oh," she said to Alicia, not even trying to conceal her disappointment. "You're home."

"Again," Amy said, picking up the teddy and handing it back to Alicia.

"Hello, Barbie," Alicia started, bouncing the teddy. "I'm Mr. Teddy."

But before Alicia could toss the bear, Miss Fairchild snatched it away.

"No!" Amy cried.

Miss Fairchild dropped to her knees beside the girl. "I can be Mr. Teddy," she said.

"Look!" She started bouncing the bear frenziedly.

"No!" Amy repeated, louder.

But Miss Fairchild just kept bouncing that bear desperately. She was so caught up in it she didn't even notice Amy picking up the Barbie. Alicia did, though. She saw what was about to happen, as if in slow motion, but she was powerless to prevent it.

Amy thwacked the doll hard against Miss Fairchild's forehead.

Miss Fairchild gasped, tears springing to her eyes. Alicia was about to ask if she was all right when Miss Fairchild lunged forward, slapping Alicia so hard across the face so hard that she saw stars.

• • •

Amy seemed to take an active dislike to Miss Fairchild after that. And the girl's affection for Norah, Alicia, and Jessica seemed to increase in correlation to her dislike for Miss Fairchild.

"No!" Amy would squeal when Miss Fairchild tried to pick her up, her little body tensing and thrashing. "Down. I not like you."

The more Miss Fairchild smothered her with attention, the more irate Amy became. Alicia realized that she rather enjoyed it, even if it made her worry for Amy, who was too little to understand how dangerous it was to make an enemy of Miss Fairchild.

"We don't speak to Mummy like that," Miss Fairchild said at first, trying to cajole Amy out of her mood, but after the sixth or seventh injury from a flying Barbie doll, she began to lose patience.

"That's very naughty, Amy," she said one day, after Amy had tried to slap her. "Now you're going to have a time-out in your high chair."

Alicia didn't dare intervene as Miss Fairchild dragged a crying Amy to the kitchen, but she bore silent witness, hopeful that perhaps her presence would temper Miss Fairchild's anger. Norah and Jessica also appeared, perhaps hoping the same. Miss Fairchild was lifting the girl into the high chair when Amy's kicking foot—in a patent-leather Mary Jane—connected with her face.

"Argh!"

Miss Fairchild released Amy, letting her tumble to the floor. She hit her head with a grotesque crack on the wooden tray on the way down.

For a horrible moment, everything was silent. Alicia and her sisters fell to their knees. Alicia scooped her up and held the limp little body in her lap. After a terrifyingly long moment, Amy began to wail.

The girls resumed breathing, looking at each other in relief. Miss Fairchild, who was cursing and holding her chin, barked, "Put her down."

Alicia stared at her. "But . . . she's hurt."

"I said *Put. Her. Down.*"

Alicia couldn't believe it. This wasn't her, or Norah, or Jessica. Amy was a baby. She was innocent. She was *hurt.* Crying! What kind of monster wouldn't want her to be comforted?

Miss Fairchild took some paper towel and wiped her lip, which was bleeding. "Now, Alicia."

After a glance at her sisters, Alicia lifted up the little girl and put her on the floor. Immediately Amy tried to clamber back onto her lap, wailing loudly. Alicia pushed her away. She'd never hated herself more. Miss Fairchild loomed over her, watching. Alicia wondered if she was enjoying herself.

Amy was now lying on the floor, red-faced and screaming. Every instinct urged Alicia to comfort the child, but she refrained for fear that it might lead to trouble. Not for her—for Amy.

"See, Amy?" Miss Fairchild said. "This is what happens when you kick Mummy. You have to learn that your actions have consequences."

After what felt like an age, Miss Fairchild left the room, and Alicia scooped the girl up again. Her sisters huddled around them and together they held Amy while she sobbed. When at last her tears had dried, they all pretended to be clumsy horses, crawling around the kitchen on all fours, crashing into things. Only when Amy started giggling was Alicia able to exhale.

They were entirely indebted to this child, she realized. She wasn't sure how or why or when it had happened. All she knew was protecting Amy had become their life's mission. They might not be able to save themselves, but by God, they were going to save her.

"If you hug Miss Fairchild, I'll give you this chocolate," Alicia said to Amy, waving the Freddo frog at her. Norah had earned it in exchange for doing someone's homework at school, and it appeared chocolate was a language Amy understood.

"Choc-at," Amy repeated, eyes wide.

"Shh. It's our secret."

"Seek-rit."

"Go on. She's coming."

It was shocking how effective it was. Amy turned and ran at Miss Fairchild, throwing her arms around her legs.

"Oh!" Miss Fairchild looked so pleased, Alicia almost felt guilty. "What a lovely hug."

"I wuv you."

She glanced slyly at Alicia, who gave her the thumbs-up.

But the problem with toddlers was that they didn't appreciate the importance of consistency. Some days Amy didn't feel like making a happy face when Miss Fairchild played a game with her. Other days, when the girls left for school, she stood at the front door and sobbed.

"How will you survive without *your darling girls?*" Miss Fairchild would say crossly.

Each day they went to school with a heavy feeling in their hearts. And though they didn't talk about it, Alicia knew that none of them could relax until the moment they turned in to the driveway at the end of the day.

"What do you think happens to Amy when we're at school?" Alicia said one day as they walked to school.

"I check her for injuries every day," Norah said. "I haven't found anything since the day she hit her head on the high chair."

But Norah sounded as uncertain as Alicia felt in her heart each time they left Amy alone at Wild Meadows. They should have listened to that uncertainty. When it came to Miss Fairchild, their instincts were seldom wrong.

"That's weird," Norah said, as they walked up the driveway after school one day. "Is Miss Fairchild in the pool?"

She held her hand across her eyes to block the glare from the afternoon sun. They followed her gaze. As they reached the top of the driveway they could clearly see a person in the water, and two beach towels on the grass nearby. It was *weird*. No one had used the pool in years, not since Alicia had arrived at Wild Meadows. And it wasn't even a particularly warm day.

"Why is she in the pool?" Alicia said out loud.

That was when they noticed that Jessica was running. Jessica had never been particularly athletic, but now she was flying down the driveway, red dust rising up from her heels.

Alicia felt the alarm ring through her even before she understood what was happening. As Norah took off after Jessica, Alicia scanned their surrounds. In the lower paddock, a tractor rolled by. The horses were having a run while Dirk looked on. Everything seemed normal. But when Alicia looked back the pool, she realized. There were *two* towels by the pool.

So where was Amy?

By the time Alicia started running, Jessica was diving into the pool fully dressed. Miss Fairchild waved and yelled uselessly as Norah dived in right behind her.

Alicia reached the pool as Jessica emerged with Amy in her arms, coughing and spluttering.

"You were drowning her?" Norah screamed at Miss Fairchild.

Their foster mother scoffed. "I was teaching her to swim."

The timing, Alicia realized, was interesting. She knew they'd be arriving home at this time. This performance wasn't for Amy—it was for them.

Dirk must have heard the commotion because when Alicia glanced toward the horse paddock he was looking right at them.

"Like you taught me to swim?" Jessica cried.

"Well . . ." Miss Fairchild looked amused. "You learned, didn't you?"

The woman wasn't even trying to deny it. She found it *funny*.

Amy coughed, then began to vomit water. Jessica carried her to the side of the pool, patting her back as she clung to Jessica's neck. She was so little, so vulnerable.

They couldn't just hope that things would turn out okay, Alicia realized. Not anymore. The stakes were too high. They needed to do something.

THE OFFICE OF DR. WARREN, PSYCHIATRIST

When I arrive for our next session, Dr. Warren *smiles* at me. It is concerning, considering where we left off our last conversation, and where he suggests this session begin, but it isn't for me to judge.

"So he let you out of the basement. What happened then?"

"Home life became a game of trying to figure out how to exist without upsetting John. I'd clean, go to church, and not talk back. Most of the time, I didn't talk at all. I tried to stay out of

John's way, but there were days when, even without saying a word, I could invoke John's wrath." I re-create these moments in my mind, watching them play out like scenes in a film. "It might have been that he'd decided I hadn't cleaned something properly, or I'd used the wrong tone when speaking to him. On a few occasions it was simply because I needed to understand who was in charge. When it happened there was no discussion, no opportunity to defend myself—he just grabbed my ear and dragged me to the basement."

I think about what Dr. Warren said last time, about how I'd blamed my mother when John mistreated me. It brings furious tears to my eyes. "My mother *always* stood by silently. The fact that she didn't even *try* to intervene was worse than being locked in the basement. After a while, my hatred of her became an outlet for my pain. A focus. A place to channel it."

"How did you channel it?" Dr. Warren asks quietly.

I shrug. "It was pretty easy. Every morning, while John was sleeping, my mother ironed him a shirt and left it hanging from a hook in the bathroom. Naturally, John was as fastidious about his shirts as he was about everything else. Before my mother married John, I doubt she'd ever ironed a shirt in her life. She certainly never ironed one for my father. So she'd had to learn quickly. Oftentimes, while he ate breakfast, John would scold her because his collar wasn't starched enough or his sleeves were rumpled. Criticizing her homemaking skills was a favorite pastime for John. At first, I'd been indignant on her behalf, but after a while, I came to enjoy it.

"One day, while my mother and I were preparing breakfast, John stormed into the kitchen and flung a shirt onto the table with such force it knocked over a water glass. He shouted at my mother, 'Look what you've done, you stupid woman!'

"My mother stared at him in confusion. Then she reached for

the shirt and held it up. A large, iron-shaped burn mark could be seen on the lower back.

"Mum was so flummoxed. 'I . . . I . . I'm sorry, I didn't realize . . .'

"I busied myself with cleaning up the spilled water.

"'You didn't realize because you're lazy and you don't pay attention. That's why you never do anything properly.'

"John was positively wild with fury. I hadn't heard him shout at Mum before. I wondered if he was going to take her by the ear and throw her in the basement.

"'This was a brand-new shirt,' he cried. 'Who is going to pay for a replacement? Are you going to get a job and start working? No—who would hire a lazy stupid woman, like you?'

"'I . . . I'll pay for it out of my housekeeping,' my mother stammered.

"Her 'housekeeping' allowance was barely enough to buy food. If she had to buy a shirt, we'd all be living on fresh air for the week. At least, Mum and I would. But it would be worth it.

"'Iron me another shirt,' John said, storming from the room.

"I managed to give Mum a tiny smirk before she hurried after him.

"From then on, finding ways to make John angry with Mum became an outlet for me when things got tough. It wasn't hard. I'd go back to a spot on the floor that Mum had already cleaned and walk on it with dirty shoes. I'd use their bathroom and 'forget' to dry the soap, so that it congealed in the basin. I'd take a few dollars from the tin where he hid his money."

Dr. Warren's pupils had dilated with pleasure.

"Mum never told him it was me. Maybe that's why I kept doing it."

"To get her back?"

I consider that. "More to prove to myself that she had *some* feelings left for me," I say. "Anyway . . . now that John's attention had shifted to her, I had more freedom. I still had to clean, go to church and refrain from talking back, but as long as I did these three things, John didn't really bother me. He didn't seem to care what time I came home from school, or who I hung out with, or what kind of grades I got.

"It was around this time that a boy in my class named Troy started to notice me. Troy wasn't particularly attractive or charismatic, and he had an irritating habit of saying 'anythink', but he had one important thing going for him: he liked me. When you feel like nobody likes you, it's hard to overstate the thrill of that. It didn't matter that I didn't like him back—or, indeed, that I actively disliked him. His interest in me was intoxicating.

"And so we'd meet before school and hang out near the sports equipment shed on the oval and kiss. He'd pass me notes and letters torn from the pages of his school diary, saying he thought about me all the time. After school, we'd hang out as a group with some of our classmates, or sometimes it was just the two of us at his place, in the garage that had been converted into a rumpus room. We'd roll around in our clothes, kissing and fondling. And after a while we took our clothes off.

"The sex wasn't great; in fact, it was on the dull side. But I enjoyed my time out of the house, being a normal fifteen-year-old, roaming the streets with my friends, riding on the handlebars of push-bikes and shoplifting from the general store. Troy was always by my side, like a faithful puppy dog. When the sun began to set, we said our goodbyes and went back to our own homes. Usually I'd find Mum was cooking and John was reading the newspaper or a book in the living room. But one day, they were waiting for me at the door. I recognized John's demeanor. His gaze was sharp, his jaw tight. The veins in his forearms bulged. My mother stood silently beside him as always.

"'Where have you been?' he asked me.

"I hated that I was nervous. 'I was . . . just hanging out with my friends.'

"John's eyes narrowed. 'Friends? Or a boyfriend?'

"I didn't reply. My mother lowered her gaze, as if this all had nothing to do with her.

"'Answer me,' he roared. 'Do you have a boyfriend named Troy?'

"Troy. He knew his name. I wondered how. 'I go to school with a boy named Troy, but he's not my boyfriend.'

"John's eyes widened dramatically. 'He's not? Then perhaps you can explain to me why you were kissing him behind the fish-and-chip shop this afternoon?'

"Now there was nothing to say. But John was happy enough to fill the silence by calling me names. Slut. Whore. Trash.

"'From now on you come straight home after school. No going to friends' houses. No after-school sport. School, home. That's it.'

"He grabbed my ear, wrenching it painfully, and with my mother watching on he dragged me down to the basement."

"Are you okay?" Dr. Warren asks.

My eyes well up. "It was just so unfair. I had no one. My father was dead. My own mother chose John. Then I couldn't have a boyfriend . . ." The tears spill over. "Every human being needs someone, don't they, Dr. Warren? One person that's in your corner. One person who's *yours*?"

Dr. Warren's gaze is fixed on mine, his mouth slightly open. He gives himself a little shake. "I . . . would say that's true."

I nod, wiping tears from my face. "And if someone doesn't have that one person?"

Dr. Warren's gaze drifts from my face as there is a knock at the door.

"Ah," he says. "That's it for today."

But he looks a little sad that I am leaving.

35

ALICIA

BEFORE

Miss Fairchild did that to me," Jessica whispered. They were in Jessica's bed, lying side by side like a row of sardines under the blankets in their shorty pajamas. Jessica was in the middle and Alicia and Norah each rested a head on her shoulder. "In the pool. She 'taught me to swim.'" Jessica grimaced as she said the words. "She told me she would catch me. She *promised*. Then she let me flail around under the water until I blacked out."

Alicia felt a tear from Jessica's face hit her cheek. It invoked a swell of fury in Alicia. She clenched her fists.

"That's fucked up," Norah said.

"Yes," Alicia agreed wholeheartedly. "So fucked up. It's child abuse. It's . . . it's attempted *murder*."

"She wouldn't have let me drown," Jessica said. "Or Amy. She would have grabbed her eventually."

"Jessica!" Alicia cried. "Tell me you're not still defending that woman. Who *cares* if she would have saved her—or you?"

Jessica's expression was tragically, desperately uncertain. "I guess you're right."

"We have to tell someone," Alicia said. "A teacher. The police."

"She'll just deny it." Jessica sniffed and propped herself up onto her elbows. "And even if they do believe us, what then? We'll have to leave Wild Meadows. We could end up anywhere. What are the chances that they'll let us stay together?"

They'd talked about this before, of course: and each time they decided to keep quiet out of fear of being separated. But this time was different. They all knew it.

Alicia glanced at Norah, who stared determinedly at the ceiling.

"It's a risk we have to take," Alicia said. "I know it's scary but . . ."

Jessica wiped her face with her forearm. "Just slow down, Alicia. We just need to keep a closer eye on Amy, that's all. Maybe we can take turns to stay home with her, like we did with the other babies?"

"And if she doesn't let us stay home?" Alicia said. "What then? We can't protect Amy if we're not here."

Alicia looked at Norah again. Her face was carefully blank, but Alicia saw the effort it took to hold back her emotions. They all knew there was no one more terrified of them being separated than she was.

"I agree with Alicia," Norah said, her gaze still fixed on the ceiling. "We *have* to tell. We've already waited too long."

Amy's face lit up when they entered the kitchen for breakfast the next morning. She dropped the piece of toast she'd been smearing all over the tray of her high chair and began waving her hands about.

Miss Fairchild huffed. "Great. Now she'll never eat her breakfast."

"Hello, Amy," Norah said brightly, picking her up out of her high chair and spinning her about. Amy giggled hysterically.

"Norah," Miss Fairchild cried. "I'm the only one who—"

"Wheeeee!" Norah cried, ignoring her and spinning Amy faster.

It would have been funny seeing Miss Fairchild's confusion, had Alicia not worried it might tip her off that something was wrong. Jessica must have had the same thought, because she chose that moment to say, "We'd better go, guys."

The moment she said it, Amy broke into heartrending sobs. "Nooooooo," she cried, betrayed. "No go!" She looked at Norah and Jessica imploringly, her face desperate.

"We'll be back after school," Alicia said, as the child put her chubby arms around Alicia's leg. When Alicia put a hand on her head, it felt warm and sweaty. By the time they'd brushed their teeth and got their bags, Amy was a gasping, snotty, red-faced mess.

"That's enough," Miss Fairchild said, prising her away. "For goodness sake, what a fuss!"

"Bye," they said to her inadequately, then they hurried from the house so quickly that Jessica forgot her schoolbag and had to run back for it.

As Norah and Alicia waited for her, they consoled themselves with the fact that with any luck, after today, they'd never have to do this again. Of course, if they were wrong, it meant they'd be making things worse for themselves. And not only that, they'd have made things a whole lot worse for Amy.

They didn't talk at all on the way to school. Not one single word. What they were doing felt too important. They needed to focus.

Norah walked with her head down, somber and stoic, like a prisoner on her way to death row. Jessica fought tears, and occasionally shed them. As Alicia walked alongside them, the idea that they could be separated today finally settled upon her chest. The last couple of years hadn't been happy, not at all. Compared to her life before that, with Grammy, they had been a nightmare. And yet. At least she'd had these two—her sisters. As Norah said the day Alicia found out Grammy had passed away, it wasn't nothing. On the contrary, Alicia realized now, it was *everything*.

"Should we go to our lockers?" Jessica asked, when they got to school.

Norah shook her head, pointing toward the principal's office. "Let's just get this over with."

They had to wait for Mr. O'Day for nearly twenty minutes. He was on the phone, and from where they sat in the small reception area, they heard every word of his side of the conversation. It might have been interesting had it not been about funding for new sporting equipment. Mr. O'Day had been the PE teacher before he'd become principal and he made no attempt to conceal the fact that he didn't have much interest in any other subjects, or anything about education in general.

Finally, he ended the call and ushered the girls into his office—a small brown room with white venetian blinds and a framed picture of Shane Warne on the wall. Opposite his L-shaped desk was a cabinet filled with sporting trophies.

He only had two seats for visitors, so Alicia remained standing.

"I've got five minutes before I'm due to judge the year two art show," he told them, with a glance at the clock on the wall. "So, what's this all about?"

Mr. O'Day didn't make it to the year two art show. Instead, he called the police, and the rest of the day's appointments were canceled.

Two police officers arrived at the school promptly, and joined them in Mr. O'Day's office.

"Hello, girls," the older cop said, pushing Mr. O'Day's chair toward Alicia. He had white hair and kind eyes. He sat down on the corner of the desk. "My name is Sergeant Grady, but everybody calls me Max. This is my colleague Constable Hart." He pointed to the other cop, who was young enough to be his grandson. "You can call him Robbie. I understand your names are Norah, Jessica, and Alicia?"

They nodded.

"It's very nice to meet you. Your principal tells me you've asked to speak to us—is that correct?"

"Yes," Norah said. "Our foster mother is abusive."

"That is extremely concerning." The sergeant's bushy eyebrows knitted together. "You did the right thing by coming to us."

It was probably part of his standard spiel, but Alicia couldn't help but find it affirming. *They'd done the right thing!* Alicia couldn't remember the last time someone had told her that.

"We're worried about Amy," Jessica said.

"Amy?" Max glanced at his colleague briefly. "Who is Amy?"

"She lives with us. Miss Fairchild adopted her six months ago. She's two."

"I see. And you've witnessed your foster mother being abusive toward her?"

"Yes," Alicia said. "And it's getting worse."

Norah sat forward. "We're worried something could be happening to her right now!"

Max held up a hand. "We've already sent a car to Wild Meadows. Our officers will probably be there by now. We can get a message to them to check on Amy's welfare."

He nodded to Robbie, who left the room. As Alicia watched him go, relief mingled with heavy dread at the idea of the police car pulling up to the door. She could picture Miss Fairchild's polite, concerned face covering up her white-hot rage at being questioned like a criminal.

"Is this the first time you've reported the abuse?" Max asked, when Robbie had gone.

"Yes." Alicia felt a pull in her chest. "We should have reported it earlier but . . ."

"What's important is that you've reported it now," Max said. "Unfortunately, I'm going to need you to tell me a little bit more about the abuse. I know it might be upsetting, so take your time. Mr. O'Day is waiting just outside in case you have any questions or are uncertain about anything."

"Well," Alicia said. "Yesterday was what brought it to a head."

"All right," Max said. "Let's start there."

"We arrived home from school to find Miss Fairchild in the pool. Amy was in the pool too, but her head was underwater. We ran all the way from the gate, which would have taken nearly a minute and her head was under the whole time. She did the same thing to Jessica when she was a child. It's a punishment for not loving her enough."

"She'll say she was teaching her to swim," Jessica said, "but she's only two years old. You don't let a two-year-old flounder under-water for a whole minute."

The policeman nodded, but he didn't look as horrified as Alicia had expected. "And have there been other instances of . . . abuse?" he asked.

"Miss Fairchild dropped her on the high chair and she hit her head," Norah said.

The policeman raised his bushy eyebrows. "She dropped Amy? On purpose?"

"Amy kicked her in the face as she was putting her in the high chair," Norah said. "Miss Fairchild let her go and she hit her head hard. Then Miss Fairchild wouldn't let us comfort her. She said she had to realize there were consequences to her actions."

The policeman nodded. "I see."

"She barely feeds us," Alicia said.

"She's obsessed with cleanliness and makes us clean for hours every day," Jessica said.

"She drinks," Norah said. "At night she roams the halls and sometimes comes into our rooms and wakes us all up."

The did their best to report each incident in detail, and Max paid close attention, taking notes and asking questions, but an hour went by and Alicia could see that they hadn't given him nearly enough. Miss Fairchild had been clever. None of her abuse had been clearcut. In every case, there was a way for her to spin it as discipline or an accident or lies. They didn't have any tangible proof. It was their word against hers. The whole thing came down to who the cops chose to believe.

"What else can you tell me?" Max said.

"She went through a period of fostering babies through respite care," Alicia said. "When she tired of them, she left their care to us. Check with the school. Our school attendance would have been fifty percent at best. It was because we were looking after the babies that Miss Fairchild fostered."

Max made a note of this.

"And there was one day she made me take Amy down into the basement when the social worker came to visit. She locked us down there for nearly an hour. That was kind of weird."

There was a knock at the door.

"Phone call for you, Sergeant Grady," Mr. O'Day's secretary said.

The police officer assured the girls he'd be right back and left the room.

"Do you think he believes us?" Jessica said.

"It's hard to tell," Alicia said. "But he'll have to investigate. He can't just ignore us without looking into it."

The door opened again. As Max reentered the room, Alicia noticed a difference in him. There was something slightly stiff about his movements, a kind of pervading tension.

"Sorry about that," Max said, resuming his seat on Mr. O'Day's desk. "That was my colleague. He's at Wild Meadows right now."

Norah was already on her feet. "Is Amy okay?"

"Don't tell us we were too late," Alicia said.

Jessica was trembling, as if she'd already decided the worst had happened.

Max didn't reassure them. His face was perplexed, his brows so tightly furrowed they almost touched. "The police at the house conducted a thorough search of the house," he said finally. "They didn't find Amy."

Alicia looked at Norah and Jessica in horror. "But where else would she be? Miss Fairchild never takes her anywhere."

"Did they check the basement?" Norah asked.

"She must be *somewhere*," Alicia said.

Max shook his head. "They didn't find any sign of a toddler at all. Not a nappy or a high chair. Not a single piece of baby clothing. Nothing."

He waited, perhaps hoping they'd have an answer for this. But they all just stared back at him, bewildered.

"That doesn't make sense," Alicia said finally. "She was there this morning when we left for school."

"Is it possible someone tipped her off?" Max asked.

"But no one knew," Norah said. "No one apart from the three of us."

There had to be an explanation. Had Miss Fairchild packed Amy up and taken her somewhere? It was possible, of course, but it didn't make sense. Why didn't she tell them what she was planning? And why pack all Amy's stuff away?

Jessica and Norah looked just as perplexed as Alicia.

"There's something else," Max said. "My colleagues have spoken with social services. The records show three children in Miss Fairchild's care. *You* three. There's no record of a toddler being placed for adoption or foster care at Wild Meadows." Max stood from the desk and paced, tired or frustrated or both. "According to our records, Amy doesn't exist."

36

ALICIA

There were no records for Amy?" Anna said. She was eating her lunch at her desk, a chicken schnitzel roll, and leaning forward as if watching a terrifying and enthralling movie. "Weird."

"I know, right?" Norah said. "It would make a great true crime podcast."

"What did you make of it?" Anna asked.

"We didn't know what to make of it. Maybe that Miss Fairchild had done something to her and then covered it up? But even that didn't fit. How would she have known that we were going to tell the police *that* day of all days? I mean, she was pretty good at reading us, but even if she had guessed, what did she do with Amy? And why didn't the authorities have any record of her?"

"Those are good questions," Anna said. She looked as confused as they had been. "Did you come up with any answers?"

"Not at first," Alicia said. "It didn't make sense."

Anna nodded. "All right. Before we get into that, I need to make you aware of a new development."

Alicia braced herself. She wasn't sure she could take any more developments. In the past few days, she'd experienced enough developments to last a lifetime.

"She's spoken to the media."

"Who?" Jessica asked, though of course they all knew.

Norah had already pulled out her phone. Alicia did the same.

It only took her a few clicks to find it. The others peered over her shoulder to read along with her.

Former Owner of "Wild Meadows" Speaks Out After Foster Home Scandal

The former owner of Wild Meadows Estate, Holly Fairchild, has spoken out about her horror at the discovery of human remains under the country home where she fostered dozens of children in the late 1990s.

"My heart breaks at this terrible news," Fairchild said. "I will assist the police with their investigations however possible and won't rest until this matter is resolved."

Fairchild also spoke out about the "crisis of displaced children" in Australia, imploring families to "open their hearts and homes to these poor, lost souls."

Asked if she has any insight into what may have taken place, Fairchild responded:

"I don't like to speculate when there is a police investigation underway. I will say that having had the opportunity to work with many traumatized foster children, the damage can be extensive. Often the victims actually become perpetrators. I've seen it firsthand. Frankly, I don't like to think about what they are capable of."

"Is she allowed to say that?" Alicia asked, when she reached the end of the article. "She's basically called us perpetrators!"

"I'm not happy about it," Anna said. "But she hasn't named you, and she's spoken in general terms, so legally speaking, she can."

It was classic Miss Fairchild. It was her way of having the last word, of letting them know that *she* was in control of the situation, like always. She needn't have bothered. No one knew it better than the three of them.

37

JESSICA

'll get the drinks," Norah said the moment they walked into the pub. Anna had another meeting, so they'd decided to grab some lunch before they reconvened in a couple of hours. Jessica had suggested they mix it up, maybe get fish-and-chips, but Norah wouldn't hear of it. Desperate to get back to the bartender, obviously. Unlike last night, the place was bustling, and the line for the bar was three deep, but Norah pushed her way to the front, unbothered by the irritated comments from people waiting.

"Good luck getting a table," Hando said, appearing behind them. Patel was by his side.

"Our lawyer told us we're not allowed to talk to you," Jessica said.

"Understood," Patel said. "And we won't ask you anything about the case. But we can talk about burgers, can't we? The local cops tell us they're the only edible thing on the menu. Apparently we need to avoid the chicken at all costs."

"Three burgers," Alicia called to Norah, who relayed the order to the bartender.

"Five," Hando said, and the bartender nodded and turned to put the order through the window.

As they waited for a table to become available, Jessica and Alicia stood awkwardly alongside the detectives. Jessica received a text message from Sonja, informing her that she needed to speak with her urgently. Jessica reached into her bag for another pill, and turned off her phone.

"Can I ask you guys something?" Patel said. "Not about the case, promise." When no one responded, she pressed on. "Why don't any of you have kids?"

People were jostling them. At the far end of the room, a horse race was playing on a large television and several men stood watching it, beers in hand. Everyone in Port Agatha must have been having lunch at the pub that day.

"I'm a social worker," Alicia said. "I have thousands of kids."

"Never thought about fostering yourself?"

"Once or twice." She shrugged. "But the timing hasn't been right."

As far as Jessica knew, Alicia had never considered fostering. Then again, Alicia might have been lying. After all, if crime novels were anything to go by, the only person more likely to commit murder than a foster child was a woman who was childless by choice.

"What about you, Jessica?"

Jessica offered her usual answer. "I would have liked to, but . . ."

She shrugged, as if to imply that she was unable to have kids. She'd found it to be the easiest response, and the one least likely to provoke any supplementary questions. The truth was, Jessica had never tried to get pregnant. Whenever Phil halfheartedly brought it up she told him they would definitely try "in a few years," and he always accepted it. It wasn't that she didn't want kids. If one had shown up in her life like a lost dog, she would have scooped it up and loved it and protected it forever. But making the decision to have one, to *create* one, was too big a leap.

Occasionally, over the years, she'd fantasized about Norah getting pregnant. Unlike Alicia, Norah had a lot of sex, and also unlike Alicia, she had a profound dislike of children. In the fantasy, Norah would birth the child and Jessica would graciously step in and raise it as if it were her own, leaving Norah to be the favorite aunty. She would perform every role required of a mother and more. She'd be fiercer, more loving than she'd ever been. Which really begged the question: if she could do that for Norah's child, why not her own?

"Have a nice chat with the barman?" Alicia said to Norah when she finally reappeared. The noise from the crowd and the television were giving Jessica a headache. She was glad she'd taken two pills before coming here.

"I was getting your drinks!" Norah said. "Talk about ungrateful . . . Hey, there's a high table—over there!"

Norah hurried toward it, almost knocking over a couple headed in the same direction. When the rest of them—the detectives included—joined her, Norah said, "For fuck's sake."

"What?" Jessica asked.

Norah pointed at the doorway, and the rest of them turned to see Miss Fairchild, neat and prim in jeans and an expensive quilted anorak, glancing around the room with a slight frown. To anyone else, she would have seemed to be assessing whether to stay at the pub or go somewhere else, but Jessica recognized it as a performance. Miss Fairchild knew they were there. Nothing in her world happened by chance.

There was a theatrical moment in which she appeared to notice them, and then she slithered through the crowd toward them as though they were friends.

"Hello," she said brightly, looking at Jessica. "Grabbing some lunch? Me too."

"Get the chicken," Norah said. "It comes highly recommended."

"We read your interview online," Alicia said. "Nice touch, putting not only us but all foster children under suspicion."

Patel and Hando stepped forward, clearly keen to prevent a confrontation.

Miss Fairchild's face tightened. It aged her, emphasizing the tiny lines around her mouth. "It's important to me that this case gets the media attention it deserves," she said. "I might not have been able to stop what happened to that child, but at least I ensure justice is done now."

"Which child?" Norah snarled. "The one who didn't exist?"

Miss Fairchild's cheeks flushed pink, and she cast a quick glance at the detectives. "The one buried under the house."

"Say her name," Norah said, stepping forward. Her fists were clenched and Jessica was grateful there was a table between her and Miss Fairchild.

"Why don't you say it, Norah?" Miss Fairchild countered. "You're the one who's been talking about her since you were a child. In fact," Miss Fairchild continued, "it really is the perfect crime, now that I think about it. You harm a poor defenseless child, bury her under the house, and then claim she was my foster child. You always were the clever one, as well as the violent one."

It happened so fast. Norah flipped the table, leaped over it, and grabbed Miss Fairchild by the lapels. Alicia responded immediately, grabbing Norah by the shoulder and attempting to restrain her. Jessica tried to do the same, but her movements felt awkward and slow, like her body couldn't quite keep up with her mind.

"All right," Hando said, several moments after he should have. "I think that's enough."

"She put her hands on me," Miss Fairchild said. "That's assault."

And there it was. They'd fallen right into Miss Fairchild's trap.

"Let's go," Alicia said. "Cancel the burgers."

"I could never control her, you know, even as a little girl," Miss Fairchild said to the cops, as Jessica and Alicia each took one of Norah's arms and pulled her toward the door. "Her sisters always covered for her. Clearly, they still do."

Norah tried to wrench free of their grip when she heard this, but this time her sisters didn't let her go.

38

NORAH

The day they told the police about Amy seemed to go on forever. After hearing the news that Amy wasn't at Wild Meadows, they were taken by car to the police station.

There, Norah, Alicia, and Jessica were shown into separate rooms and asked to tell their stories again. They answered a seemingly endless number of questions. What did Amy look like? When did she arrive? What was her daily routine? What specific interactions with her did they remember? Norah couldn't figure out how this information could possibly assist them in finding her, but after a policewoman offered her a chocolate bar in exchange for answering the questions, Norah decided to go along with it.

"So no one saw Amy besides the three of you?" the woman asked. "No one at all?"

It was shocking to realize that it was true. It was something she'd never considered before. They rarely had visitors. No friends. No family. And Miss Fairchild had been so reluctant to take Amy anywhere, saying that she needed to stay close to home in order to "bond." The only people who ever visited the house were social workers, and the last time Sandi came Jessica had been told to take her to the basement.

"*Scott!*" Norah cried suddenly. "Scott saw her. Several times."

"Scott Michaels?" the woman asked.

"I don't know his last name, but he's my social worker," Norah said. "Awful guy."

Norah waited for the woman to leave the room or make a call or tell someone, but she didn't. Her expression barely changed.

"The thing is," she said, "my colleagues have spoken to Scott, and to Sandi Riley, but neither of them had any knowledge of a toddler at Wild Meadows."

Norah shook her head. "Sandi never saw her because Miss Fairchild made Jessica hide her in the basement—but Scott *definitely* saw Amy."

Norah thought for a moment. Scott and Miss Fairchild were friends. He would lie for her. But Norah didn't understand why he'd have to. And why was there no paperwork for Amy? Why would Miss Fairchild suddenly pack up Amy's things the morning they'd decided to go to the police? It didn't make sense!

The policewoman looked as frustrated as Norah felt. "No one else saw her?"

Norah shook her head. "I don't think so."

"All right," she said. She put a hand on Norah's, which perhaps was meant to be reassuring. Norah snatched it away.

"Wait!" Norah felt it in the back of her brain. "There was

someone . . . Dirk! Dirk saw her! Dirk looks after the horses at Wild Meadows. He came to Amy's birthday party to take back the horse I stole."

The policewoman brightened at this. "Dirk Winterbourne?"

Norah nodded, though she didn't exactly know his full name. "Yes! Ask him—he'll tell you."

Finally, the policewoman nodded and headed for the door. Before she left, Norah added, "Make sure they've searched the house thoroughly. Check the rubbish bins, too."

Norah felt encouraged. Amy had to be somewhere. And when the police spoke to Dirk, they'd have to start taking the sisters' claims seriously. She just hoped they moved quickly enough to find Amy, wherever she was.

Around lunchtime, they were shown to a lunchroom at the police station, where they were greeted by a social worker they didn't recognize.

Her name was Genevieve, and she wore Doc Martens and a pretty floral dress. She brought them salad rolls and more chocolate bars to eat but she didn't know anything about the case, so Norah had to sit by the cracked-open door to eavesdrop on the police in order to get information.

"Their stories are consistent," Norah heard Max saying to someone.

"They may have planned it," another cop said.

"Possibly," he said. "Yet they're not identical. They each described the events in different ways, but the events are the same."

"Okay, but—"

"I believe them, Jerry. I've always thought something wasn't quite right with that Wild Meadows woman."

They stopped talking then, and Norah heard a new, third voice speaking.

"You need to see this," the voice said.

Norah leaned closer to the door.

"Are you girls thirsty?" Genevieve said. "I can get you something to drink from the vending machine."

"Shh!" Norah said.

"Where did you find this?" Norah heard Max say.

"Wild Meadows. In the basement."

Norah peeked around the doorframe and came face-to-face with Max, who was walking toward them. In his hand was a knitted doll with blond hair and blue eyes. AMY was written across her chest.

"That's the doll I found in the basement the day Amy and I were locked down there," Jessica said.

Max frowned. "You've seen this?"

Jessica took the doll. "I thought it was weird that Miss Fairchild had a doll called Amy because it's definitely older than our Amy."

Max looked at the doll. "So it's not possible . . ." He paused, winced. "It's not possible the doll *is* Amy?"

"It's a *doll*," Norah said slowly, as if she were talking to an idiot, which apparently she was. "Amy is a human."

Max exhaled. He looked sad. As if he wanted to believe her, but it was impossible.

"What about Dirk?" Norah said. "Did you speak to him?"

"My colleague did."

"And?" she demanded. "Did he tell you? About Amy's birthday party? The pony rides?"

Long exhale. "Dirk has no knowledge of a little girl called Amy living at the farm."

"Bullshit!" Norah cried. Clenching her fist, she slammed it

into the wall, which buckled slightly; it was barely thicker than paper.

Max didn't seem concerned. "He did say . . ."

"What?" Jessica asked.

"He said he had seen you three playing with a doll that matched the description of the child."

Norah felt the rage rising in her body like the tide. It pulsed so hard she felt like she might burst out her skin.

She slammed her fist into the wall again, and again. She punched it until her knuckles bled, until her fist broke clear through the flimsy plasterboard. Then she went searching for something else to punch.

39

ALICIA

Shit. Shit shit shit. *Shit.*"

Alicia paced back and forth on the tiled side porch of the old pub. The chatter of diners inside floated out through the open windows, but the streets were deserted apart from the odd car driving through.

"Did you hear her? She's going to press charges against Norah for assault."

"And I didn't even get a punch in," Norah said miserably.

Norah and Jessica sat on an old church pew that was pressed up against the brick wall. Alicia expected that Jessica would be beside herself, but she wasn't. She was quiet. Almost spaced out.

"Jessica!" Alicia stared at her. "Do you understand what just happened? Norah has a CCO! She'll go to jail!"

"I understand that," Jessica said.

"Then why aren't you freaking out? Are you on something? Why am I the only one who's panicking?"

Jessica shrugged. "I'm sorry I can't summon the correct level of stress for you, but I assure you I'm concerned. What do you want from me?"

Alicia sank onto the pew beside them. "Sorry. I'm just . . . worried." She glanced at Norah. "But we'll work it out. Maybe Anna will be able to give us some advice."

They sat there for a few more minutes before Alicia realized what was bugging her.

"Did you guys find it weird that Miss Fairchild didn't seem anxious? I mean, if the body is Amy, it's pretty incriminating for her."

"The body *isn't* Amy," Jessica said.

"Unless it is," Alicia said.

"Alicia, would you listen to yourself?"

"Hear me out. Miss Fairchild was the adult in the house when Amy lived there. If the body is hers, she'll have some explaining to do. What will she say? That she didn't know Amy existed? That we smuggled her into the house, murdered her, and buried her without Miss Fairchild's knowledge?"

Jessica opened her mouth as if to dispute this, but before she could speak a voice said, "Pretty close."

They all turned toward the door. Patel and Hando had joined them on the porch without them noticing.

"Her current story is that she had to stop fostering babies because you three were jealous and often became agitated or even violent with the smaller children," Patel said. "She says if there is a child buried on the property that you girls are responsible." Her gaze flickered to Norah. "Norah specifically."

"Bullshit!" Norah sprung from her seat. "*She* was the one who jealous! She was the one who became agitated with the babies!"

Alicia stood and put a hand on Norah's shoulder.

"But her testimony is compelling," Patel pointed out. "You three had troubled childhoods and Norah has well-documented issues with violence. We've also seen enough to know that the three of you would do just about anything to protect each other. A lovely trait among sisters—but also a pretty powerful motivation to lie."

Alicia sank back against the brick wall. Once again, Miss Fairchild had managed to paint herself as the victim. They were still three foster kids, troubled and angry and inherently suspect.

Patel exhaled. "I just want to know what happened at Wild Meadows," she said, sounding frustrated. "I *want to know* whose bones were buried under the house."

"So do we." Jessica's voice was quiet but intense. "That's why we came here."

"Then why didn't you mention Amy from the start?" Patel exclaimed.

"We did." Jessica rose to her feet. "We *did* mention her. Twenty-five years ago, we risked everything to tell the police about Amy and no one believed she was real. Now, we get a phone call out of the blue telling us there's a body, and suddenly we're supposed to understand that now you accept she was real all along? You should be apologizing for the mistake the police made twenty-five years ago!"

Patel had the decency to look abashed at this. Hando, too, looked uncomfortable.

"So you think the bones are Amy's?" Norah asked.

Patel shrugged. "It's possible."

"Well, if there's one thing to learn from what happened twenty-five years ago," Alicia said, "it's that *we* are the ones who are telling the truth."

40

JESSICA

BEFORE

Despite appearing to doubt their story, the police were kind—perhaps because they were children. In the three hours they'd been at the station they'd been treated to an endless supply of soft drinks and chocolate, and an officer had bandaged Norah's hands so they resembled large white boxing gloves. She'd done some damage to the wall, but she hadn't got into trouble. One of the benefits of the hole was that they could now hear the conversations happening in other offices clearly. It was obviously a slow day for policing, because one hundred percent of the discussions revolved around them.

"The girls have a history of trauma," someone was saying. "The foster mother says they're all troubled and regularly invent things."

"But the part about extended time off from school was true." This was Max talking. "How does Holly explain that?"

"School refusal, apparently. She wanted them to go but they said no."

"Did she tell the school this?"

"No. The school had them down as sick days."

A long sigh. Norah swung one of her boxing gloves in the air in front of her, her eyes narrowed. "School refusal," she muttered angrily.

"Let me speak to the boy again," Max said. "To double-check."

"We've already spoken to him twice."

"I'll triple-check then."

Norah's boxing gloves shot upright, like a cheer. "Good old Max."

"Are you saying you believe these girls, Sarge?" the other voice said.

A chair scraped across the floor. "I'm saying these are serious allegations that need to be investigated. If their story is true, a child is either missing or dead. Even if they are troubled, it doesn't mean they're lying."

A few seconds later Max appeared in the doorway.

"Thanks," Norah said. "For triple-checking."

He looked surprised, then smiled. "These walls are thinner than I thought." He sat on a vinyl chair and let out a long breath. "Look. We've searched the house again from top to bottom and found nothing. Dirk is still claiming he's never seen her. And there's no record of Amy ever coming to the home. She wasn't legally adopted, she didn't come through the foster system, and she doesn't match the description of any missing children." He looked dejected. "Where else could she have come from?"

The three girls turned to each other. Not one of them was able to answer his question.

41

NORAH

Norah wasn't sure she believed in heaven, but if it existed, she thought it would resemble this fenced-off patch of dirt, with these four giant hysterical dogs.

She'd been out back collecting her dogs when Ishir had appeared.

"I was wondering where you went!" he cried, beaming at her. "Shall we throw sticks to the dogs for a bit?"

Of course Norah wanted to throw sticks.

"Banjo—fetch!"

Ishir tossed a stick in the air and Banjo leaped like a clumsy elephant. Not to be outdone, Thong, Converse, and Couch also leaped, their mismatched levels of height and coordination resulting in a cheerful dog pileup on the grass.

"Ishir!" An irate-looking waitress poked her head outside. "What the fuck are you doing? There's a full house in here. Get your ass back inside or I'm quitting!" She retreated without waiting for a response.

"Again?" Ishir said to the dogs, who all nodded.

Norah couldn't remember when she'd last enjoyed herself so much. She particularly enjoyed admiring Ishir's flexing biceps. Today he was wearing a bow tie decorated with Bert and Ernie on it. The man had style, no doubt about it.

"Do you want a turn?" he asked Norah.

"No, no," she said. "You're doing a great job."

"Must be weird," he said, between throws. "Being back here after all this time."

"It is."

"Not *good* weird, I'm guessing?"

He tossed the stick again as Norah contemplated this. At this moment, at least, it wasn't *bad* weird.

"I think my sisters are more freaked out than I am. I get it. Some scary stuff happened to us here. But for me, the scariest thing was always the prospect of being separated from Alicia and Jessica. Honestly, coming back here without having to fear that . . . it feels kind of good."

He watched her thoughtfully, seemingly unaware of the four dogs thrashing around at his feet.

"Besides," she added, "I don't blame Port Agatha for what happened to us. It's hardly the town's fault. I kind of like it here."

He threw the stick. "Not gonna lie, I was hoping you'd say that, because I've got a very old car, and I'm not sure if it could cope with driving back and forth to Melbourne every week."

Norah felt a zing in the center of her chest. "You're not very good at playing it cool, Ishir."

"No," he agreed. "Never have been."

"How's it working for you?" she said, in her American Dr. Phil voice.

"Well, I'm divorced," he said. "And I had two serious girlfriends before I was married, and one since. All of them dumped me." He threw the stick again. "So I'm gonna say not well."

"I've never married," Norah told him. "I date occasionally, mostly to get odd jobs done around the house for free. I broke the nose of my last date and sent him sexy pictures in exchange for not going to the cops."

Ishir winced. "Did it work?"

"Naturally." She was about to offer to show him when she noticed his blush.

"This is fun," he said. "Being out here with you."

Norah could see he meant it. It was extra sweet as she hadn't even shown him her boobs.

"Here . . . your turn." He handed her the stick. "Go on. Try it. It's fun."

Norah threw the stick and watched the motley crew crash into one another in their eargerness to fetch it. They looked as happy as she was feeling.

"You might be interested to know," Norah said, "that not playing it cool is working very well for you this time."

The dogs went crazy around them as they grinned at each other like idiots.

"Ishir, you asshole! Get back behind the bar before I call your mother!"

Ishir's grin faded. "Well," he said. "I guess our date is over."

"That was a *date?*"

"I hope it was."

It didn't resemble any date she had been on before. No meal, no exchange of awkward personal information, no list of odd jobs that needed doing.

No nudes required. No videos.

She didn't hate it. She didn't hate it at all.

42

ALICIA

Jessica had parked across the road from the pub, in the police station parking lot. As the three women crossed the road, a beaten-up old station wagon pulled up next to their car. A man in a baseball cap emerged from it.

"Dirk," Jessica said quietly, but there was no one else around, so her voice carried.

Alicia peered at the man. Wow, she thought. It *is* Dirk.

He hadn't aged well. The hair visible beneath his cap was still red, but there were flecks of gray, and though he was a relatively young man, his posture was stooped. He slammed the door and glanced at them over the roof of the car, smiling quizzically. He clearly didn't recognize them.

"Oh. My. God," Norah said, a few seconds behind, as usual.

"Do you remember us?" Jessica asked. "I'm Jessica. These are my sisters, Alicia and Norah. We're the foster kids that grew up at Wild Meadows."

She sounded so calm. As if she'd slowed herself down to .75, like

Alicia often did with a podcast or audiobook. Considering she was normally at least a 1.5, it was a big improvement.

Dirk's smile vanished abruptly and his eyes darted around the parking lot.

Interesting, Alicia thought. *He's nervous.*

Jessica, strangely, didn't seem nervous at all. "Can I ask you something?" she said. "The little girl the police questioned you about all those years ago. Amy. Did you really not see her?"

Dirk dug his hands into his pockets. "Look—"

"It's important," Jessica persisted, cutting him off. "Think back."

Dirk glanced toward the police station, then back at Jessica. "If I did see her," he said, "why would I lie about it?"

"You tell us," Jessica replied. "Maybe you were rewarded for lying? Or blackmailed? Or maybe *you* did something to her."

Alicia's gaze, which had been on Jessica, suddenly bounced back to Dirk. She'd always assumed he'd lied for Miss Fairchild; it had never occurred to her he might be covering his own tracks. She hadn't thought he'd be capable of harming Amy himself. Had she been wrong about that?

"I didn't do anything to her," he said, "because I never saw her."

"Bullshit!" Norah called. "If the bones turn out to be Amy's, you'll have blood on your hands."

"Hey!"

They all turned. Detective Tucker was leaning in the entrance of the police station. His relaxed posture suggested that he'd been watching them for a while.

"You ready, Dirk?"

Dirk started walking toward the station.

"If she made you lie," Jessica called after him, "it's not too late to say so."

Dirk kept his head down and his stride swift. Alicia started to wonder if Jessica might be on to something . . .

They were climbing into the car when they heard someone calling their names.

"Alicia! Jessica! Norah!"

Alicia sighed. Running into old acquaintances wherever they went was one thing about small towns that she would be glad to leave behind.

It was Zara. Her hair was braided in two plaits today, reminding Alicia of a Dutch milkmaid. It was a pretty color—cool brown glinting blond in the sunshine.

"Oh, hey, Zara," the sisters muttered with varying degrees of enthusiasm.

All Alicia wanted was to get in the car with her sisters and call Meera. Not only did they need Meera's help, Alicia needed her friend's voice to soothe her, tell her everything was going to be okay.

"Your turn to speak to the cops?" Alicia asked.

Zara nodded, her gaze fixed on the door that Dirk had just walked through. "Who was that?"

"Dirk," Norah said. "He used to look after the horses at Wild Meadows."

"Why's he talking to the cops?" Zara asked. "Is he a suspect?"

"I'm not sure they have suspects yet," Alicia said, "since they haven't identified a cause of death. Maybe it was natural?"

Zara raised an eyebrow. "A child buried in an unmarked grave under a foster home? Natural causes?"

Zara asked a lot of questions. Alicia started to wonder if she was an investigative journalist.

"What's Dirk's last name?" Zara wanted to know.

The sisters looked at each other.

"Winter-something?" Alicia said, pulling it from some part of her memory that she hadn't known existed. "Or maybe that's wrong. I don't know."

Zara got out her phone and began to type something into it.

"We need to go," Jessica said. "We're back on with our lawyer in ten minutes. Good luck with the cops, Zara."

Zara thanked them, still tapping away at her phone, and Alicia, Jessica, and Norah piled back into the car with the dogs. But as they pulled onto the street, Alicia saw Zara getting back into her own car rather than going into the police station. *Why had she lied?* Alicia wondered. *And who was she lying for?*

43

JESSICA

"Okay," Anna said when they resumed the Zoom meeting back at the cottage. "So what happened after you finished giving your statements to the police? Did you go back to Wild Meadows?"

Jessica shook her head. "A social worker took us to a respite home."

Anna wasn't taking any notes now. Jessica started to feel self-conscious, worried that she wasn't making sense. She'd taken another pill half an hour ago, after the interaction with Miss Fairchild, and she was now feeling floaty and relaxed.

"We stayed there for three months, while they looked for a permanent home that would take all three of us. They couldn't find one, and we refused to be separated, so we went to a group home, where we stayed until we aged out. Because of our 'trauma', we received on-going weekly counseling until then." She smiled wryly at her sisters. "Norah and Alicia hated it, but I quite liked it. Having someone just listen to me like that, giving me their undivided attention? I'd never experienced that before."

"And Miss Fairchild wasn't investigated further?" Anna asked.

Jessica shrugged. "Not to my knowledge. But after that day we never heard much more about it."

"Wow." Anna appeared gratifyingly appalled, eyes wide as she shook her head. "Okay, let's recap . . . You reported Miss Fairchild's abuse of Amy to the cops, but they found no sign of her in the house and no record that she existed. Then they found a doll with her name on it and decided . . . what?"

"That Amy was a figment of my imagination brought on by childhood trauma," Jessica said. "My therapist thought that Amy was the little girl inside me, the one who yearned to be loved and cared for."

"And they asserted that all three of you had the same delusion?"

Anna sounded incredulous, as if they'd been stupid for going along with it. Maybe they had. While it wouldn't have been the first instance in history of three different people imagining the same thing, it was extraordinarily rare. Jessica had often suspected that, faced with three adolescent girls who swore blind the child existed, the therapist had been forced to dig deep to find a plausible explanation.

"And you believed this?"

Alicia shrugged. "Everyone said the same thing. The police. The social workers. Our therapists. Everyone we trusted. And given the fact that there wasn't a single shred of evidence that Amy was real, what were we supposed to think?"

"You never considered the possibility that your foster mother may have killed her and hidden both her body and any sign that there'd been an infant in the house?"

"No," Jessica said.

"Why not?"

"Because that would've meant that Amy was dead."

Anna was quiet for a moment. "But now," she said, "a little girl's body has been found underneath the house."

"Yes."

She frowned deeply, fiddling with a locket around her neck.

"What is it?" Norah asked.

"I was just thinking." Anna shook her head. "If this body turns out to be Amy, it will be a monumental cock-up for the cops in Port Agatha. When it comes out, it's bound to cause a political shitstorm."

"I hadn't thought of that," Alicia said.

"Maybe not," Anna replied, sitting back in her chair. "But I guarantee *they* have."

THE OFFICE OF DR. WARREN, PSYCHIATRIST

"By the time I turned fourteen," I tell Dr. Warren, "I'd noticed John was looking at me differently. He'd comment on even the most modest of my clothes, calling them sluttish. He talked about me being a young woman and having to be mindful of men's sinful thoughts—as if I could control them. He watched closely while I cleaned—too closely. Sometimes he'd ask me to go back and redo something that required me to bend over. It was revolting."

Dr. Warren tries to look aghast, but his exhilaration shines through.

"Mum noticed it too. I caught her watching him watching me. It made me hate her even more than him. It was around that time when John started visiting me in the basement. Whenever it happened, I thought about my mother upstairs. Sitting in her chair or washing John's underclothes while her husband defiled her daughter. She knew. She must have known.

"I didn't want it to happen, let me be absolutely clear about that. Not for a single solitary moment. But when I thought about how foolish it made my mother look, how humiliating it was for her and the pain it would cause . . . it helped a little. It gave me the strength to endure it."

Dr. Warren leans forward with his elbows on his knees like a child at the movies. His eyes are hooded, his cheeks flushed. "John sexually assaulted you?"

"Yes."

"And you blamed your mother for that too?"

I nod. "It was her job to protect me from monsters. He was just the monster, doing what monsters did."

Dr. Warren writes something on his notepad. I wonder if he was quoting me for his thesis on mother-daughter issues.

"I had just turned fifteen when I realized I was pregnant."

Dr. Warren's jaw drops.

"It was the most terrifying thing that has ever happened to me. John had locked me in the basement for twenty-four hours without food and water just for answering back—what would he do when he found out I was pregnant? Fear of him finding out occupied most of my thoughts, but I was surprised to notice another emotion cropping up alongside this. Pleasure. Not about the baby; I was excited because I'd finally found a way to cause my mother even more pain and humiliation.

"'I'm pregnant,' I announced one morning at breakfast.

"John looked up from his plate. By that point, I'd managed to conceal my pregnancy for nearly five months. It was easier than I expected. When no one pays any attention to you, you can hide quite a lot. Even if they were having sex with you, as it turns out. Eventually, I realized that if I didn't tell him, John might not ever realize that I was pregnant.

"As my comment registered, John's gaze dropped to my stomach. Unlike the last few months, when I'd dressed in oversized, baggy clothes, that morning I'd made no effort to conceal my growing belly.

"My mother stood by the sink, water dripping from her rubber gloves onto the kitchen floor.

"'No,' she whispered. But she could see that it was true.

"John's expression told me I had good reason to be terrified. His lips tightened, his nostrils flared, and his giant, fat hands trembled. The fact that neither of them asked who the father was spoke volumes.

"'You filthy little whore,' John said, rising to his feet. The quiet menace in his voice was more frightening than if he'd been shouting.

"I had prepared myself. I'd packed my bag and it was on the porch. I knew John would kick me out for being pregnant, despite the fact that it was his fault. Mum would do nothing to stop him, but she'd probably feel sufficiently guilty that she'd manage to connect me with friends in Melbourne or find some money to help me get started.

"The timing of my announcement was important. I needed plenty of daylight if I was going to walk into town (I doubted John would give me a ride after what I had to say), then get a bus to Melbourne. There, I'd find a women's refuge, get on welfare, and then find a job and a place to live.

"I'd thought about this day and night since the moment I realized I was pregnant. How could I have predicted that when John found out, he wouldn't kick me out? I should have known he'd do the opposite. Put me somewhere he could keep an eye on me."

"The basement?" Dr. Warren guesses.

"Bingo."

He smiles. Then he catches himself, straightens his face, and nods somberly. "I'm so sorry."

"This time, I was in the basement for months. My mother brought me food and drink, even a few books, but she rarely spoke to me. John didn't visit at all, which was a not-insignificant blessing. He had told everyone I'd been sent off to boarding school. It was genius. No one would think to question it. When I was old enough to have finished high school, John could say I'd gone away to university, then moved overseas. If my mother and John had been more sociable, it might have been hard to hide me, but as they rarely had visitors it was possible that I could spend the rest of my days in the basement and no one would think to look for me."

Dr. Warren's face lights up. "Being locked in a basement for months on end can have serious psychological consequences for anyone, let alone a pregnant teenager," he cries.

"I realize that," I say, and he has the grace to look sheepish.

44

ALICIA

It was getting late, and Alicia was tired. Beside her on the couch, Jessica looked wrecked. Meanwhile, Norah continued to hound Anna with questions.

Even though the idea that Amy was *not* imagined had crossed Alicia's mind in the past few days, it felt too enormous to process. Alicia could have spent a hundred years reflecting on it, and it still might not have sunk in. Norah, meanwhile, had already moved on to what it meant for them now.

"What I don't understand," she was saying to Anna, "is how we'd even know it was Amy's remains under Wild Meadows. How could they identify her, if there are no records?"

"Given what you've told us, there *is* a way," Anna said. "If the child had six toes, that will show up in the coroner's report."

"Of course!" Alicia said quietly. "I hadn't thought."

"And if it *is* Amy," Norah continued, "Miss Fairchild will be charged?"

"Not necessarily," Anna said. "When a body has been buried for so long it can be hard to determine the cause of death, so it is often very difficult to make a case for murder or manslaughter. If, indeed, Miss Fairchild did murder her."

"But the fact that she denied Amy's existence . . ." Norah said.

"Is compelling, definitely," Anna said. "But let's take this one step at a time."

"Okay but . . . are you . . . feeling confident?" Norah asked. "I mean, you don't think we could be blamed for anything, do you?"

"My job is to make sure you aren't," Anna said. "Oh, one more thing: Does Dirk Winterbourne continue to deny having seen Amy?"

"As far as we know," Alicia said. "That was always the weirdest part for me. If Dirk had seen her, why didn't he say anything? The only thing I can think of is that Miss Fairchild had something on him."

Anna paused, looking thoughtful. "What if I told you I knew a reason he might lie?"

"What?" Alicia said.

"You weren't the only one talking to the police at lunchtime. I also had a conversation with a cop I know who has connections in Port Agatha. He told me that the detectives have been speaking to known sex offenders in the area at the time." Anna raised her eyebrows. "And one of them is Dirk."

Alicia, Norah, and Jessica were in the living room of their cottage, gathering their things before setting off on the two-hour drive back to Melbourne.

"It's so strange, talking about Amy after all this time," Alicia said.

"Strange" wasn't the right word. She wasn't sure what the right word might be, but "harrowing" felt closer. All day, she'd felt on the verge of tears, and after yesterday's episode the last thing she wanted was to start crying again.

"Were we stupid, believing we'd imagined Amy?" Norah asked. "I remember thinking it was ridiculous, at first. But it seemed to be settled. Maybe we should have tried harder to make them listen?"

"We were kids," Alicia said, to herself as much as Norah. "We *had* to believe what they told us."

"Maybe this body turning up is a good thing?" Norah said. She looked anxious even suggesting it, wringing her hands. "I mean, if she has six toes . . ."

"Then it's only the beginning," Jessica said. "You heard Anna. Even if they prove Amy existed, it doesn't mean that Miss Fairchild killed her. And the body's so old, it might be impossible to prove."

Alicia frowned at Jessica. It wasn't what she said; it was that her tone was off. The lack of emotion. She seemed . . . flat. She seemed *dazed.*

"Are you all right, Jess?" Alicia asked.

"Yes. Why?"

"You look kind of spaced out."

"Thanks a lot."

A phone began to ring.

"It's been a long day," Alicia said as she rummaged in her bag. "Why don't we stay here another night and drive back home tomorrow when we're fresh?"

Norah nodded her agreement, but Jessica shook her head. "Let's just go home," she said. "We'll feel better when we're back in our own beds."

Alicia located her phone and raised it to her ear. "Alicia Connelly speaking."

"Alicia, hi, it's Sonja—Jessica's business manager?"

"Hi, Sonja." She raised her eyebrows at Jessica.

"I'm sorry to bother you, but is Jessica there?" Sonja asked. "I haven't been able to reach her."

"That's weird," Alicia said. "Maybe her phone's on silent. She's right here—I'll put her on."

Alicia held the phone out to Jessica, who, oddly, took a step back. "It's just Sonja," Alicia told her. "She said she hasn't been able to reach you on your phone."

For a moment, it looked like Jessica wasn't going to take the call, but then she did. "Hi, Sonja."

Alicia couldn't hear what Sonja was saying, but she could make out her high-pitched tones of worry.

"Sorry about that," Jessica said into the phone. "Um . . . yep . . . Okay . . . I don't know . . . Hmmm."

Usually Jessica sounded so authoritative and commanding when she was in business mode. Today she sounded detached. Her posture was that of a teenager—slumped and uninterested.

"Oh," Jessica was saying. "Ah . . . Okay." Then, as she noticed Alicia and Norah watching her, "Sonja, I'm sorry, but I . . . I can't do this right now."

Then without so much as a goodbye, Jessica ended the call.

"What's going on?" Alicia said.

Jessica waved her hand airily. "Work stuff. Too boring to go into. You're right—it's been a long day, and I'm tired. Let's stay the night."

"I'll get my stuff from the car," Norah said, heading for the door, presumably before Jessica could change her mind.

"Are you sure you're okay?" Alicia asked Jessica.

"I'm fine; I just need a good night's sleep."

"All right," Alicia said. She could use that herself. "I'll just call—"

"Meera," Norah said.

"Yes," Alicia said, surprised. "How did you know?"

"No, I mean . . . *Meera.*" She pointed.

Alicia turned to the doorway.

And there she was. In jeans and a trench coat, her hair was pulled up in its signature messy bun. "Thought you could use a lawyer on the ground," she said, smiling. "Or a friend."

The tears Alicia had been holding at bay all day didn't stand a chance.

To Alicia's relief, her sisters played it cool—even Norah. They greeted Meera, thanked her for recommending Anna, and refrained from commenting when Alicia suggested they go into her bedroom so they could talk (although Norah's facial expression did speak volumes).

"I can't believe you came here," Alicia said, closing the door behind her.

"Why not?"

Meera sat on the bed, while Alicia paced the room. She felt rattled by Meera's unexpected arrival. Panicked. Thrilled. "Because . . . because why would you?"

Meera shrugged. She looked like a doll, with her long curled eyelashes, her high cheekbones, her bow lips. "Because we're friends. That's what friends do."

"Are we *friends*?"

It wasn't like Alicia to be like this. She chalked it up to the emotion of the weekend.

Meera chuckled. "Sure. Stop pacing, would you? You're stressing me out. Sit down."

Alicia caught her reflection in the mirror on the wall. She was a wreck. She ran her hands through her hair to try to smooth it, but the effort proved staggeringly ineffective. Then she sat next to Meera on the bed, but her heart continued to race. It was Meera's presence. Somehow it both comforted her and made her nervous simultaneously. Her knee began to jiggle. "Sorry."

Meera laughed. "For God's sake," she said, shaking her head. Then she leaned over and kissed Alicia on the lips.

45

JESSICA

After Meera and Alicia disappeared into Alicia's room, Jessica decided to retire to her own. It had been a good idea to stay another night, she decided. It wouldn't have been safe for her to drive with all these thoughts spiraling in her head—not to mention the Valium in her system. Sleep would give her some respite for a few hours. Under the circumstances, it was the best Jessica could hope for.

She lay on the scratchy bed linen and closed her eyes, trying to find an aspect of her life that she could focus on without feeling positively ill. There wasn't one. It had happened so quickly—the unravelling of Jessica's carefully structured life. Or had it? Perhaps it had been slowly falling apart for a while.

According to Sonja, the situation was looking pretty dire. A half dozen complaints since yesterday, all about pills going missing from bathroom cabinets and bedside tables, and now Debbie was threatening to go to the police as well as the media. Normally Jessica would have run toward a disaster like this, desperate to get on top of it before it got on top of her. But today she didn't have it in her. If she was honest, today she actually *wanted* things to implode—and to take her down—so she wouldn't have to deal, to be responsible and hold it all together. Because then she would have peace.

At the edges of her consciousness, Jessica became aware of a hushed, disagreeable conversation taking place outside the cottage. A marital argument, perhaps. She and Phil rarely argued. They were polite—too polite. Maybe they needed to argue more. Connect more.

"What is the matter with you?" an irritated voice said.

Jessica couldn't help but tune in. Even through her fog, someone else's misery was a siren.

"Dirk?" the voice said. "Did you hear me?"

Jessica sat upright. It wasn't just the name Dirk that had caught her attention; it was the person saying it. Miss Fairchild.

She got to her feet and crept across the room to peer through the window.

"What was I supposed to think?" Dirk said. "You lied to me."

"Oh, come on." Miss Fairchild laughed nastily. "Really? You're really saying . . ."

Jessica didn't hear the rest, because she was already striding out her door and into the living room. It may have been the Valium that stopped her from overthinking, or panicking. Or maybe it was the fact that, even after all these years, Jessica was powerless to resist Miss Fairchild's magnetic pull.

She threw open the cottage door. "What are you doing here?" she demanded.

Dirk and Miss Fairchild turned to face her, clearly startled.

Miss Fairchild recovered first, a warm smile spreading across her face. "Jessica! What a lovely surprise."

"What are you doing here?" Jessica repeated. She didn't return the smile.

Dirk was already walking to his car, replacing his baseball cap on his head.

"Dirk wanted to talk to me," Miss Fairchild said. "We decided to meet here. I didn't know you were staying in this place."

"Why did he want to talk to you?"

Miss Fairchild shrugged, but Jessica saw a flash of irritation cross her face. She lowered her voice. "I think he might have a guilty conscience. Did you know he is a sex offender?"

Jessica nodded. "Our lawyer told us."

"She did?" Miss Fairchild looked surprised. "What else did she tell you?"

"None of your business," Jessica snapped.

It felt wrong, speaking to her former foster mother like that. For a moment, Jessica thought Miss Fairchild might reprimand her. Instead, she smiled. "It hurts to see you so upset with me, Jessica. I know the other girls don't like me. I *understand* it. They had a terrible childhood and I was the scapegoat." She shook her head sadly. "But it was different with you and me. We were *connected*."

Jessica raked a hand through her hair, losing her resolve. "We were."

"I've kept an eye on you, you know," Miss Fairchild continued, still smiling. "I couldn't help myself. I've been so proud of your success. You must have heard me, cheering you along."

Jessica stared at her. She felt both appalled and touched by what the woman was saying, and also strangely detached from it, as if it had nothing to do with her. Perhaps it didn't.

"I've been worried about you, too," she went on. "Addiction is common among foster kids. A way to escape the pain of abandonment."

Now Jessica felt herself reattach to reality. Her expression must have given away her shock, because Miss Fairchild put a hand on each of Jessica's shoulders.

"Of course I know about it," she said. "I'm your mother, Jessica, in every way that counts. I know everything about you. I always have."

Jessica stepped back, away from Miss Fairchild's touch.

"Don't do that," Miss Fairchild said, stepping forward. "Let me help you, darling girl. Let me bear some of your load. Shh. It's okay to cry. Let it out."

She reached for Jessica again, and this time Jessica didn't have the strength to back away. Instead, she surged forward into her mother's arms and started to cry. How she *wanted* her mother.

More than anything, she wanted her mother.

46

NORAH

Norah was relieved when everyone retreated into their bedrooms so she could finally do the same. There, she lay in the
middle of her bed, surrounded by dogs, and turned her mind to the
subject she'd been avoiding all day.

Kevin had texted twice more, saying how much he was looking
forward to her video. With the second message, he sent links of
some examples he'd seen online. Norah had had to turn them off
before she'd finished. She wasn't a prude, but it was really quite
repulsive. Some of it looked painful. The idea that it came from
weaselly Kevin made it all the more repulsive.

It's a transaction, she told herself. *No big deal.* And yet, somehow,
she found she didn't believe it.

*I suspect your skewed idea of sex and its power stems from your
childhood.*

Her therapist's comment had echoed loudly in Norah's ears all day. Though she'd never admit it to Neil, she was starting to think he had a point. As a child, Norah had had very little power. She'd had to use every means at her disposal to keep herself safe, to have some agency in her life. It just so happened that "every means at her disposal" meant sex and violence.

It was true that, as an adult, she had more tools in her kit. She had money—not a lot, but enough. She had food in her fridge. She had the dogs to protect her and her sisters to support her. In most situations, it was possible for her to do things differently from how she'd always done them. Pay for someone to do odd jobs for her. Tell people to go away rather than hit them. Save sex for—what had Neil said?—mutual pleasure. After those few moments this afternoon with Ishir and the dogs that afternoon, it was certainly an idea that she could get behind—in the future. But in the meantime, she had a problem she needed to deal with *right now*. And once again, as in childhood, she was powerless.

She pushed the dogs off her and sat up. The room was small and devoid of props, but she pulled the throw from the bed and arranged the pillows on top, propping her up her phone on the coffee table. Then she stripped off and sat down. The dogs were watching curiously from the bed.

"A little privacy, please?" Norah said.

They all ignored her, of course.

"Guys," she said. She'd thought she was speaking in her usual conversational tone, the same tone she used when they'd eaten one of her shoes, or killed the neighbor's rabbit. Instead, it came out scratchy, pitchy, rising into a squeak like someone starting to cry.

She was, she realized, starting to cry.

By the time she'd noted her own tears, the dogs were already getting up off the bed and circling around her on the floor, before pressing their great hefts against her comfortingly. It only made things feel more hopeless. She began to sob in earnest, her entire body heaving with it. "Stop it," she said to the dogs. "Stop comforting me. I have a video to make and I can't do it with you three lying on the set."

She wiped her face with her forearm and stood. She'd have to let them out. It was better for everyone if they didn't have to see what she was doing. She stepped into her jeans and T-shirt, and walked through the living room. The moment she opened the front door of the cottage, the dogs burst out into the night in search of nocturnal animals to torment. Norah was about to shut the door again when she saw them.

Miss Fairchild. And Jessica. Hugging.

47

ALICIA

Meera's skin was baby-soft. She smelled of oranges. It was madness, how good it felt to kiss her. Better than anything Alicia had ever felt.

"I can't believe you came here," she said between kisses. "How did you know I needed you? *I* didn't even know I needed you."

Meera's smiled. "Who said I knew? Maybe I needed *you*."

She started to undo the buttons on Alicia's shirt. "Is the door locked?" she asked.

Alicia nodded, then grabbed the remote control and turned the TV on. "To block out the noise."

Meera laughed. "Your poor sisters."

She climbed onto Alicia, kissing her playfully. Then Meera lifted her hips, and Alicia pulled off her jeans.

"Alicia," Meera said when they were naked, their bare legs intertwined. "You are so fucking gorgeous."

Alicia's kisses slowed. "No I'm not."

Meera pulled her closer. "You *are*. You know that, don't you?"

Alicia shook her head.

"There are so many great things about you," Meera said, her mouth traveling around Alicia's body. "You're funny . . . you always do what you say you will . . . you enjoy feedback, even if it's not positive . . . you speak up, when no one else is prepared to . . . you care about vulnerable people . . ." Her mouth was on Alicia's breast now. "You have amazing breasts . . . particularly this one. To be honest, it's my *favorite* breast."

Meera rose up to kiss Alicia's lips, then stopped short.

"Al," she said. "Why are you crying?"

"Shit." Alicia wiped at her face. "Shit, sorry."

"Don't be sorry," Meera said. "Just tell me what's going on."

But Alicia was already sitting up, retrieving her shirt from the floor. "Nothing. I just . . . I can't do this."

As she pulled on her clothes, Alicia hated herself. She should have known this would happen. She couldn't have a normal relationship. She was an idiot to get swept up—and, worse, to allow Meera to think something could happen between them.

Meera pulled her own clothes on and sat silently on the bed beside Alicia.

"I can't talk about it," Alicia said, preempting Meera's questions.

Before Meera could respond, there was a knock at the door.

"Alicia?" It was Norah.

"Not now, Norah," Alicia called.

"I'm sorry if you're having kinky lesbian sex, but it's an *emergency*."

"Norah," Alicia replied. "For God's sake—"

The door opened. Guess it wasn't locked after all.

"I *said* it was an emergency," Norah told her. "I need you to come out here. Now."

48

NORAH

NOW

After rousing Alicia and Meera, Norah flew back outside and ran toward Jessica and Miss Fairchild.

"Get your hands off her!" she cried, breaking them apart with such force that Miss Fairchild hit the stone wall of the cottage hard. Jessica would have fallen backward in the opposite direction had Norah not caught her elbow and righted her.

"You violent little thug!" Miss Fairchild gasped. She sounded winded. "You can't help yourself, can you?"

Norah was also out of breath. She tasted bile. She looked at Jessica, who was teary and shamefaced. It was hard to tell from her expression if she was happy or sad to have been interrupted.

Alicia and Meera emerged from the cottage. "What the hell is going on?" Alicia demanded.

Miss Fairchild hesitated. The presence of Meera had rattled her, Norah realized. She'd always had different personas for outsiders, and it was funny to watch as she floundered, unsure what mask to wear.

"I was talking to Jessica when Norah assaulted me—*again*."

"I was protecting Jessica," Norah said. "Miss Fairchild was *hugging her*!"

Alicia's gaze moved to Jessica. She looked as appalled as Norah felt.

"Jessica didn't need protection," Miss Fairchild said. "She was just fine—weren't you, Jessica?"

They all looked at Jessica, who gaped back at them like a little girl.

Alicia walked over and put an arm around her shoulders.

"I think you should go, Miss Fairchild," Alicia said.

Miss Fairchild held her hands up, perhaps in an attempt to appear reasonable for Meera's sake. "Listen. I know things ended badly between us, but don't you think this could be an opportunity—now that we've been brought back together again after all these years?"

"Yes," Alicia said. "It's an opportunity for us to get justice for Amy."

Norah came to stand on Jessica's other side. Miss Fairchild watched them, her face twisting bitterly. "For God's sake, when will you girls ever let up about *Amy*? The police already decided she was nothing but a fantasy."

"When they identify the body as Amy's," Norah said, "which they *will*, when the coroner sees her extra toe, you're going to have some explaining to do."

"Except they won't identify her—because it's not Amy." She sounded so sure of herself.

"Who is it then? Some other child you killed?"

Miss Fairchild took a breath, as if suddenly overcome by emotion.

"Do you really think I'd kill a child? What kind of monster do you think I am?"

She looked to Jessica for help. The fact that she expected support from Jessica after everything she'd done filled Norah with sudden rage.

"What I want to know is how you knew to get rid of Amy that day," she said, narrowing her eyes at Miss Fairchild. "Did you know we were planning to report you, or was it just a coincidence?"

"Oh." Miss Fairchild's gaze flicked to Jessica, and for a moment she seemed almost amused. "You didn't tell them?"

Jessica's cheeks flamed. Norah wasn't sure what was going on, but she took a protective step in front of her sister.

"You girls always seemed so perplexed when I knew things," Miss Fairchild continued, seeming happier now. "Meanwhile, the school was always going on about how smart you were, Norah!"

Norah glanced back over her shoulder. Jessica's head remained down.

"I had an informant, of course. Jessica told me everything. *Everything*. Right up until that final day."

"What?" It took a moment to reframe her memories. And then she realized: it was obvious. All the little things that no one knew but the three of them. Of course Jessica told her. How else could she have known?

She turned to face her sister. "You *told her*?"

She recalled the day they'd reported Miss Fairchild. Jessica running back inside for her schoolbag. *Jessica* had tipped her off that she needed to erase every trace of Amy.

"How could you *do* that?" Norah cried.

A tear dripped off Jessica's chin.

"You three might be thick as thieves now," Miss Fairchild said, clearly enjoying herself, "but Jessica was loyal to me before she even met you. She probably always will be." She looked triumphant.

Norah's fists began to clench.

"Just to be clear," Alicia said to Miss Fairchild, "there's only one person we blame for any of this, and that's you."

Miss Fairchild rolled her eyes. "Lucky me," she said. "Getting to be the scapegoat for all of your troubles!"

She gave an odd little laugh as she walked a few paces toward her car.

"You're only a scapegoat if you didn't actually do the thing you're being accused of," Norah said.

Miss Fairchild stopped, turned. "Which is what? Killing a child?" She laughed. "What I want to know is, if I'm supposed to be a child killer, why did I let the three of you live?"

It was a good question, Norah realized. One that none of them had an answer for.

"The truth is," Miss Fairchild continued, turning back toward her car, "I'm as keen as you are to find out who is under that house and how they got there."

49

JESSICA

barely touched her," Norah said to Meera, who was already asking questions.

"She hit the wall," Jessica pointed out, closing the door to their cottage. But she didn't care. At the moment, she found it hard to care about anything. She sat on the arm of the sofa, wrapping her arms around herself where Miss Fairchild's arms had just been. She could still feel the warmth of her skin. Still *smell* her.

Alicia looked at Meera. "What happens if she claims Norah assaulted her?"

"The only witness is Jessica, so she can say what she wants."

Meera's face was completely straight. Alicia smiled. Norah gave her a high five.

"The other incident is trickier," Meera continued. "A report has been filed. But we can talk about that later."

"Jess," Alicia said, her eyes resting on her, "about what Miss

Fairchild said out there, I meant what I said: Norah and I could never blame you for telling Miss Fairchild we were going to report her. Never ever."

Jessica looked at Norah, whose expression was far less forgiving.

"She groomed you to please her, ever since you were a little girl," Alicia continued, more loudly, as if to make up for Norah. "You think we would blame you for that?"

"You may not blame me, but I blame myself." Jessica's eyes filled. "I blamed myself even when I thought we'd imagined Amy. But now . . ." Her voice cracked and she stopped, took a breath. "If hers is the body under the house, it's my fault."

"No," Alicia said, shaking her head. "No."

Jessica was nodding. "It is. I never intended to tell her. When I went back into the house, I was just going to get my bag. But then I saw Miss Fairchild sitting with Amy, singing to her." She wiped away a tear with her fist. "I was jealous. I knew how to ingratiate myself with Miss Fairchild. And so I did what I always did: I told her what we were planning to do. I'd done it all my life. All those times you wondered how she knew stuff—it was me." Now she was sobbing. "I didn't expect her to kill Amy. She didn't have a lot of time, but she probably had enough. And all because I was jealous of a toddler."

Everyone was quiet. After a moment, Norah opened her mouth to speak.

"Don't . . ." Jessica held up her hands like stop signs. "Please don't say anything. I'm not ready. I think we should all go to bed now. We can talk in the morning."

She felt like a zombie—like she was sleepwalking—as she closed her bedroom door. Oddly untethered, she seemed to be feeling everything and nothing at once. It reminded her of having a local anesthetic for stitches, how you could feel the doctor tugging your skin but you couldn't feel the pain. But with it went the knowledge that once the injection wore off, the pain would hit. Jessica didn't know if she would be able to withstand it.

She sat on the bed. She needed sleep. Deep, dreamless sleep. On her bedside table sat a just-in-case vial of Valium and a bottle of water. She didn't pause to think; she just tipped two pills into her hand, popped them into her mouth, and washed them down with the water. She was about to lie back down when she changed her mind and reached for the pills again. Tipped out a few more. And a few more after that. A swill of water and the job was done. Finally. Sleep was coming.

THE OFFICE OF DR. WARREN, PSYCHIATRIST

The next time I see Dr. Warren, he is asking questions before I even sit down.

"So you were in the basement," he says. "What was the plan for when the baby came?"

"That's what I wanted to know. My mother didn't seem to have any idea.

"'I'll ask John,' she said when I asked, which was her answer to everything. Sometimes I wondered what the hell she was thinking about. I'd started to notice bruises on her, more and more each time. On her arms mostly, and occasionally her face. Once, she had a ring of bruises around the base of her throat. So it was possible that she was thinking about that. She was so entirely under John's thumb . . . which meant I was too.

"'Don't lock the door,' I'd beg every time she left.

"'I'm sorry,' she always said, before latching it shut.

"When I pressed her, she told me the plan was to say the baby was hers. It felt weak to me. Mum seemed too old to have a baby—though she was in her mid-forties, so I supposed it was possible.

"'But what's going to happen when I go into labor?' I demanded. 'Who will take me to the hospital?'

"When she finally responded, I wished I'd never asked.

"'You'll give birth here,' she told me. 'I've been doing some reading about home birth. It's how most women give birth in India and Africa. It's going to be fine.'

"'Will you listen to yourself?' I cried. 'What would Dad say if he knew you had locked me in a dungeon and were planning to deliver my child in secret? What if I go into labor and you don't know because I'm down here? The baby could die. *I* could die!'

"She looked me right in the eye and for a second I thought I might have reached her.

But then she turned and walked up the stairs.

"The door was closed. Latched. And the last piece of my sanity smashed into a million pieces."

Dr. Warren just sits there, shaking his head. "This wasn't in your file."

"Well, no," I say. "It wouldn't be, would it?"

"So you had the baby at home?" he says. "In the basement?"

"I went into labor a month before Mum thought I would, but considering I'd had no ultrasounds to confirm my due date, that wasn't a huge surprise. I'd had cramping on and off all day—Braxton-Hicks contractions, Mum said, after consulting her library book. I knew it was more than Braxton-Hicks. A woman knows. Equally, I had no interest in telling my mother that I was in labor. I'd have sooner delivered the baby dead than allow her to assist me.

"When labor began in earnest, it was hard and fast and blindingly painful. The pains got worse and worse until I thought I might die . . . but then I reached down and felt her tiny, warm head. I can't even begin to describe the experience to you—it was awful and wonderful, and . . . and I'd never felt so vitally important."

Dr. Warren inhales deeply, shaking his head. "You gave birth alone, in the basement?"

I nod. "Her name came to me as I held her to my chest. Amy was a character in a book I'd read. In the book, her mother said she'd chosen the name for its meaning—'beloved.' I'd never heard anything more perfect."

I reach up and flick away a rogue tear.

"I had no scissors to cut the cord, so Amy remained attached to me until my mother brought my breakfast in the morning."

"Wow," Dr. Warren says. "An experience like that. I can see how that would change you."

"It does," I say. "It did. But not nearly as much as what happened next."

50

NORAH

"Meera?"

Alicia and Meera were headed back to Alicia's room when Norah stopped them.

"Before you go and do whatever it is you lesbians do, could I have a word?"

"Can't it wait, Norah?" Alicia asked. "It's been a long day."

"It's just . . ." She felt awkward suddenly. Norah wasn't used to feeling awkward. "I could use some legal advice."

"It's fine, Al," Meera said, sitting back down on the couch next to Norah. "Is Anna not working out?"

"It's not that," Norah said. "Anna's great. It's about . . . something else."

She shot a glance at Alicia, who looked panicked.

"What have you done?" Alicia asked, looking defeated. She fell into the armchair.

"It's not a big deal," Norah said. "But remember that guy I punched on Friday? He's asked me to make a porn video."

Alicia whimpered, dropping her head into her hands.

But Meera was unflustered. "Alicia, there's a notepad in my bag, can you grab it?" Then she looked at Norah. "Let's start at the beginning."

51

ALICIA

NOW

W hat's going to happen to Norah?" Alicia asked Meera, when they were finally back in Alicia's bedroom.

It was after midnight by the time Norah and Meera had finished talking. Meera had been reassuring, as she always was, but now that it was just the two of them, Alicia wanted to understand what this really meant for her sister.

"As far as the CCO goes," Meera said, "it will depend on the judge. But given the extenuating circumstances—specifically, the fact that she'd just learned about the bones being found under the foster home in which she'd spent her childhood—I'd hope the judge would be lenient."

"And what about Kevin?"

Alicia seethed even saying his name. She wanted to punch that weasel-ferret man in the face for what he'd done—and felt oddly glad that that was exactly what Norah had done, even if it was what had got her into this mess. More than anything, though, she felt weak with gratitude that Norah had decided to confide in Meera before sending him the goddamn porn video he was requesting.

Norah had been quite matter-of-fact in her reporting of events to Meera, but Alicia knew her well enough to see how rattled she was. Even though Norah was perhaps the most dangerous person Alicia knew, she was also one of the most vulnerable. And no matter how old they were, Alicia would never be able to turn off her instinct to protect her sister. Neither, she knew, would Jessica, she knew.

"Kevin messed with the wrong girl," Meera said evenly. "And we're gonna nail his ass to the wall."

Despite everything, Alicia smiled. "Is that a promise?"

Meera smiled back. "Have I ever let you down?"

"No," Alicia said. "Which makes me feel so much worse."

She sank onto the bed, which she was planning to offer to Meera for the night. It was the least she could do. "I'm so sorry about all of this. You really got more than you bargained for when you came here. Dysfunctional sisters, criminal charges, a run-in with my monster of a former foster mother."

Meera remained standing. "It makes sense," she said thoughtfully.

Alicia wasn't sure what she was referring to. There were so many possibilities. "What makes sense?"

"The fact that kindness, or hearing anyone say nice things to you, would make you cry, after the childhood you had."

Alicia didn't respond.

"When cruelty becomes familiar in your tender, adolescent years, of course you start to become comfortable with it. You believe you deserve it. But you don't."

Now Meera sat down on the bed too. Alicia risked a look at her. It was a mistake. Her brown eyes were too warm, too full of understanding. Tears began to well in Alicia's eyes immediately.

"What I'm telling you is nothing you haven't told a hundred foster kids, Al. And you know what else you tell them? That they will learn to become familiar with kindness if they open their hearts to it."

Alicia looked at the carpet. It was very hard to shrug Meera off when she was speaking the truth. Alicia thought of all the foster kids she'd worked with who'd been unable to process kindness. One of her long-term cases, a teenage boy called Marco, used to punch himself in the face reflexively every time someone gave him a compliment. Marco had done quite well in therapy. The last time she saw him, she'd told him it was good to see him, and he'd grinned in response.

"I know you're not a fan of therapy," Meera said. "But if it helps you to move forward, isn't it worth it? It's going to be pretty hard for us to have a relationship if I can't even say a nice word to you."

Alicia glanced up in surprise. "A . . . relationship?"

"Yours and mine," Meera clarified. "Our relationship. And all your other relationships, I guess. It can only be a good thing, right?"

Alicia stared at her. Surely, after everything that had happened, she wasn't sticking around? There was only so much a person could take, right?

Alicia opened her mouth to tell Meera this, but her throat clogged with tears. Meera tugged her shoulder, and Alicia fell against her, heaving.

"You are beautiful, Alicia," she said. "Kind. Loving. Smart." She paused, and Alicia felt her smile. "And it has to be said, I fucking *love* your right breast."

She was still crying when they began kissing, and when Meera started to peel off Alicia's clothes. This time, she cried and cried . . . but she didn't push Meera away.

Afterward, lying with her head on Meera's shoulder, Alicia felt bone-tired. Yet sleep wouldn't come. It was as if there were a fly in the room: something was buzzing around in her head and she yearned to swat it away.

"What is it?" Meera asked, when Alicia finally sat up.

"It's Jessica." Alicia turned on the lamp. "I'm worried about her. She didn't seem herself tonight. I want to check on her."

Meera patted her leg and smiled. "Go on," she said. "Go check."

Walking into the living room, Alicia bumped into Norah.

"What the hell?" Alicia cried. "What are you doing?"

"Checking on Jessica."

"You too?"

Norah nodded. "She doesn't seem right. She won't be asleep . . . let's go talk to her."

And so they barged into Jessica's room with the confidence of sisters. But to their surprise, Jessica *was* asleep. The hallway light illuminated her, curled up on her side, hands clasped in prayer under one ear. Drool shimmered down the side of her face. She was *snoring*.

"We can talk to her in the morning," Alicia said.

They were about to close the door, when Norah said: "Did she vomit?"

Alicia opened the door again. On second look, she saw that Norah was right. It wasn't drool on her face. It was vomit.

As they crept toward her, Alicia noticed a bottle of pills on the bedside table. She hurried over and seized it. Benzodiazepine.

She flicked on the bedside light. Jessica's lips were blue.

"Call an ambulance!" Alicia shouted at Norah. Turning, she slapped Jessica hard across the face and waited for her to sit up angrily and ask what the fuck they were doing. She didn't. Her eyes remained closed. The snoring sound they'd heard was actually more of a gurgling. "Jesus. Tell them to hurry!"

Jessica was rushed out of the ambulance, straight into Emergency. Even Alicia, who'd traveled in the ambulance with her, hadn't been able to keep up with them, and was stopped at the double doors when she got there.

Meera had followed the ambulance in her car, with Norah in the passenger seat. Now the three of them stood in front of a tired-looking, ponytailed emergency nurse in scrubs and sneakers who was examining the empty bottle of pills.

"Ada Rogers," she said, reading the name on the label aloud. "Any idea who that is?"

Alicia and Norah shook their heads. Alicia had never heard of Ada Rogers.

"Were you aware your sister was abusing benzos?"

They blinked at each other stupidly. The humiliating thing was that they'd always considered themselves so close. Closer even than biological sisters, they'd tell people. They felt each other's feelings before they felt them themselves. It had been a source of pride; a badge of honor.

And yet they hadn't known.

It was true Alicia had thought Jessica was acting strangely. She'd even asked if she was on something—but she hadn't really meant it. Why had she allowed herself to be so easily reassured? Why hadn't she pushed it? Jessica had been unnaturally calm; Alicia should have *known* something was wrong.

"Are you sure this is the drug your sister took?" the nurse asked.

"No," Alicia said. "But this is what we found at her bedside."

"Was she taking any other substances that you're aware of? Any opioids?"

"I don't think so," Alicia said. She looked at Norah, who shrugged.

"Alcohol?"

"No," they said together.

A gurney came flying through Emergency and they all had to squeeze against the wall to allow it to pass. When it was gone, Norah said, "She's going to be okay, right?"

"It depends on how much she has taken," the nurse said. "An overdose of benzodiazepines is very serious. It can produce severe and prolonged respiratory distress. Her breathing rate wasn't great when she arrived."

Alicia found it hard to hear the words. She was too focused on the nurse's serious expression. She hadn't immediately reassured them. She wasn't smiling and telling her Jessica would be okay. She looked sober. Guarded. It scared the crap out of Alicia.

"But she's not going to die, is she?" Alicia asked.

The nurse's expression didn't change. "We will do everything we can for her. But at this point we can't rule out the possibility that the overdose may be fatal." Now her face softened into something like sympathy. "I would suggest you call any close family members as soon as possible."

52

NORAH

NOW

Norah and Alicia slept on the plastic seats in the waiting room. Meera left at some point to feed the dogs, and returned a little while later with blankets and pillows and bottles of water. Now she'd gone for coffees.

"Ew," Norah said to Alicia, wiping her shoulder. "You drooled on me."

"Nothing your dogs haven't done to me before," Alicia said defensively.

"But they're *dogs!*" Norah said emphatically. She was about to describe all the reasons this was more disgusting, then stopped.

Jessica.

She shot to her feet. "Where's that nurse?"

The nurse had been their lifeline when they brought their sister in. Norah appreciated that she didn't try to placate them with false hope, and for this reason trusted her implicitly. The last time they'd spoken to her, she'd told them Jessica was breathing with assistance, but hadn't regained consciousness.

Phil had his phone on silent, so they hadn't been able to reach him until this morning. He was on his way now.

"Do you think she meant to—?" Norah started, but Alicia cut her off.

"Absolutely not," Alicia said. "She would never have done that to us."

Norah shrugged. "Maybe you're right."

"But that's the problem, isn't it? She wouldn't do it to *us*. She's always thinking about what other people want, never about what she wants."

"Guess who taught her that?" Norah said.

Alicia looked around for the nurse, but she was nowhere to be seen.

"Hey," Meera said, appearing with a tray of takeaway coffees. "I got these from the service station but it should still be better than the stuff they serve here."

Norah grabbed a coffee, took a sip, then immediately spat it out. It tasted horrible. "Thanks, Meera," she said. She didn't want to be impolite.

Alicia took a coffee and kissed Meera on the mouth. Norah wondered if they were dating. She hoped they were. Alicia was different with Meera around. She stood taller. They had the subtle chemistry of people with a deep connection—their movements felt in sync, their words blended artfully.

Norah liked Meera. She'd driven Norah to the hospital, exceeding the speed limit enough to show an appreciation of the gravity of the situation but not so much as to risk more tragedy. She hadn't offered Norah any baseless assurances. She'd brought coffee (it wasn't her fault it was disgusting). Norah could handle having her around. She just prayed Alicia wouldn't fuck it up.

"Hey, Norah," Meera said. "Take a look at this."

She handed Norah her phone, which displayed a news article. Norah scanned the headline.

Primary School Vice Principal Quits
After Pornography Extortion Scandal—
Leaked Text Messages Released

Norah looked up. "Meera!"

She raised her hand to give the woman a high five, but Meera was unavailable because Alicia was already kissing her. Under the circumstances, Norah let it slide.

"More to come, regarding legal charges," Meera added, when she came up for air, "but at least he won't be working around children anymore. He's still blocked from your phone, isn't he?"

Norah nodded.

"Good. Keep it that way, okay?"

Norah nodded again, feeling the tight sensation in her chest loosen for the first time in days.

"Did you speak to Phil?" Meera asked Alicia, when they broke apart.

She nodded. "He's on his way."

"Great," she said. "And how's Jessica?"

"We were about to go looking for an update."

"I'll go," Norah said, already walking in the direction of the nurses' station. She'd just reached the desk when her phone began to ring. She lifted it to her ear. *"What?"*

The nurse at the desk looked up, startled. Norah shook her head, pointing at the phone and rolling her eyes.

"Norah?" the voice said.

"Obviously."

"Uh . . . it's Detective Hando. I know it's early, but we've just heard from the coroner and wanted to give you an update. We've tried to get in touch with your sisters but haven't been able to reach them."

"Alicia's phone is dead and Jessica overdosed on Valium, so it's just me."

She couldn't quite work out if she was trying to be shocking, or lighthearted or even amusing. Judging by the silence that followed, Hando wasn't sure either.

"Norah, I'm so sorry. Is Jessica all right?"

"I don't know. I'm at the nurses' station now trying to get an update."

She looked at the nurse, who nodded and picked up a phone. She didn't need further details. It was a small country hospital; there was hardly an abundance of patients who'd overdosed. Norah heard her ask for an update on Jessica Lovat.

Alicia and Meera appeared at Norah's side.

"We were hoping you could come in to the station," Hando said, "but under the circumstances . . ." He trailed off uncertainly.

"It's Detective Hando," Norah said to Alicia, covering the phone. "They've heard from the coroner and want us to go in."

"We should check with Anna," Alicia said.

"He said it's important," Norah said.

"I can go with you," Meera said. "Stand-in legal counsel."

"Jessica hasn't woken up, but she remains stable," the nurse at the desk broke in.

"The station isn't far," Alicia said. "We could be back here in five minutes if we need to be."

"Fine," Norah said. "Meera can drive."

THE OFFICE OF DR. WARREN, PSYCHIATRIST

I can't wait to get to my next session with Dr. Warren. The thing about sharing a story like mine is that it doesn't just stop when you're not telling it. It continues to play out in my mind continuously. It is a relief to be able to speak it out loud.

Dr. Warren seems just as happy to see me. He has moved our seats a little closer together, and there is a box of tissues on the window ledge. I find these small gestures touching.

"The plan was for me to breastfeed until John said I was allowed to leave," I begin. "Then I would go to the city, and never return. But I didn't see how I could do that. My daughter's attention was like heroin. She had fair, wispy hair, blue eyes and a dimpled chin. She slept well and didn't fuss. My mother was smitten with her too. When John wasn't home, she and I would spend hours cooing at her. Mum knitted little stuffed animals for her. She even knitted her a life-sized doll with blond hair and blue eyes that looked exactly like Amy, with Amy's name written across her chest. Amy loved her grandmother, but there was no competition when it came to who she loved most. Me. No one came before me.

"With Mum visiting the basement so often to see Amy, I started looking forward to the sound of the door opening. But then, about six weeks after Amy was born, the door opened late one night. It was late. Usually my mother visited during the day, when John was at work. I shielded my eyes from the light as I watched the stairs for her legs. But they weren't my mother's legs descending. They were John's."

Satisfyingly, Dr. Warren puts a hand to his mouth. It is hard to believe he is an actual psychiatrist. He looks like someone watching a scary movie.

"John had been drinking," I continue. "It was always worse when he'd been drinking. The fact that I'd recently given birth didn't help matters, nor the fact that it had been a while since he'd visited. Somehow, he'd become more depraved. More disgusting. And my pregnancy had provided the perfect justification for what he was doing. Because I was dirty. I was a whore.

"While I could never say his drunkenness was a good thing, it was probably the reason he forgot to latch the door properly when he left that night. From where I lay downstairs on the mattress, I saw it creak open, allowing a thin strip of light through.

"I moved quickly, wrapping Amy in a blanket and collecting our things into a sheet, tying the ends in a knot to create a makeshift bag. I crept up the stairs then dashed through the kitchen and let myself out the back door. I didn't have any particular plan. I could go to Troy's place, I figured, and hide out in his rumpus room until I worked out what to do next.

"I was halfway down the porch steps when I heard a soft cough behind me. When I turned, my mother was standing on the porch in her nightie. 'Take this,' she said.

"In the moonlight, I saw she was holding the tin of money John kept hidden in the rice.

"She pressed it into my hand. 'Good luck,' she said, kissing Amy's head."

Dr. Warren looks a little teary. "That was brave of her."

I snort. "It was for Amy, not for me. When it was just me,

she wouldn't even unlock the bloody door to the basement. Then Amy comes along and she risks everything to give us their entire savings?"

Dr. Warren's silence tells me I've made my point.

53

ALICIA

NOW

They arrived at the police station at the same time as Bianca, Zara, and Rhiannon.

"You got here fast," Patel observed as they entered the foyer together. "Why don't we head into the meeting room?"

"Hando told me about Jessica," Patel said to Alicia as they walked down the corridor. "How is she doing?"

"No change."

The room she led them to looked like any other crappy meeting room—ugly blue carpet, shiny pine table, a whiteboard at one end.

"What happened to Jessica?" asked a voice behind them.

Alicia whirled around. It was Miss Fairchild.

"Don't," Alicia said, holding up a hand. "Don't you *dare* say her name."

Meera put a hand on her shoulder. "Al."

"What do you mean?" Miss Fairchild looked surprised and irritated. She didn't like not knowing things. "Where is she?"

A small part of Alicia wanted the woman to be aware of what she'd done. Another didn't want to give her the satisfaction of knowing the power she still held over Jessica.

"Alicia?" Miss Fairchild prompted.

"She doesn't want you to know, you stupid woman," Dirk said, appearing behind her.

Miss Fairchild glared at him, incensed. "How dare you?"

It was chaotic in the little room, with everyone talking. "Which ones are the police officers?" Meera whispered to Alicia. She hadn't yet introduced herself as their legal counsel.

"Dirk," Patel said. "This is a private—"

"I just have something to say," he said. "About Amy."

Now Dirk had the floor. You could have heard a mouse whisper in the room. Even Meera's professional mask slipped a little as she gaped at him with interest.

"I lied," Dirk said. "I did see her."

The silence that followed seemed destined to last forever. It was too big, too complex a statement. It rattled in the room. Every time Alicia opened her mouth to say something, the words evaporated into the air.

"This is a significant admission," Patel said finally. "Are you prepared to put it in a statement?"

Dirk nodded. He turned the baseball cap he was holding around and around in his hands.

"You can't be serious!" Miss Fairchild exploded. "The man is a sex offender. He's probably the one who *put* the body under the house!"

"I'm not a sex offender," Dirk said. "My only crime is hooking up with a fifteen-year-old when I was eighteen. We were in a bar, so I assumed she was of legal age. Unfortunately, her dad was a barrister and I was found guilty of having intercourse with a minor." He exhaled slowly. "I moved to the country to get away from all the talk. I've always loved horses, so it was the perfect job. I was supposed to stay one hundred meters or more away from kids." He spoke directly to Alicia, Norah, and Jessica. "Your foster mother was annoyed with me after I let you ride the horses and she did some research. The day Amy supposedly disappeared, Miss Fairchild paid me a visit."

"She blackmailed you?" Norah asked.

"For heaven's sake," Miss Fairchild said. "The police are investigating him. Of course he's going to come up with a story to cover his ass!"

"She didn't tell me much," Dirk continued, "just that there had been a mix-up with the adoption paperwork and it turned out she'd had the little girl illegally for six months. She told me the girl was already on her way to her new family, but if the police had questions just to say I knew nothing. If I did that, she said, she wouldn't have to tell them I'd been *fraternizing with the adolescent girls at the farm*." Dirk put on a very strange woman's voice for this last part. "That was fine by me; I didn't want to be caught up in anything regarding a little girl, given my record."

He looked up at them with new clarity, as though his speech had taken him somewhere else. "I read about the body being found under Wild Meadows last week. I should have gone to the cops straightaway, but . . . I don't know. I thought they'd point the finger at me. I've been wrestling with it for a week. I came to see you last night to tell you but I was intercepted by you-know-who. Anyway, I wanted to tell the truth, so there it is. I'm sorry."

"All right," Hando said finally. "We appreciate you sharing that,

Dirk, and as Detective Patel said, we'd like you to make a formal statement. Detective Tucker will take care of that with you now." He nodded at Tucker, who led Dirk from the room.

Alicia's feelings were piling up too quickly for her to process.

Anger at Dirk for lying.

Gratitude toward him for telling the truth now.

The knowledge that they'd been gaslit their whole lives.

The thrill of finally being able to prove it.

Meera spoke up. "My name is Meera Shah," she said. "I'm acting as legal counsel for Alicia and Norah today."

Hando and Patel exchanged a glance. "Noted."

"You brought a lawyer?" Miss Fairchild said. "Sounds like you're feeling guilty about something."

"As I said on the phone," Hando sound loudly, as several voices rose in protest, "we've asked you here because the forensic anthropologist has finished examining the remains. As you may or may not be aware, there was a request to pay careful attention to the feet, looking for evidence of a sixth toe, or a deformity that would indicate that there had once been a sixth toe."

"And . . . ?" Alicia could barely breathe.

"They found no evidence of this," Hando said. "The feet appear to have developed normally."

Alicia and Norah and Meera looked at one another.

"I don't understand," Zara piped up. "Why would there be a sixth toe?"

"Amy had six toes on her left foot," Norah said, her gaze still on the detective. "Are you sure they checked the correct foot?"

"Who is Amy?" Rhiannon said.

"There's more," Hando said. "They also estimated the child to be under the age of one."

Silence. Norah looked as baffled as Alicia felt. Alicia didn't know what to say. "It doesn't make sense."

The only people in the room who didn't look confused were Hando and Patel. Patel chose this moment to step forward with her piece of the puzzle. "Perhaps the most significant finding was that the bones are older than we initially thought," she said. "Their best estimate is fifty years. Certainly longer than twenty-five."

Alicia had no words. Norah wiped her face with her palm. Everyone in the room looked stunned, with the exception of Zara, who looked quite . . . animated. It was jarring. Alicia was about to ask if she was all right, but Zara got in first.

"Okay, so I don't know if this is significant," she said, "but *I* have six toes on my left foot."

THE OFFICE OF DR. WARREN, PSYCHIATRIST

"So you disappeared into the night with the baby and a tin of cash?" Dr. Warren says. "How far did you get?"

"Not even to end of the driveway," I say. "Mind you, it was a long driveway. I was almost at the gate when I heard the engine of John's car roar to life. There was no point in running, nowhere to hide. Within seconds, the headlights illuminated us. I turned to face them, as the car approached.

"My mother was in the passenger seat. Her eye was swollen. John got out of the car and came at me like a train, grabbing my shoulders and shaking me so hard I dropped my bag and had to clutch Amy to stop from dropping her too.

"'Where is my money?' he roared. His eyes were glazed with demented fury. Of course it was about the money. It would have hurt his pride to see me get away but ultimately it would have made his life easier. The money was another story.

"'Give me the tin, you bitch!' he said, pushing me again.

"I stumbled, then flew at him in a rage, pummeling him with my free hand. 'You are disgusting,' I cried. 'Preying on vulnerable women and little girls while pretending to be a man of God. It's so sad. How can you live with yourself?'

"After the shock of the first few punches wore off, he gripped me by the shoulders tightly enough that his nails bit into my skin. Then he held me at arm's length, preventing any more of my pathetic punches from landing. I hadn't noticed my mother getting out of the car. When she came to stand by my side, I thought it was a sup-portive gesture—until she snatched Amy from my arms.

"'No!' I cried. But she didn't listen. Her face was determined as she carried Amy back to the car. 'Mum, plea—'

"John slapped me so hard I saw stars, tasted blood.

"'Mum,' I tried again, weaker now, but the next slap was harder, knocking me to the ground, stealing my breath.

"John spat at me. 'Whore.'

"He bent over, pulling open my makeshift bag and withdrawing the tin of cash. After checking to see it was all there, he spat again, and returned to the car.

"'Don't hurt her,' I called after him weakly, but he wouldn't have heard because the engine was roaring to life again. 'Please! Don't hurt Amy.'

"He did a U-turn, then drove away back to the house. I never saw Amy again."

54

NORAH

It was just so unexpected, so out of left field. For a moment, Norah couldn't see how it fit. Everyone glanced at one another. Hando kept blinking, then shaking his head, then blinking again. Rhiannon and Bianca were open-mouthed. Miss Fairchild looked as if she were having a mild stroke.

It was Patel who broke the silence.

"You have six toes?" she said to Zara.

"Hold up." Patel looked utterly lost. "You're Zara, right?"

Hando stepped in. "I interviewed Zara. She wasn't on our list. She read about the body in the newspaper."

"I didn't know you *had* a list until I arrived and bumped into Rhiannon and Bianca," Zara chipped in.

"But how did you know that you'd been at Wild Meadows?" Patel asked.

"When I was adopted, my parents were told that I'd come from a foster home in Port Agatha. When I turned eighteen, I tried to get in touch with the person who facilitated the adoption, but his contact details were old. So I came back to Port Agatha with my parents and we asked around. That's where I heard Miss Fairchild's name. But of course, you were in Melbourne by then." Zara looked at her. "I've tried to get in touch for years. I emailed and phoned. You never got back to me."

Miss Fairchild had been silent through all of this. Her chest rose and fell with what looked like deep, anxious breaths.

"I kept tabs on Port Agatha. I saw that the home had been sold. Then I saw the news about the body underneath. I decided to drive up here to see what I could find out."

"And you have six toes?" Norah said, still stuck on that important fact.

"I did have," she said. "One was removed just after my third birthday, when I'd been living with my adopted family for nearly a year. Which meant I was at Wild Meadows around the time I was two."

As she spoke, Zara was undoing her shoelaces. It sent Norah back to the day they met Amy, on the floor of the living room in Wild Meadows. Miss Fairchild removing her little sock. Now, Zara removed her own sock, showing a tiny silver scar between her pinkie toe and the next one. A tiny telltale bump, in the exact spot where Amy's toe had been. "Am *I* Amy?"

Norah looked at her closely.

"Do you have any pictures of yourself soon after you were adopted?" Alicia asked.

Zara got out her phone. "Here's one from my first Christmas with my family. I use it as my profile pic on Facebook. I would have been about two and a half."

Zara thumbed her phone for a moment, then handed it to Alicia, who only looked at it for a second before lowering the phone. She closed her eyes; her hand found her heart. She lifted the phone again for another look.

"Oh my God," she whispered, handing the phone to Norah. "Oh. My. God."

Norah took the phone. Stared at it.

"Amy," she said to the phone. Then she looked up at Zara. "You're *Amy.*"

"Which adoption agency did your parents use?" Alicia asked her.

"Are you police detectives now?" Miss Fairchild said, finding her voice suddenly. She looked at Patel beseechingly.

"It wasn't an agency," Zara replied, ignoring her. "It was a man. Scott something. Mitchell or Maxwell or—"

"Scott?" Norah cried.

"Scott Michaels?" Patel said, ignoring Miss Fairchild.

"Who is Scott Michaels?" Meera whispered to Alicia.

"That's it!" Zara said. "Scott Michaels. Do you know him?"

"Scott was our social worker," Norah said. "He and Miss Fairchild were friends."

Everyone looked at Miss Fairchild then. She rolled her eyes and looked away, as if this were a stupid conversation that didn't interest her. She'd pulled her phone out and started typing something into it.

"But if you are Amy . . ." Norah said, looking at Zara. "whose is the body under the house?"

There was a short silence that made it clear that no one knew the answer. Then the silence was broken by Miss Fairchild, who suddenly began to wail.

55

ALICIA

NOW

S he lied," Miss Fairchild said. "She said Amy was with a good family. All these years, I've pictured her, living with them. Being loved by them. But she lied."

"Who lied?" Patel asked, looking exhausted, though it was barely nine in the morning.

"My mother."

"Wait," Zara said, confused. "Are you talking about me? I *was* living with a good family."

Alicia was as lost as Zara, and so were the cops, apparently. Miss Fairchild looked stricken, her lip trembling, her face wet with tears. She looked small, suddenly, like a child. It was shocking, seeing her in this light. Alicia had to remind herself not to feel sorry for her.

"What happened to the baby?" Miss Fairchild asked suddenly. "Did the body give any hint as to . . ."—she winced—"how she died?"

"The coroner reported a flat depreciation at the back of the skull consistent with a blow or fall," Hando said.

Miss Fairchild shuddered. Her hand went to the back of her own head, and fresh tears poured from her eyes. Patel and Hando exchanged a look.

Patel came and sat beside her. "You know, we've been asking these girls about their upbringing at Wild Meadows. But they're not the only ones who grew up in that house, are they?"

Miss Fairchild shook her head, her eyes cast down, her lips pressed together.

"I'm sorry," Hando said, "but I'm going to have to clear the room of everyone except Miss Fairchild."

"But we need to hear this," Alicia cried.

"I understand," Hando said, meeting Alicia's eyes. He didn't look like the enemy anymore. "And you will. But we need to hear it first."

Alicia, Norah, Meera, Zara, Bianca and Rhiannon filed out of the meeting room and back into the foyer, which was too small to contain the six of them as well as the intensity of their feelings—not to mention the questions that remained.

"We need to bring Scott Michaels in," Alicia heard Hando shout to someone. "Dirk Winterbourne is in room four. And can you arrange for Zara to come back in later this afternoon to give a statement? Her parents too."

"Okay, I need more information," Zara said. "I am Amy—and you thought I was the body under the house?"

Alicia shrugged. "We thought it was possible."

"May I ask why?"

"You may," Alicia said. "And we will explain everything. But there's someone who I think should be with us for this. Someone who will be very glad to see you again."

She looked at Norah, who nodded in agreement.

THE OFFICE OF DR. WARREN, PSYCHIATRIST

"What did you do after John and your mother took Amy?" Dr. Warren asks.

"I walked into town and waited until morning. Then I intercepted Troy on his way to school, and I told him everything. We ran all the way back to Wild Meadows. She greeted me at the door."

"Who?" Dr. Warren asks.

"The woman I would never again call my mother."

Dr. Warren can barely contain his delight.

"She seemed nervous. I knew immediately something had happened.

"'Where is she?' I cried. *'Where is she?'*

"She tried to put her hands on my shoulders, but I threw them off. Her eyes were full of tears. 'Where is who?'

"I began to scream. I screamed so loud and for so long that I must have blacked out. It was a mercy, because those few minutes of being unconsciousness were the last ones moments I can remember when I wasn't in pain."

"She pretended Amy had never existed?" Dr. Warren asks.

"Only because I had Troy with me. To make me look crazy. But later, after he left, she told me that some ladies from the church had come for her. She said they'd taken her to a good home."

"And you believed that?"

"After everything that had happened, I didn't think my mother would have stood by while John killed my baby. But it turns out that's exactly what she did."

Dr. Warren closes his eyes for a moment as he takes this in.

"The reason I became a foster mother was because I was looking for a replacement for my daughter. But it was never the same. None of the girls were Amy. The trauma of it all . . . it sent me mad, I guess."

A knock at the door.

"Time's up," comes a voice from outside. There's a buzz, and the door opens. The guard enters to escort me back to my cell. "Let's go."

Dr. Warren stands too.

"I'll see you in court," he says, and then the door clanks closed between us.

56

JESSICA

NOW

When Jessica opened her eyes, she didn't have the privilege of the foggy confused feeling that people in movies seemed to experience after waking up in a hospital. She knew where she was. She could feel the oxygen tube in her nose, she could smell the antibacterial soap, hear the hum of the medical equipment around her. She also knew that she'd brought it all on herself.

While her surroundings were not a surprise, the person at her bedside was. Phil. He sat on the side of her bed and brushed a piece of hair back off her face. "Hey."

She wasn't sure why she suddenly felt shy, seeing her husband of fifteen years sitting there.

"Phil . . . what are you doing here?"

"Where else would I be? I came as soon as Alicia called. I would have been here last night if I had known." He smiled sadly. "The nurse told me you'd overdosed on Valium."

"I'm sorry," Jessica said, because really, what else could she say? "You must be . . . I don't know . . . shocked."

He scrunched his face up, almost a grimace. "Honestly . . . I found a bunch of pill bottles at home a few months ago with different people's names on them. I should have said something."

Jessica was taken aback. She'd thought she'd hidden it so well. She was so organized, so efficient, so in control. She'd imagined that everyone—Phil included—would be blindsided to know what had been going on.

"What?"

"I didn't know the extent of it, obviously. But you haven't seemed yourself for a while."

"Why didn't you say anything?"

"I should have." He focused on the bed rail, running his fingers along it. "I wish I had. I just . . . I thought you'd get through it— bounce back. You have your ups and downs. My job is to be calm. I know you need that." He shook his head, sighed. "When I found the Valium, I knew I should bring it up. But you seemed stressed out, and I didn't want to upset you. I thought that if I just stayed calm . . . I don't know. That sounds idiotic." He let go of the bed rail and exhaled heavily.

"Actually, it sounds familiar."

Jessica felt ill. Had she unwittingly created a home environment like the one in which she'd grown up? An environment where you had to assess the lay of the land before you felt safe to speak? An environment where, after a while, you stopped speaking completely?

"I grew up in a house where I was constantly trying to assess if it was safe to say something," she heard herself saying. "Where I held myself responsible for my foster mother's feelings—good and bad.

I know it's too much pressure to put on a person. But that's exactly what I did to you."

Jessica thought back to when they'd first worked at the restaurant together. The way he always rushed ahead to clear a table for her if she was busy. The way he stood behind her when a difficult customer complained. The way he was always right there, silently supporting her. She'd been too consumed by her pain to notice how he really felt.

"I'm so sorry." She started to cry. "I'm so, so sorry."

"Shh, it's all right." He reached for a box of tissues and plucked a couple out. "It's all right. Thank you for telling me about the house you grew up in. It makes sense now."

He handed her the tissues and Jessica wiped her eyes and nose. "I can tell you more about it . . . if you want to know."

"I do," he said, reaching for her hand. "Very much."

The sound of her sisters in the corridor drifted into the room. A moment later, Jessica heard a gasp.

"She's awake!" Alicia cried. "Norah, she's awake!"

Her sisters thundered to her side. Alicia was beaming but Norah's eyes, Jessica noticed were full of tears.

"You scared the shit out of us," Alicia said.

Norah gave Jessica a light punch in the arm. "Idiot."

"Sorry," Jessica said.

Norah nodded, blinking back her tears. "You should be," she said gruffly. But she gave Jessica a quick kiss on the head.

"I should have known it was only a matter of time before you two showed up," Phil said, lending levity and ease to the moment, as usual.

"You mean *four* of us," Alicia said.

Jessica hitched herself up in bed. She assumed Meera would be with them, which made three. "Four?" she said.

"Meera's just grabbing some coffees. And we brought someone else we thought you'd like to meet."

They stepped apart dramatically to reveal Zara.

Jessica smiled, confused and a little underwhelmed. "I know I've had a drug overdose but I remember that I've met Zara before."

The three of them came further into the room. There was something odd about their expressions.

"What's going on?" Jessica asked.

"Jessica," Alicia said solemnly, "we'd like to introduce Amy."

"I'll leave you girls to it," Phil said.

He was almost at the door when Jessica said, "Wait, Phil. Stay."

She continued to stare at Zara. She didn't completely understand. But at the same time, she did.

Phil hesitated in the doorway. "Are you sure this isn't family stuff?"

"It is," Jessica said. "And you're family."

Phil made no further protest, he just returned to Jessica's bedside.

Jessica looked from Zara to Norah to Alicia.

"Right," she said. "Fill me in."

57

JESSICA

NINE MONTHS LATER . . .

When they'd found out the baby under the house was likely Miss Fairchild's daughter, Jessica had almost felt sorry for her. They'd been unable to get total certainty around it, as both John and Miss Fairchild's mother had long since passed away, but without any solid proof, the police had concluded that John had caused the death of baby Amy and buried her.

It had been nine months since Miss Fairchild was charged with kidnapping (even though she hadn't actually been the one to "take" Amy, she'd knowingly kept a child obtained illegally, which legally amounted to the same thing) and perverting the course of justice (for blackmailing Dirk and lying to the police). It was six months since she'd been held on remand after being caught trying to flee the country. During the time she'd been in jail, she'd reached out to Jessica several times, asking her to visit. Alicia and Norah had been adamant that Jessica shouldn't go, but in the last month, Jessica had told them that she felt ready, and they supported her, as they always did.

Jessica could not have been better prepared for her visit, as least insofar as logistics went. She'd almost been too focused on the preparations, however, because it wasn't until she was following the guard down a wide corridor toward the visitors' room that she truly considered what she was doing.

If Jessica ever needed a Valium, it was now. Her anxiety was palpable. Unfortunately, now that she was in recovery, it was out of the question.

After leaving the hospital in Port Agatha, she'd been transferred to a drug rehabilitation center in the city. With client after client coming forward to report drugs missing from their homes, it had been futile to deny it, so Jessica handed the reins of Love Your Home to Sonja and issued a statement apologizing for the harm she'd caused. She would be stepping away from the day-to-day running of the business to seek help. She'd even called Debbie Montgomery-Squires to apologize personally.

Rehab had been much harder than Jessica had expected—both the detox aspect *and* the humility part. She'd thrown herself into it, like the good student she was, following every suggestion, completing every activity, determined to be the best and most enthusiastic at recovery. Still, even six months later, she continued to crave the feeling she got when the pill slid down her throat. The knowledge that calm was coming. Now, her therapist told her, they were shooting for a different type of calm. A less chemical type. A more reliable type. And today's visit was part of that.

Jessica heard a buzzer, and the guard opened the door. Inside, Miss Fairchild sat at small table.

Last night, when she'd had dinner with Norah and Alicia, they'd discussed what it might be like, seeing Miss Fairchild. Norah was curious as to whether she might have been beaten up in prison. Alicia wondered if she would have lost weight or become ill. Jessica had steeled herself for the oddness of seeing her in prison clothing. Oddly enough, the prison uniform didn't look bad on her. Her hair was pulled back into a ponytail, which suited her, made her look younger. If it weren't for her bitter expression, she might have looked pretty.

"Jessica," she said tearfully, getting to her feet. "Thank you for coming. I knew you would."

Jessica sat down in the seat provided, ignoring the other woman's outstretched arms.

After a moment, Miss Fairchild sat too. "Can you believe they put me in here?" she hissed. "Like a criminal?"

"You *are* a criminal," Jessica said neutrally.

Her neutrality was important, she'd learned. She'd spent the past six months learning about narcissists. She'd read books and listened to podcasts and had therapy, all designed to help her understand the abuse she'd suffered and acquire the skills which would allow her to take back control of her own life. (Phil had read the books and listened to the podcasts too. "It's like a sick, tragic book club," he'd said cheerfully, as he arranged a cheese and fruit platter.)

Miss Fairchild looked betrayed. "For goodness' sake. Not you too."

"I'm just stating facts."

Miss Fairchild leaned forward, her eyes narrowed. Jessica was familiar with this stance. It was designed to intimidate her. It was so interesting watching it happen, knowing what it all meant.

"*I've. Been. Maligned,*" Miss Fairchild said.

Jessica mimicked her stance, leaning forward. Showing she

wasn't intimidated. "So you didn't illegally procure a child, and then send her away when she didn't meet your needs?"

Now Miss Fairchild groaned. "Listen to yourself. *Procure! Meet my needs!* Dramatizing everything. You're as bad as the media."

The media had been swift in condemning Miss Fairchild. Rightly so. To someone as image-obsessed as she was, this was bound to drive her crazy.

"Scott was the one who brought her to me. How was I supposed to know it wasn't legal?"

Scott, it seemed from Miss Fairchild's emails, was public enemy number one in her eyes. After Zara had named him as the one to facilitate her adoption, the police had brought him in. Once he'd realized he was going to jail, he hadn't even *tried* to protect the identities of those he'd worked with. He admitted to everything, but even so, he would be going away, and for a lot longer than Miss Fairchild.

"I'm just sorry that we weren't able to charge her with anything regarding her treatment of you three girls," Patel had told the girls just last week. The police had kept in touch over the past few months, and the sisters discovered the police weren't the enemies they'd perceived them to be. "Unfortunately, with the house gone, and a lack of supportive evidence, it was very difficult to build a compelling case."

In the end, it didn't really matter. Miss Fairchild was paying the price regardless.

"So you thought it was legal to return a child you'd planned to adopt and then pretend she never existed?" Jessica said to her.

Miss Fairchild rolled her eyes. "Why are you even here if you're just going along with the popular narrative that I'm a monster?"

Jessica wasn't surprised that her former foster mother wasn't accepting any responsibility for her actions. Still, there was something shocking about seeing how readily she could deflect her own guilt and paint herself as the victim.

"I'm here because I want to understand something," Jessica told her.

"What?"

"I know you had a daughter named Amy when you were a teenager. Your stepfather killed her, as far as we know. Ten years later, you fostered me. Why? Was I meant to be a replacement for Amy?"

Miss Fairchild's expression changed. She seemed thoughtful.

"Not a replacement, no," she said. "No one could ever replace her. Maybe it was my attempt to make it up to her? When I returned to Wild Meadows after my mother and John died and heard that there was a little girl who needed me it felt like a sign. A second chance." Miss Fairchild's expression was so pure Jessica had to force herself to keep her guard up. "I'll never forget the moment I saw you. The connection I felt. I loved you in an instant. And you loved me back!"

"I did," Jessica acknowledged.

"But then you started loving other people. Friends at school. Norah and Alicia."

"You brought all of them into my life. What was I supposed to do?"

"You were supposed to love *me*!" Miss Fairchild cried, so loudly that the guard stepped forward and told her to keep her voice down. When she spoke again, her voice was softer. More miserable. "Norah didn't love me. Alicia didn't love me. The respite babies didn't love me. Even my own mother found someone else to love. The only person who ever loved me and only me was Amy. My daughter.

"It was Scott who suggested that instead of fostering I adopt a baby. He told me that for a rather large fee, he could fast-track an adoption with a healthy baby who would attach easily. He could even find one who looked like me, he said. I went along with it in good faith. I didn't know the details."

Jessica stared at her. "I assume you know the details now?"

Miss Fairchild just rolled her eyes.

"Scott took kids from foster care and sold them," Jessica said. Miss Fairchild knew this, of course, but Jessica wanted to spell it out, so she had nowhere to hide. "He told the parents, usually vulnerable young women or parents from a non-English-speaking background, that they had lost custody permanently and would never see their kids again."

Miss Fairchild shook her head, her lips pursed. "He took kids from parents who were ill-equipped to look after their babies. I would have given Amy a better life. But she decided she loved you girls more than me. It was so demoralizing, Jessica."

"So you *gave her away*?"

"I had no choice! You told me you were going to report me to the authorities! I called Scott. He came immediately and took Amy and placed her with another family—the family who raised her. I'm told they were good people. So it all worked out in the end."

Jessica stared at her. "It didn't *work out*. Zara was *stolen* from her birth parents. Sold to you and then to another family. She has been displaced and a set of parents lost their child!"

Miss Fairchild shrugged. "What was I supposed to do?"

"You were supposed to be an adult!" Jessica cried. "And do the right thing! You were supposed to provide security, consistency, and love! If you weren't capable of that, you had no business having children in your care."

Miss Fairchild started crying noisily. But they weren't tears of realization for what she'd done, Jessica realized; they were tears of self-pity.

Jessica had had enough.

When she stood to leave, Miss Fairchild's tears dried in an instant, replaced by icy coldness. Jessica was no stranger to Miss Fairchild's changing moods, but even so, the speed with which the transformation occurred was chilling.

"Jessica," she said slowly, her gaze settling on her stomach. "Are you . . . ?"

Jessica paused. "Yes. I'm pregnant. Five months along."

One surprising upside of rehab was how it had brought her closer to Phil. As she was only allowed visitors on a Sunday, and she didn't have the use of her phone, they found an old-fashioned way of connecting: writing letters. In his letters, Phil told her all the things he'd wanted to say to her throughout their marriage. That he found it hard to connect with her when she wouldn't ever stop moving. That he knew she wasn't okay all those times she insisted she was. That he yearned to have the kind of bond with her that she had with her sisters. In response, Jessica told him things she'd never talked about before—describing her childhood, her addiction, how she was haunted by her innermost thoughts. She explained that her sisters had been her safe place, her family, growing up. She apologized for not widening that circle to include him when they married. And she promised that things would be different when she came home.

By the time she had finished with rehab, they'd said everything they needed to say. They were able to start over. A month later, Jessica was pregnant. And while the prospect of having a baby still terrified her in many ways, she found her terror was balanced by the moments of joy she and Phil experienced. Such as when they'd learned the week before that they were having a baby boy.

Miss Fairchild was still taking it in. It annoyed Jessica that she still felt the yearning. Longing for a reaction to her news from the woman who'd been a mother figure to her. Maybe she would always feel it. But unlike in the past, her reaction wasn't going to control her. Because she knew now that Miss Fairchild hadn't been a mother figure. She had been an abuser. And Jessica wasn't going to be manipulated by her anymore.

"Were you going to tell me?" Miss Fairchild demanded.

Jessica turned and walked to the door, gesturing to the guard that she was ready to leave. "No," she said, "why would I?"

"Why would you?" Miss Fairchild blustered. "Surely after everything I deserve to—"

The door buzzed and Jessica pulled it open. Miss Fairchild was still talking as Jessica walked out. The click of the door shutting securely behind her felt like a new beginning. One she was finally ready for.

58

NORAH

A YEAR LATER . . .

Norah walked into the pub. It smelled warm and yeasty and the air felt shot through with deep-fryer oil. Larry sat at the bar, nursing half a pint. Behind the bar stood Ishir. Apart from the two of them, the place was empty.

"I'm back!" Norah announced.

Larry looked over briefly, then immediately went back to his beer. But Ishir beamed. His mustache rose up at each corner, making him look like a circus ringmaster. Norah had grown to adore the delighted way he greeted her arrival.

"Where are the dogs?"

"Already out back," she said. "They couldn't wait to see Banjo."

"He missed them," Ishir said. "It would really be much better if they—and you—were here all the time."

As he'd warned her, Ishir was terrible at playing it cool. As Larry still hadn't offered to buy the pub, he'd been stuck in Port Agatha, and he'd been begging her to move there too. Norah was considering it. With her job she could work from anywhere, and the dogs adored it here. She'd also found a kickboxing class in the area that she loved, which really helped channel her difficult emotions. There were a lot of reasons in favor of moving—not the least of which was Ishir.

In the past, she wouldn't have considered living so far away from Alicia and Jessica, but since her stint in jail she'd realized that it wasn't impossible. She'd spent eleven days in prison as a result of her assault on Kevin. It could have been a lot longer had Anna not represented her and had the women's prison not been over capacity. It wasn't so bad, on the whole. Not dissimilar to Wild Meadows, really, except she hadn't been locked under the stairs and didn't have to worry about something happening to her sisters. Jessica would have loved the schedule. Prescribed times for personal hygiene, phone calls, and "leisure." The food wasn't great, but it was only eleven days. Norah had emerged with a clean slate. Four months after leaving prison, it was still clean. And the best part of the whole experience? Thanks to Anna and a female judge, Kevin got four months for extortion, and would never work around children again.

After that, leaving Melbourne didn't seem so unthinkable. It was only a couple of hours' drive. And, despite everything that had happened in Port Agatha, she had to admit that there was something about the town that felt like . . . home.

But she hadn't made any decisions yet.

Ishir poured Larry a fresh pint and placed it on the bar in front of him. Then he lifted the hinge on the counter and came around the bar to kiss Norah. She loved the way his mustache tickled her top lip.

"Is that your phone," he said against her lips, "or are you just happy to see me?"

Norah fished her phone out of her pocket. It was Meera.

"I have news," she said. "We found Zara's parents. Her biological parents."

"No!" Norah cried.

"Here's what we know. They were newlyweds and had just emigrated from Russia to Australia when Zara's mother discovered she was pregnant. They were in their early twenties, and confessed they didn't know much about caring for a baby. Zara was taken into care after a neighbor heard her crying. Apparently they'd left her home alone while they took a night class, learning English. They were told if they took a parenting course she would be returned to them, but they never saw her again."

"Wow."

"They returned to Russia a decade or so later. They're having a FaceTime with Zara later today."

"I hope Scott gets extradited to Russia to face them," Norah said. "I bet they'd love a few minutes in a cell with him."

Meera laughed. "I'll see what I can do."

They ended the call, and Norah walked back to the bar to see Ishir had pulled them a couple of beers.

"Larry, can you hold the fort for a few minutes?" he asked.

Larry continued staring at the television, as if he hadn't spoken.

"Awesome, thanks," Ishir said. Then he turned to Norah. "Come on. Let's go play with the dogs."

And so they did.

This, Norah realized, was home.

59

ALICIA

What do you think your grandmother would say if she could see you now?"

Eliza did that thing where she cocked her head and waited. Alicia hated it when she did that thing. She hated Eliza's stupid office with its calming blue paint and soft furnishings. She hated her neat gray hair and pressed beige slacks. She hated the way Eliza wouldn't let her deflect her feelings with sarcasm. She hated the fact that, in nearly every session over the past year, she'd cried.

"I think," she started, "Grammy would say she was proud."

And there she went, blubbering like an idiot.

Eliza didn't even need to push the tissues toward her. These days, Alicia just grabbed the box on her way in the door and held it in her lap. She took one now and dabbed at her eyes.

Eliza smiled her calming smile. "I think you're right."

Eliza charged Alicia $185 for making her cry, and then, like the sadist she was, Alicia made an appointment for the following week.

For all of the suffering Eliza caused her, Alicia had to admit, there was something addictive about the sessions. Each time she left the psychologist's office, Alicia felt lighter.

Back home, Alicia heard the hum of life as soon she put her key in the door. Meera was in the kitchen making a salad. Aaron was sitting at the counter, demolishing Meera's beautifully prepared charcuterie board as if it were McDonald's.

"How'd it go?" Meera asked, shaking a jar of dressing.

"Awful." Alicia kissed her. "I talked about myself and my problems for fifty minutes. Now I feel dreadfully sorry for myself." She shut the fridge without taking anything out.

"Serves you right," Aaron said, "for forcing foster kids to go to counselling."

"Touché. Look, I think it might be . . . useful. I will say I feel much better about certain things now."

"What things?" Aaron said, loading what must have been seven dollars' worth of prosciutto on top of a cracker.

"None of your business," she said, sitting on the stool beside his. "And leave some of that for me. Where's Theo?"

"Napping," Meera said, and then she lifted her head slightly at the sound of movement. "*Was* napping."

"I awake!" the little boy called. "Awon?"

Theo was now talking so much it was hard to imagine he was ever silent. His favorite and most oft-used word was Aaron—or Awon, in toddler-speak.

Aaron sighed, standing. "I guess I have to do everything around here," he said, rolling his eyes.

Alicia snorted. Nothing brought her more joy than Aaron giving them cheek. A child comfortable enough to give their carer cheek is a secure child. At least, she hoped that was the case, now that they'd officially adopted him. She, on the other hand, wasn't quite as secure. She was already feeling that low tug of dread when she thought about the fact that Aaron was leaving to go to university in the new year. He had come into his own in the last six months.

"Sit down and finish eating your inheritance," Meera told him. "I'll get Theo."

Aaron sat back down.

It was during the car trip back to Melbourne from Port Agatha that Alicia had managed to verbalize to Meera what she'd been unable to stop thinking about.

"Meera, I'm wondering if you would consider representing me if I petitioned to legally adopt Theo and Aaron?"

Meera, of course, knew exactly how she would go about it, and outlined the process in detail. It wasn't until they were nearly back home that she said, "Your application would be stronger if you adopted as part of a couple."

She cocked an eyebrow.

And so it was decided. Given their connections, and the fact that they had both undertaken all the required checks and training, the process was relatively straightforward. Theo had struggled with the adjustment, but having Aaron with him had done wonders for his integration into their family.

Being thrust into parenthood of a teen and a toddler had also done wonders for Alicia. To her great surprise, she loved being part of a family. Loved the banter in the kitchen as they made dinner. Loved telling Aaron to clean his room. Loved moaning about Theo drawing on the walls *again*. Loved that moment at the end of the day when Theo was asleep and Aaron was in his room, and she and Meera curled up on the couch and heaved a silent, satisfied sigh at having made it through another day. Alicia remembered Grammy releasing that sigh when she returned to the living room after putting her to bed. This was what parenthood was meant to be, she realized. Nothing at all like what she'd experienced at Wild Meadows.

"Aaron!" Alicia cried, as Aaron picked up an entire cube of quince paste. "What the—"

"Dare me to eat it?"

"No!" she said. Then, she reconsidered. She glanced over her shoulder to make sure Meera wasn't around. "Actually, go on."

He didn't hesitate, just crammed the entire thing in his mouth. Almost immediately he started making gagging faces. Alicia began to laugh uncontrollably.

As he ran to the rubbish bin to spit it out, Alicia felt that unfamiliar feeling again—the one that bowled her over at least once a day, and always at the strangest times. When Theo hit his head and held his arms out to her for comfort. When Aaron had a girl over and asked if they could hang out in his room. When they all ate dinner in front of the TV. When Aaron did something dumb like eat an entire cube of quince paste. The feeling was gratitude mixed with a little horror. The feeling was: *We could have missed this.*

"Alicia?" Aaron said, once he'd rinsed his mouth out with water and returned to his spot on the stool. "Remember when I said I was lucky that Trish was keeping me until I finished school, and you said I wasn't lucky because it was the least I deserved?"

"Yeah, mate."

"I'm lucky now," he said decisively. A momentary pause. "Right?"

It was in that pause she saw the lasting wounds of his upbring-ing. Despite the bravado, the sarcasm, the cheekiness, he still needed that reassurance. Alicia's role was to give it to him. It was a role she relished more than she could describe. The best role of her life.

"Sorry," she said, rumpling his hair. "But that'd be us. *We* are the lucky ones."

60

HOLLY FAIRCHILD

Dr. Warren was a tough nut to crack. Overworked, underappreciated, and provided by the state to assess the mental capacity of criminals, he'd well and truly checked out by the time he met me. It made sense. After all, how many forensic evaluations can one complete before one starts to phone it in? It made me nervous at first, though. He was my only hope. If it weren't for his strange fetish, I might have been done for. But it worked out in the end. I was happy to entertain his perversion. If mother-daughter issues turned him on, I could provide. Now my defense is in the bag: mental impairment, thus not criminally responsible.

Yes, I had to tweak the details of what happened. But I wasn't going to be held responsible for something that was my mother's fault. Besides, the first part of my story was true. My mum *was* entirely useless after my father died. John *was* part of a church that stepped in to help. As for the rest . . . I just gave Dr. Warren what he wanted.

John wasn't the disciplinarian I described, and he never locked me in the basement or sexually assaulted me—*heaven forbid!*—but what he did was worse. He *stole my mother.* Then they fell hopelessly, disgustingly, in love. They married *less than a year after my father died.* And then, while my head was still spinning from all of this, they had a fucking *baby.*

From the moment Amy was conceived, she was more important than me. Mum rested constantly "for the baby." She barely left the house. She started knitting for the baby . . . *knitting!* She made a bunch of soft animals and even knitted a life-size doll, adding Amy's name to it after she was born. She started eating organic food—which was *not* a thing back then—while continuing to feed me fish fingers and whatever other rubbish she had in the freezer. And apart from me and John, she didn't tell anyone that she was pregnant, suddenly superstitious that something would happen to her perfect, magical, second-chance child.

When the time came, she had a drug-free home birth rather than the epidural-assisted hospital birth she had with me. Worst of all, she gave birth to a daughter, making me entirely redundant.

"Aren't you a darling girl?" Mum would say as she stood over the bassinet, gazing at her. "How I love you, darling girl."

It made me sick.

One night, Mum and John left me to babysit for a few hours, which frankly wasn't the greatest parenting choice, given that I was barely a teen. They'd made a big deal of it, saying, "Your big sister is babysitting," to Amy a million times in a silly baby voice. We were all referred to in reference to our relationship with Amy by then. *Amy's* mummy. *Amy's* daddy. *Amy's* big sister. As if we'd ceased to be anything else. As if we hadn't existed before she came along.

Mum thought babysitting would be a good way for me to bond with Amy. I thought it would be a good chance for me to ignore her and watch TV. It might have been okay had she not kept crying. She cried until her little face was red and her legs were scrunched up against her belly. *Not so cute now, are you, darling girl?* I thought, as I peered down at her.

Did I mean to hurt her? Well . . . I won't say it didn't feel good to throw her against the wall. I won't say it didn't feel good to put an end to the crying. I won't say it didn't feel good to see Mum's and John's faces when they saw what I'd done.

Mum was the one who buried her. In secret—to "protect" me. She told John she couldn't bear to lose two children. For God's sake. I assumed she'd taken her to the woods or something, not buried her under the damn house! Then again, if she hadn't buried her under the house, I never would have dreamed up this teen pregnancy story. Thank you, Mummy. Thank you for everything.

Acknowledgments

When this book was in its infancy, I had the privilege of speaking with a dozen women who were raised in foster care in Australia. I will forever be changed by these conversations. Without them, I couldn't have *begun* to appreciate the feelings of bewilderment, displacement and powerlessness that result from being taken away from your home and placed with strangers when you are a young, traumatized child. What perhaps moved me most was each women's unprompted assertion that she was lucky. *Lucky* because she was able to remain in contact with her biological brother. *Lucky* because she wasn't sexually assaulted more than once. *Lucky* because her foster parents were kind to her. It inspired me and broke my heart in equal measure. They were receiving so much less than any child deserves. But in their minds, they were lucky.

I am so grateful to the foster parents and social workers who took the time to speak with me. For every villain in the foster care world there are a hundred heroes working tirelessly to help these kids and fight this broken system. We need more heroes. These children belong to all of us, and as long as the system is failing, so are we.

At its heart, this is a book about sisters born from different wombs. I was able to write about this with some authority because I have experienced this kind of sisterhood. Sasha Milinkovic, Emily Ball, Emily Makiv, Kena Roach, Jane Merrylees, Danielle Sanders—thank you for showing me that the greatest love story of all is friendship.

The book is infinitely richer for the team of people who worked on it—with Jen Enderlin, to whom this book is dedicated, at the helm. Thank you, team.

At St. Martin's: Brant Janeway, Erica Martirano, Katie Bassel, Kejana Ayala, Christina Lopez, Kim Ludlum, Brad Wood, Lisa Senz, Tracey Guest.

At Pan Macmillan Australia: Alex Lloyd, Ingrid Ohlsson, Katie Crawford, Praveen Naidoo, Charlotte Ree, Tracey Cheetham, Ali Lavau, Brianne Collins, Claire Keighery, Candice Wyman and Christa Moffitt.

And as always, special thanks and gratitude to my literary agent, Rob Weisbach.

You can't write about foster care without reflecting on your own family of origin. I will always be grateful to my parents, Geraldine and Trevor Carrodus, for giving me a childhood home where I felt safe and loved—so safe and loved that they had to sell the family home and move into a one-bedroom apartment to get us to move out. I didn't understand the privilege of that at the time. I do now.

To my brothers, Simon and Chris Carrodus; and my sisters-in-law, Nikki and Therese; thank you for giving me nieces and nephews. If anything ever happens to you, I'll take in every last one